GROWING UP
LUCKY

A Young Magician's Travels in the American Civil War

The Willard Show c. 1935

GROWING UP
LUCKY

A Young Magician's Travels in the American Civil War

Based on the true life adventures of
James Michael "J.J." Willard

BILLY M. COPELAND

ELM GROVE PUBLISHING
San Antonio, Texas

ISBN 978-1-943492-40-4 (hard back)
ISBN 978-1-943492-41-1 (soft cover)

Cover design © 2018 by Jim Villaflores
Illustrations © 2018 by Marvin Tabacon

ELM GROVE PUBLISHING

San Antonio, Texas
www.elmgrovepublishing.com

This book is dedicated to my wife,
Madeline Willard Copeland,
whose grandfather this book is about

Our two sons, who are the great grandsons of James Michael Willard

Christopher Scott Copeland,
born June 2, 1960

and

Forest Clark Copeland,
June 6, 1963 to December 9, 1994

And to the Many Friends whose names I have used freely, placing them in an era

in which they would have loved to have lived–and been as lucky as James!

Contents

Lucy Mae Keefer Willard

James Michael Willard and son Harry F. Willard

Preface

James Michael Willard was a real person. He was a magician who traveled throughout the United States and Canada. He married Lucy Mae Keefer and they had four children—three boys and a girl. He died on June 23, 1936; he is buried in St Frances de Salle's Catholic cemetery in Houma, Louisiana.

I was born on June 30th, 1936. I married his granddaughter on June 29, 1957.

We started our search in 1987 for information about the Keefers and the Willards.

We found the Keefer ranch in Chico, California in 1988 or 1989. We also had the pleasure of meeting a young lady who had done a thesis on the Keefers. She had done a lot of research and put together many facts.

There is a picture of James M. Willard with his son Harry F. Willard to the left. We believe that it was taken in the 1920s or early 30s.

I ran into a complete wall about who James Michael Willard's parents were so when that happens, you go about telling a story out of your imagination, which is really all this book is, with a lot of facts put in. You, the reader, will just have to try and figure out where is fact and where is my imagination. Have fun!

Chapter 1

The Long Journey South

In the distance a whippoorwill was making its nightly noises as the wagon ground slowly through the dense fog. There was an eerie feeling as if there was something about to happen, but the young boy who was nine couldn't tell what it was. James Jr. sat silently beside his father, James Sr., who was driving the two horses. The wagon was a medicine wagon, and on the side it said "Willard's Magic Elixir." James Jr., his father, mother, and two sisters had left Brooklyn, New York 40 days ago and were going to New Orleans to meet with family members. The year was 1861 and war between the states had already begun. There was tremendous tension as they traveled through many of the areas. At each town his father would stop and sell some of the magic elixir, which really was just molasses and alcohol and some ingredient that his father kept secret, maybe Cayenne Spice. It was brown. His dad had lots of bottles of molasses in the wagon and would pick up wood alcohol when he needed it. He would buy empty bottles in some towns. James was always amazed at why people would buy the stuff. What was so funny was that most of the people buying it were ladies in their 40s or older.

James Jr.'s dad pulled the horses to the side of the road, and with his finger told James Jr. to be quiet! As they listened they could hear wagon wheels grinding on the road coming toward them. The sound got closer and closer and the fog seemed to make the sound come from all around them. James Jr. held his breath. Then a man on a horse appeared, then another and another. When they finally got close enough James could see that they were Union soldiers. As they went by, the officer who was leading the column tipped his hat to James Jr.'s father. James Jr.'s father tipped his back!

As they went by there were four wagons, three cannons and about 100 men, with about 20 of them on horse back and the rest in the wagons or marching. In the fog they appeared as if ghosts from another life, and then they disappeared as if they had returned to their other world. It gave James Jr. a very eerie feeling. The sounds of the wagons and cannons disappeared quickly, gobbled up by the fog. James Jr.'s dad took out a small book and made notes in it. After finishing writing, he hid the book in a small compartment in the floor of the wagon.

They pulled back on to the road and continued through the fog. The chill now seemed to engulf them and James Jr. pulled his coat closed and wrapped his arms around his body to try and get warm again. James Jr. wondered about the book his father had written in, because he had been doing that the whole trip. Every time they passed Union soldiers he would make notes in the book, then hide it back in its secret place.

As the horses' hoofs made clunky noises on the soft dirt of the road James was thinking about what his father had done. Coming from Ireland with a wife and one daughter with no money and just the thought that he did not want his family to starve. James Jr.'s father had worked in many jobs and his mother had cleaned houses for the rich until they had saved enough to buy a wagon and two horses. Then using the molasses formula that they had brought from Ireland they started traveling through New England selling the "Magic Elixir." His father had done well, but now it seems that his brother who was in New Orleans said they should come down there, that there were lots of Irish and they would have many friends. James Jr.'s uncle also said that living conditions were much better in the south, and that they could buy a home for very little. James Jr. had been in quite a few fights with the "wops" and the "spics" and his dad didn't like that there were different gangs for each ethnic group and that they all fought for territories! James really didn't want to leave his friends but what is a nine-year-old supposed to do?

The sun started to break behind them; now the fog really took on an eerie look. The trees seemed to have shapes of giants lurking in the distance, waiting just to grab them if they wandered off the road. James moved closer to his Pa, who in turn put his arm around James Jr. and pulled him close. There was a bond between the two that can only be between a father and son.

James Sr. saw a clearing along the road and pulled the wagon into it. There was a creek running next to the clearing. James Jr. unhitched the horses and took them down to the creek to water. Taking off their harnesses he put hobbles around their ankles so that they could graze but couldn't run off. The horses started eating the lush grass as soon as they finished drinking. James Jr. then gathered wood for a fire, and some rocks to put around the fire. As soon as he had all the wood in place his father came over and lit it. While his father was erecting the tripod over the fire, James Jr. took the coffee pot down to the creek and filled it with water. James Jr. handed the coffee pot to his father who put some coffee in it from a tin, then hung the pot by a chain from the tripod over the fire.

Within just a few minutes James Jr. started to smell the aroma of the coffee as it started to heat up. James Jr. got a table from the side of the wagon and set it up. Then he got several chairs and put them around the table. That completed the chores that were his responsibility to do, so he sat in one of the chairs and watched his father.

Momma Willard got out of the back of the wagon. She stretched, putting her arms high into the air as if reaching for the top of the trees. Then she bent over from the waist and almost touched her head to the ground. Elizabeth Willard was a fine looking lady and was very agile for a woman who had already produced three children. She came over to James Jr. and gave him a big hug and a kiss on the forehead. Elizabeth then went over to James Sr. and they embraced and kissed then she sort of danced off into the woods with James Sr. giving her a friendly pat on the rear. She laughed as she went and her laughter always made James Jr. feel good. Her laughter seemed to just bubble up from inside her and sounded like music. When she laughed her bright blue eyes seemed to sparkle and the freckles on her skin looked like they were dancing. James Jr. would do stunts and somersaults sometimes just to make his mother laugh.

Madeline appeared from the rear of the wagon, sleep still in her eyes and a frown on her face. She stuck her tongue out at James Jr. and then went over and hugged James Sr. Madeline was eleven, two years older than James Jr. and she was always trying to boss him around, but, alas, it never worked. James Jr. had a mind of his own and normally ignored her. He loved Madeline and she loved him neither ever thought about it. A younger brother and an older sister have a different bond than other children. Had their ages been switched the bond would have been different. She headed off to the woods.

James Jr. heard a voice from the back of the wagon. It was Gloria his younger sister. She is only six and had a hard time getting out of the wagon. James went to the back of the wagon and put his hands under her arm pits and lifted her out. Gloria hugged him and ran over to her dad and hugged him and then ran to the woods. Gloria was James Jr.'s delight, she was more like her mother than Madeline. Madeline had long dark hair like James Sr. and very fair complexion, where as Gloria took after her mother, she had reddish hair and freckles and dancing eyes and a devil may care personality. Back in Brooklyn James Jr. was always getting her out of trouble. She would get nose to nose with the "wop" girls even when they were bigger than her and she would stand her ground. Which always got James Jr. into a pushing match with the other girls' brothers. Tempers would flare and words would be said, but that was normally the end of it. It seemed sort of like a game that they all played, the Irish tempers against the Italian tempers.

Elizabeth came back out of the woods went down to the creek and washed her face with the creek water and with a brush she pulled from her dress washed her teeth. She had very pretty teeth and was proud of them and brushed them at least twice a day. She always made sure each of the children brushed their teeth twice a day! She would scold James Sr. cause he always had a cigar and would tease him that she wouldn't kiss that dirty mouth until he had washed it. That always worked and James Sr. would get out his brush and do his teeth, then bare them to her and say, "Now, is that cleaned enough for a wee tiny kiss, me dear?" Then they would both laugh.

James Sr. already had the large frying pan out and bacon that he had sliced from a slab frying in the pan. Elizabeth took over and turned the bacon then got out some flour and a rolling pin and went over to the table and mixed up the flour with water and some yeast and baking soda and made biscuits. Something about biscuits cooked over an open fire just made them taste so much better. She then removed the bacon from the pan and put it on a plate and put eight eggs into the pan and scrambled them. Breakfast was ready. Both girls as if by magic appeared from the woods at the same time and went directly to the table. One thing that the Willards all had in common, they loved to eat! After breakfast the girls would do all the clean up. It was their job. Madeline actually did most of it, but she made sure Gloria did a share of it. James Sr. and James Jr. crawled into the back of the wagon and went to sleep. It was about 7 am and they would sleep until noon. Well James Jr. would probably sleep longer if he was allowed to. Most of the time he was allowed to and wouldn't wake up until the wagon was rolling again. The two girls usually would tease him with a feather or a string across his nose,

but with his good nature he didn't get mad about it.

May 1, 1861 the wagon bumped along the road and each side were corn fields. The stalks were about two feet tall. Black birds were flying everywhere as if saying to the Corn, "Hurry Up, We're Hungry." Their caws could be heard from the distant trees that surrounded the fields. James Jr. sat next to his dad and thought how great the world was. Funny how in Brooklyn, New York he never knew so many different birds existed. Now he saw red birds, blue birds, black birds, gray birds and yellow birds. He had hated leaving Brooklyn, but now he was glad they had. In his wildest imagination he could never have thought how beautiful the country was.

So far his greatest delight had been in Pennsylvania, where he had seen a deer for the first time. The grace and speed that the deer ran with just amazed him. Then when they saw a doe with two fawns, and a big buck with lots of antlers! Well it just made him glad that his dad had decided to make this trip.

The wagon rolled past a hand painted sign that said, Welcome, You are Entering Johnson City, Tenn. James Jr. had to laugh out loud, because the town had a total of five buildings. A general store, a saloon and 3 houses. But the town was bustling, there were about seventy or a hundred people milling around doing different things. On the porch of the general store sat about ten men, some were smoking and others apparently were chewing tobacco, cause they spit every minute or so.

Across the street at the saloon another ten or twelve men were either standing or sitting and again doing the same thing, smoking or chewing. From inside you could hear the sounds of a piano, playing some slow music, but of course the sound went through the whole town. Horses were tied up to hitching post and buggies were everywhere. James Jr. wondered why so many people were in this small quaint little town. James Sr. found a place for the wagon that would be easy for every one to see, because he was going to try and sell some elixir while they had so many potential customers. He told James Jr. to undo the horses and take them over near the creek so they could drink and then let them graze on the grass. James Jr. immediately started doing what his dad had told him to do, but he sure wondered why so many people were in town.

He unhitched the horses from the wagon. The ladies climbed out and immediately headed for the general store. He asked Gloria if she wanted to go to the creek with him, but she said no, she wanted to go to the store. The horses seemed glad to see the creek and immediately started to drink. That is when James noticed another boy about his age with two horses that were grazing. After tethering the horses so they could graze, James went over to the other boy.

The boy said his name was William A. Ferguson and that his folks owned some land outside town. He was a nice young man and he was ten. Sort of spoke with an English twang to his words. Said everyone was in town to find out about the war and to send a letter to the capital that they would like for Tennessee to join the Confederacy. It seems every one felt that each state should have the right to make its own laws and not have one big government telling them what to do. Heck, if the federal government could tell them they couldn't have slaves. What would be next? Tell them they couldn't raise tobacco or that they couldn't make liquor? James asked William if his family raised tobacco or made liquor and William said no, but they felt they should have the freedom to do so if they wanted to. What William said made sense to James, but he still didn't know what all this talk about war was and what the heck, it didn't affect him anyway.

James and William spent the next few hours talking. William was amazed at what James told him about New York and Brooklyn. He had never been to a city that big. They had gone down to Knoxville once, but, heck, it only had a couple thousand people and no real large buildings. They had fun chasing squirrels from tree to tree for awhile, then coalized the squirrels were just playing with them.

Suddenly James and William heard a lot of noise coming from town. They both tethered the horses and ran to see what was happening. Two men were in a big fist fight in front of the saloon. A crowd had gathered around them and were agitating them to keep fighting! James Jr. asked someone why they were fighting? The guy said one was for staying in the Union and the other was for joining the Confederacy. They started by having "words" then ended up in the fight! Two other men started having words and then they got into it. Now there were four men fighting and then six. Two of those fighting were twins, one twin was for the north and one twin was for the south, so they were fighting each other. James Sr. came over and put his hand on Jr.'s arm and told him they should go. James Jr. said goodbye to William and they headed over to the wagon!

The ladies had returned from shopping and had prepared a lunch from some of the things they had purchased. They had it spread out on a blanket on the far side of the wagon, away from the commotion of the saloon. There was fresh bread, fresh tomatoes and some salami. James Jr. ate two sandwiches and really enjoyed it! After eating James Sr. told Jr. to get the drum out and they started preparing to sell some elixir.

James Jr. lowered the back gate on the wagon and pulled the drum out. He then got a chair and sat in the chair and started beating the drum, rat-a-tat, rat-a-tat, rat-a tat, rat-a-tat. It was always strange to James Jr. that just beating this drum would cause people to come over to the wagon, but it always did. In about three or four minutes there were about two dozen people just standing there. James Sr. was inside the wagon getting prepared to give a show.

Mother Willard and Madeline came out; mother Willard had her mandolin. It was a Spanish mandolin that she had learned to play in Ireland. She always said that she had actually learned to play it from a Spanish lady that had come to Ireland from Spain, it had six strings. Madeline played the violin. They started playing a real Irish song, some called them "jigs". You couldn't hear them without wanting to dance! When they started the second song a couple started dancing and then a couple more came over and started to dance. Everyone seemed to be really enjoying the music. James Jr. kept the beat going with the drum.

Mother Willard and Madeline had played about five songs and there was a real crowd either dancing or watching. James Willard Sr. came out on the tailgate and put his arms up in the air. They quit playing and every one got real quite. James Sr. was an impressive looking man, long tailcoat, white shirt, bow tie, he only stood about 5 feet 8 inches tall but on the tail gate he looked much taller.

James Sr. started producing items in his hands faster than the people standing around could see. First was a flower, it just seemed to come from nowhere, then various items and they all appeared as if by magic. James Jr. sat in amazement of his fathers ability to do this magic. The audience was also amazed and it really kept their attention. Then James Sr. produced a bottle of Willard's Magic Elixir. For one small quarter you could have this magic potion that had been brought from the far reaches of India, given to James Sr.'s father in Ireland by a magic man from India. It will cure almost anything and will make you forget that you have any aches and pains, give you longer life and wonderful sight! Gloria came out of the wagon with her box of bottles of the elixir and started going through the crowd. She looked so cute that James Jr. always thought that some people bought a bottle just to see her curtsy and tuck the money away!

This crowd was a good one, they were buying lots of bottles from Gloria. She had to go back in the wagon and get another load. James Sr. thanked everyone and got off the tail gate. Mother Willard and Madeline started playing music again. Gloria kept going through the crowd selling, she was so good at it! It was really a good day, they made $12.00! One guy drank a whole bottle and then bought three more. He then grabbed a lady that was there and started to dance to the music! Madeline and Mother Willard played five more songs and then quit. The crowd was gone as fast as it had gathered.

They spent the night there and could hear the piano coming from the saloon until late in the night. The next morning they loaded up and headed out toward Knoxville. They had been told that there was a real nice lake just before you got to Knoxville, and that would be a nice place to spend the night.

Large mountains could be seen to the left, they seemed to be on the far horizon. James Jr. sure hoped they didn't have to go over those mountains. The horses seemed to have a brisk step about them this morning. James Jr. guessed it was because they had a lot of rest back at Johnson City. James Jr. asked his father about the mountains and were they going to have to go over them? James Sr. said no, that they were going to stay north of the mountains and would miss them except for the foothills that they were now going through.

James Jr. asked his father how long it would take them to get to Knoxville? James Sr. responded with a day and a half. They would stop before dark if they could find a good place to camp with water and grass for the horses. It seemed to James Jr. that the hills were getting steeper and steeper.

At about four in the afternoon they came upon a real nice creek with deep water and lots of grass. James Sr. pulled the wagon into the clearing and they started the preparations for the night. James Jr. took the horses from the wagon and took them to the creek. The water in the creek was crystal clear and James Jr. could see some fish. He ran back and told is Dad. James Sr. got some string out of the wagon and a hook and then caught a couple of grasshoppers. He put one on a hook and then he put a cork on the string and threw it as far out in the creek as he could. It had no sooner hit the water when the cork went under and James Sr. pulled in a nice fish. It must have weighed about one half pound!

He handed the string to James Jr. and he tried his hand. As soon as the cork hit the water it disappeared. He pulled the fish to the bank and then his dad helped him take it off the hook. This was the first fish James Jr. had ever caught in his life! He shouted with glee. The three women came running to see what he was shouting about. He threw out the string again and again the cork went under the water. He pulled in another fish. Gloria immediately started catching more grasshoppers and James Jr. kept fishing. Within just

20 minutes, they had ten fish and Sr. told Jr. that was enough. Now young man, you have to learn how to clean your catch. They took the fish over to a flat rock. James Sr. showed Jr. and Gloria how to cut the head off and then with the knife how to remove the scales. Then how to fillet them so that there were no bones. The first one Jr. tried to do, he had a hard time cutting the head off, but he picked up removing the scales real fast. When he filleted it he got a few bones in but the second one he did real well. Gloria took the fish down to the creek and washed them. That girl isn't afraid of anything!

What a meal they had that night! Momma Willard fried the fish just right and there was enough that they all got their fill. With onions and fried potatoes, it was one of the best suppers they had on the whole trip. After supper the girls got their instruments out and played a few songs. At the urging of Madeline, James Sr. told some stories about Ireland and his folks.

When James Sr. talked he had a very heavy Irish Brogue that made you hang on to every word he was saying, "Twas a long time ago and twas on the eastern sare of our green homeland there was a full moon and my gramps sade thet the night was one of those nites that make the skin crowl up the back of yre neck, tha wind it was blowing with all it's mite, with no warning a hack at the door. The whole bunch of us just sat and wondered who would be so crazy to come out on this nite! He opened tha door and looked out, but, no one was thar! So he shat the dor and crossed back to the table, and again there was a hack at tha dor, again he crossed and opened tha door, but, again, thar was no one thar! As he started to close the door he heard the 'Banshee' cry! That is when me gramps knew that something bad had happened! But, not wanting to go out on such a nite, they had to wait 'til the next morning, and tha is when they found out that my gramps father had passed away, that it was him who was hacking at their door to tell them goodbye! Or maybe it was the little people tha was delivering the message for his father. So mi children always know, that as Irish ye are connected to all yr kin and if you hear the 'Banshee' it only means that one of us has passed to the other side. Now, give your Papa and Momma a hug and off to slep, we have a hard day tomara."

The girls and Momma Willard got in the wagon, James Sr. and Jr. got a couple of blankets and pillows and slept outside near the fire. James went to sleep looking up at the stars wondering what a Banshee sounded like, hoping he never would hear the sound, because he loved his Momma, Papa and sisters! James Jr. awoke to the smell of bacon frying and the sounds of birds singing. It was early but the sun was already up, though not very high, still on the eastern horizon. He went over to his father and got a good hug, that always started his day right. Then he went into the woods and did the necessities. Coming back he went to the creek and washed his face and hair and brushed his teeth, this really helped him to wake up. He then went looking for the horses. They had strayed off a little bit during the night! He took them to the creek and let them drink and then hitched them to the wagon. The girls were up and Gloria came over to him and gave him a hug! He hugged her back and she was gone to do the chores that were assigned to her. Each of the children had certain things they had to do each morning. No one question why. They knew why and they did them without complaining. Chores are just a part of family life and Momma Willard had it down to a science and the family ran very smoothly.

After breakfast they loaded the wagon and got started again. It was the beginning of a wonderful day.

After crossing the French River they were on a plain and the land became fairly flat. Entering Knoxville James Jr. was surprised at the size of the city. There was actually a farmers market. Some land had been donated by two of the citizens in 1853 to be used as a market place for the farmers. There were several vendors there selling fresh produce and one actually selling tobacco. James Sr. pulled the wagon over to the west part of this square and parked. This gave them a good advantage to passing traffic to later sell some of the elixir. He told James Jr. to unhitch the horses and take them to the river to water and see if he could find an open field so that they could graze.

James Jr. took the horses and started walking toward the river. He was amazed there was a real big Presbyterian Church which sat on some land donated by a James White in 1790. Then there was Blount College for some reason James Jr. thought this was unusual for a city in the south to have a college. And being a child of curiosity he had to find out more about this college. He would after he had the horses settled.

Approaching the river James Jr. saw something he had never seen before, black men in chains! They were huddled up against a barn where a platform was out in front of them. There were black men all sizes and shapes and then James Jr. saw the other side of the barn. What James Jr. saw the other side it made him almost sick to his stomach. On the other side of the barn were black women chained together along with black children. After looking for just a few seconds, James Jr. started running toward the River and caused the horses to have to trot! He just couldn't get away from there fast enough!

When the horses finished drinking he took them down a road about a quarter of mile, hobbled them in a clearing which wasn't far from the river, as the river round its way close to this clearing. He was going to leave t hem and then thought better of it. He had seen some characters in town that made him think that if he left the horses, well, they just might be stolen. The grass was real green and tall so he figured that if they ate for an hour or two they would have plenty. He started looking around to see what he could entertain himself with for a couple of hours. He walked through thin woods to the river making sure that he could see the horses all the while. At the river he was amazed that there were several barges going both ways, up river and down river. The ones going up river had eight or ten men with long poles and they were actually pushing the barges up river. Watching them James Jr. figured that was pretty hard work. The barges going down river actually sat deeper in the water as if they were fully loaded. The men seemed to be just guiding them, not really having to work very hard. Every few minutes James Jr. would check to see if he could still see the horses. He waved at the men on the barges and some of them waved back at him. He wondered where the loaded barges that were going down river were going and what they were carrying. James Jr. suddenly looked up and the sun had moved a long way. He hadn't realized that almost 3 hours had passed and he knew his father would be looking for him if he didn't start back. He un-hobbled the horses and headed back toward the market square. He wished there was someway to avoid the slave market, but it was the only street he could take.

On the way back as he passed the slaves, he noticed something that again shocked him. There with the black women were two Indian women with children, they were chained up with the black women. James Jr. stopped and gazed at the Indian women and children. These were the first Indians that he had actually seen. No one had ever told him that Indians were slaves also. He made a note in his mind to ask his father about this.

When he got back to the square there was no one around. He figured that his father, mother and sisters were off looking around the town. He tied the horses to the wagon and headed toward the college. He needed to get some answers about this college. Elizabeth Willard had made sure that all her children could read and write and she also tried to teach them about other things that she felt they would need to know. She always said that she hoped one or more of her children would go to college someday.

Going past the Presbyterian church, James Jr. decided to go into the graveyard that was part of the grounds. There he discovered the graves of some men that had played a big part in Knoxville. "William Blount", marker said Born March 26th, 1749, died March 21st, 1800, appointed by George Washington as Superintendent of Indian Affairs for the southwest territory in 1790. James Jr. wondered if the college was named for him or if he had donated the land for the College and that was why it was named Blount College.

He also found the grave of James White, but it didn't say

much. The grave of A Dr. Samuel Carrick, the churches first pastor and the first president of Blount College. James wondered if Carrick had come to Knoxville from Carrickfergus, Ireland. From the history his mother had taught him he knew that Carrickfergus was where the first presbytery was organized in Ireland. James Jr. had learned a lot from his mother about the different churches of Ireland. It seemed as if she knew every bit of history about religion in Ireland, which was funny since they were Irish Catholics. Even while traveling on Sundays she would have them read from the bible, which for Catholics in the 1800s was unusual, since most did not read or write. The church really was against Catholics reading the bible on their own. The priest didn't think the average person could understand what the Bible taught or said. This didn't stop Elizabeth Willard; she wanted her children to read the bible and she wanted them to understand it. She made James Sr. get on his knees and pray with her and the children, he was a man that didn't normally kneel to anything! Admittedly James Sr.'s prayers were not usually very long, and sometimes he reverted to a very heavy Irish brogue and spoke very quickly! All three kids would snicker and Elizabeth would say to James Sr., "Now James, do it again with a little sincerity in that voice of yours, God is listening and you want him to hear!" She always had a smile on her face during this admonishing of her husband.

James Jr. walked toward the building that he thought was the college, when he entered the gate he was surprised to find a sign: Original Home of Blount College Now Administration Offices of Eastern Tennessee University So what James Jr. had thought was Blount College was actually Eastern Tennessee University. He went inside the building anyway just to see what was there. He found a plaque inside that gave him the history. Blount College was named after the then governor of Tennessee and that in 1807 the college had been renamed Eastern Tennessee College and then in 1840 renamed Eastern Tennessee University. Looking at other documents he found a map that showed what the buildings were up on the hill, the library, the dormitories and the class rooms.

As he walked up the hill he could see men dressed in gray uniforms and men in blue uniforms. This made James Jr. wonder what was going on. He noticed that the men in gray and the men in blue didn't even speak to each other. James Jr. stopped one of the men in blue and asked him why some were in blue and some in gray. The young man told him that this was a religious institution that did military training and that a lot of the men wanted to be with the union, so they wore the blue and a lot of them wanted to be with the Confederates so they were in gray. He also said that Tennessee was voting tomorrow as to which way the state would go, and that if it went to the Confederates that everyone in blue would leave the next day and that if it stayed in the union then all the gray would leave. James Jr. thanked him for his kindness and went on up to the large building.

James Jr. entered the building and saw a sign over one door that said Library. He went in that room and just stood there with his mouth open, he had never seen so many books in his entire life. He didn't even know that many books were in existence. An older man came over to James Jr. and asked him if he could help him. After regaining his composure he told the gentlemen that he was just looking and that some day he hoped to attend this university with all its books.

The gentleman introduced himself and ask James Jr. to come over and sit down and tell him about himself and his family. James thought that was very kind for a scholar to want to know about him and his family. James Jr. and the gentleman talked for almost an hour and suddenly James Jr. saw how late it was when the gentleman struck a match to light a lamp. He thanked the gentleman for his time and all the information and headed back to the wagon on the square.

When James Jr. arrived back at the wagon, his father, mother and sisters already had everything set up for the show. James Sr. told him to start to beat the drum. They had a wonderful crowd and his father performed more magic than usual because the crowd kept applauding! Gloria made four trips for more bottles and at the end of the evening they had made almost $20.00. The whole family was really happy. James Sr. decided that they could splurge, so he took them all to the boarding house and bought supper. You could tell by the laughter how much the ladies enjoyed eating someone else's cooking. James Jr. really enjoyed it because he had steak and potatoes and fresh green beans and even some cooked carrots. Then a real "big" piece of apple pie with whipped cream. He was so full he wasn't sure he could walk back to the wagon. It was really unusual for his father to spend $3.00 for a meal for all of them. This was the first time they had eaten in a boarding house since they had left Brooklyn.

James Sr. told James Jr. to take the horses over to the livery stable and house them for the night and to tell the man to give them plenty of hay. He gave him a dollar to pay the man. James Jr. took the horses, and it seemed that they were smiling to be able to be in a stall with lots of hay to eat. They both started eating as soon as they were put in the stall. He told the man that he would pick them up in the morning, the man said that would be fine, but he wouldn't open till 6 a.m. James Jr. went back, brushed his teeth and kissed his mom and dad goodnight and crawled into his bed roll, he was asleep before his head hit his pillow, it had been a long day. James Jr. awoke out of a sound sleep to the sounds of gun fire. He didn't move. He stayed wrapped in the bed roll, more gun fire and a lot of yelling, whooping and carrying on. He could hear all kinds of men's voices. Finally deciding that the gun shots were not a threat he rolled out of his bed and put his shoes on and looked for his father. He found his father and asked him what was going on? A rider had come into town early and said that the Tennessee legislature had voted the day before to secede from the Union and to join the southern states which were seceding from the union. That was voted on May 6, 1861.

Since Knoxville was full of people dressed in gray and blue James Sr. told him to hurry and go get the horses. He wanted to get on the road as soon as possible. By this time the ladies were all up and dressed and mother Willard was already starting to cook breakfast. James Jr. asked his father the time and was told that it was 6:15 am, which was good cause the livery stable would be open. He hurried to get the horses. They seemed happy to see him and it looked like they were full and had been watered already. He thanked the gentleman and headed back to the wagon.

When he got back to the wagon he immediately hitched the horses to it so they were ready to go. Then he sat down and ate three eggs, some sausage and two pieces of bread with a cold cup of fresh milk. The milk sure tasted good. It was the first milk he had in three weeks. They finished loading the wagon and were on their way out of town by 7:30. The first thing was to cross the river, but here they were lucky because there was a bridge.

"Where are we heading?" James Jr. asked his father. "We are going to Chattanooga! It will take about 3 days but we may be lucky and do it in two." They were no more than five miles out of town when they had to pull off the road to let some soldiers in gray uniforms pass. Must have been five hundred of them. They looked sharp and they had four cannons and a bunch of wagons. A lot of the soldiers were riding in the wagons but there were also a lot of them walking. Those walking had rifles slung over their shoulders with butt end of the rifle behind their backs. James Jr. thought that the officers really looked good with all their gold braids. After the soldiers had passed, James Sr. took his little book out from its hiding place and made notes and then put it back. This made James Jr. wonder since his father had done the same thing on the whole trip when they passed union soldiers. James Jr. was going to ask his father about it, but about that time two riders came riding by at full gallop. This distracted him, so he forgot to ask. James Jr. asked his father why they were riding so fast. His answer was, "I don't know lad, but they sure had a burr up their tails."

The trip to Chattanooga had been easier than they thought and now only two days later they were pulling into the town. This was a town that had railroads that were very important. Since they had traveled along the south side of the Tennessee river they could see the mountains for both days of their travel. The mountain that was to the southeast was called Missionary Ridge, while the one that was due south was Lookout mountain. They had come in on the east of town and James Sr. looked for a field that had grass and water that was easy for them to camp at. They found it near a creek and settled in for the night.

The next morning they had breakfast and James Sr. walked into town to see what was happening. He came back in a little while and told them that he really didn't like the looks of things there. The town was full of rough looking characters and that he felt they should just pack up and head on toward the City of New Orleans. They followed the road south of the Tennessee River until they came to Brown's Ferry and took the road south through the Sand Mountains. James Sr. told James Jr. that they would stay south of the Sand Mountains and that their next town would be Albertsville. They would go to Birmingham and on to Tuscaloosa and then into Mississippi.

Albertsville turned out to be a real small little place with only a trading post and a couple of houses. They didn't even spend the night there. James Sr. would decide to head on out to Birmingham.

It took them over a week to get from Chattanooga, Tenn. to Birmingham, Alabama. When they approached the edge of Birmingham, James Jr. knew that this was a large city!

About two miles outside of town they saw a bunch of soldiers that were marching as if they were being trained. They would march one way and then turn and march another, then stop and turn around and put their rifles down and then put them back on their shoulders. The whole time James Jr. could hear someone shouting at them, and he guessed the person was giving them orders. About three men were over on the side mounted on fine looking horses. James Jr. figured that they were officers.

They drove slowly into the city, and it was a city. James Jr. figured it was as large as Brooklyn, but he wasn't sure. They found a livery stable and James Sr. then looked for a place for them to stay.

WILLARD'S
MAGIC ELIXIR

He found a big lot that was vacant with a bunch of trees and lots of bushes. James Sr. thought that would be a good place and it was only about a block from the river, so they could get water to cook with and a lot of wood so they could have a fire. It was pretty late in the evening, from the sun, James Jr. figured it was at least 5 pm, but in the spring it was sort of hard to tell since the sun seemed to stay up longer. He unhitched the horses and started to the river, but James Sr. stopped him and gave him a dollar and told him to take them to the livery. So he took them and again these horses were so smart they knew they were going to have plenty of feed and water for the night.

James Jr. left the livery stable and then sort of wondered around the city for a little bit, it seemed everywhere he went there were solders in gray. On the streets were ladies that were really dressed up. Silk dresses that blossomed out from tiny waists. He wondered how they got their waists so small. Heck some of them were as small around as Gloria and she was only 6. They had red cheeks and red lips, and as the soldiers passed them they would always stop and take their hats off until the ladies had passed. This seemed to James Jr. like a big waste of time! He guessed the ladies liked it though, they seemed to always giggle after they had passed the soldiers. The soldiers would hit each other on the back and then look over their shoulders to see if the ladies were looking.

When James Jr. got back to the wagon it was already set up for a show. He got his drum and started beating it. And again he was amazed at how fast a crowd gathered to see why he was beating a drum. They really had a good show that evening, and Gloria sold almost $30.00 worth of elixir. His father said they would have to find a place to buy more bottles tomorrow, the people seemed to really to enjoy the music and James Jr. even saw some of those ladies in the fine dresses dancing with soldiers.

James Sr. was so happy, he asked them if they would like to spend the night in a boarding house. Well there was no one that had any objections to such a luxury. They got some clothes and headed over to the boarding house. For Elizabeth Willard this was going to be a real treat, a meal she didn't have to cook and to take a bath in a real tub, with hot water, she felt like she was in heaven. The girls also felt that way. James Sr. got two rooms for the night with supper included for $10.00. The kids were in one room that had two beds and the mother and father in a room that had a private bath. The kids had to use the bath at the end of the hall, but heck that was okay with them.

They all bathed and then went down for supper. The lady running the dining room was a very large lady who looked like she really liked to eat. For the second time on this trip James Jr. really ate too much, but this time he only had to walk up the stairs to his bed. It had been a very long day and they all went up to bed as soon as they finished supper plus a few funny stories by the big lady. She had such a good spirit and laughed so easy that they all had a good time. James Jr. really enjoyed watching his mother and father laugh and the lady seemed to be doing her best to tell stories that they would enjoy.

When they went to the room, James Jr. was lucky in that he got to have a whole bed to himself. He undressed down to his underwear which was unusual because when they were camping out he always slept in his clothes, so crawling into the clean sheets really felt wonderful. He was asleep in no time.

They had been gone from Birmingham for two weeks, they had only spent one night in Tuscaloosa, Alabama where James Sr. had gotten directions as to how to go from there to New Orleans. They had been lucky when they had reached the Tombigbee River because there was a ferry and it only cost them a quarter to cross. James Sr. had been worrying about that river ever since they left Tuscaloosa. Now they were just a few miles from Meridian, Mississippi. It was getting toward dark and James Sr. found a nice clearing along side a creek and decided that they had gone far enough for one day and that the horses needed to rest.

After watering the horses in the creek, James Jr. hobbled them so that they could eat and move around freely, but not too far. There was a lot of lush grass for them to enjoy.

James Sr. already had the fire going and Elizabeth was cooking supper. The girls had the table set up and the chairs out. All of a sudden without any warning three Indians came out of the woods on their horses. Well, needless to say this scared the women so much James Jr. thought they had turned two degrees whiter! One of the Indians got off his horse and went over to James Sr. They talked in low tones, and then James Sr. asked Elizabeth if they had enough food for these men to eat with them. Her color returned and she assured them that they would be welcomed. One Indian spoke really good English and told them that they were part of a Cherokee tribe that had broken away from the big tribe. Their families were a few miles away and they were hunting for deer to feed their families. They did not have on war paint. The other two Indians never spoke a word except in Indian to the one that did the talking. He told James Sr. that his name was Fast Wolf and that the other two were Little Bear and Feathered Owl. He also told James Sr. about a tribe of the Cherokees that were in western Louisiana near the Sabine River and that his brother was there; that if James Sr. ever got there to just tell them he had met Fast Wolf and the tribe would welcome him. After supper the Indians thanked Mrs. Willard for the meal and got on their horses and left. James Jr. was surprised at how cordial they had been. They had heard so many stories about Indians in Brooklyn that they all thought they might end up being scalped!

The next morning when they awoke, there hanging in a tree was the back quarter of a deer. No one heard them but the Indians had returned during the night and paid them with deer meat for giving them supper. This made James Jr. wonder how they had been so quiet that not even his mother and father heard them, especially since he and his father were sleeping outside the wagon in bed rolls. James Sr. took the meat to the creek, washed it off real good, then put salt all over it and wrapped it up in a cloth. This would preserve it for a couple of days, but James Jr. figured they would be eating

MILLARD'S
MAGIC ELIXIR

deer meat tonight. They loaded up the wagon and were gone right after breakfast.

After the events of the night before, it reminded James Jr. of the Indian women he had seen in the slave market and he asked his dad about it.

James Sr. said that when runaway slaves were captured and they had been given safety by the Indians or were living with an Indian woman that the slave catcher would take the Indian captive and make them slaves. He thought that slavery was awful and that the practice was awful. Most of the time the Indian women knew nothing about these laws, but that even the Indians had slaves. They would have war parties and capture men and women from other tribes and make them slaves. He told James Jr. that actually a lot of the slaves had good masters that took care of them and since most had come from Africa that they had no schooling and if they were released then they wouldn't really be able to take care of themselves. James Sr. told James Jr. that all the commotion wasn't really about slavery, because there were thousands of slaves in the north and that there were actually a lot Negro freemen that owned slaves. But to be fair, James Sr. said that there were also a lot of people that treated their slaves very badly and that it didn't matter whether the owner was black or white. After how nice the Cherokee men had been to them, James Jr. thought about how bad slavery really was and that those Indian women he had seen might have belonged to the same tribe as Fast Wolf.

It took them about two hours that morning to get everything together and be back on the road to Meridian, Mississippi. They were lucky in that the road was pretty good and that there had not been any rain for the last few weeks. The air smelled so good, pine and the odor of wild flowers. This morning the horses seemed to feel that they were in a hurry to go somewhere and James Sr. was holding them back, because if not they would have gone into a trot. It was as if the horses were wanting to hurry up and get to New Orleans. James Jr. figured the horses were only reflecting what the whole family felt.

Leaving Meridian, Mississippi the landscape seemed to change completely. In Meridian they had only sold about $4.00 worth of elixir, not a very good audience. Now instead of large pine trees completely surrounding the road there were large fields with just patches of woods.

The fields were lined with rows and rows of plants. James Sr. told James Jr. that the plants were cotton. Then they came to some corn fields. One of the fields had a lot of stakes by each plant and James Sr. said they were bean stalks and that as the plant grew they would wrap it around the stakes.

Every field had Negroes working in them and usually a man on horseback along with them, sometimes the man on the horse was a black man, but most of the time it was a white man. Every one of the workers had hoes and were chopping weeds in the rows between the plants. James Jr. wondered if these people were happy.

Their routine for the next several days was pretty much the same. They would find a patch of woods with water and camp for the night and then travel all the next day until it was toward the evening, then find another place to camp for the night. The one thing that was really bothering them was the mosquitoes. It seems the further south they went, the thicker the mosquitoes. Lucky James Sr. had been warned, so he had bought a mosquito net in Meridian. At night they would pitch this net like a tent and everyone would sleep under it. A few of the mosquitoes got inside, but a good swat would take care of them. They seemed to like Madeline the best. She was swatting all the time. James Jr. had a little fun with her, he would slap her back and say, "Boy that was a bigun!" Most of the time there wasn't even one there, but it was fun! They made a game out of it, no one knows who got the most swats in.

They finally reached Columbia, Mississippi which is on the Pearl River. Columbia was a nice little town and it was a loading town for barges. Barges would carry the crops from there down to the Gulf of Mexico and over to New Orleans. They parked the wagon on a small square and James Sr. went down to the docks. James Jr. took the horses down to the river to water. Momma Willard and the girls went to see what they could find.

James Sr. came back excited because he had found an Irishman that owned a barge and it was only half full and leaving for New Orleans the next morning. He offered to take them on the barge for only $10.00. This would save them several long days on the road. Everyone got excited about traveling down the Pearl River on a barge. They immediately packed up and headed for the river.

The barge captain was Sean McMurty, he was a large man with big arms and big smile. He had eight other men working for him. McMurty spoke with a very heavy Irish brogue. He had a Frenchman as his first mate and the Frenchman spoke with a heavy French accent. There was also a Negro who had come from Jamaica and he spoke with an English accent. The other men spoke mostly American with no noticeable accents. They had loaded the wagon and horses in the back of the barge. The horses were not too happy about this, but they soon adapted.

In the very middle of the barge was a small house and it contained the cook stove. Elizabeth Willard got provisions from the wagon and went into the small house and prepared supper. She cooked plenty for all hands, and Madeline and Gloria helped her and in no time they had quite a dinner prepared. They brought it upon deck and the men lined up to eat. These men ate like they had never had a home cooked meal before, each and everyone of them thanked the ladies for a wonderful and delicious meal. James Jr. heard one of them tell captain McMurty that they should give them free passage in exchange for the lady cooking all the meals. Sean McMurty agreed and went over to James Sr. and asked him if he would be agreeable to having Mrs. Willard cook two meals a day in exchange for the passage. James Sr. asked Elizabeth if she was agreeable to this and she said she was. So now the ride on the barge was free, except the girls would have to cook. After supper the black man washed all the dishes and cleaned up with the help of one of

the other men.

The ladies went to bed in the wagon and James Sr. and James Jr. put their bedrolls on the deck. The crew had sleeping places all over the barge; several were sleeping on top of the boxes that were the cargo in the front.

James Jr. awoke to the sound of a bell ringing and for a few minutes couldn't figure out where he was. Then he remembered that he was on the barge. Sean was giving instructions to the men and they were untying the barge from the dock. This was exciting, they were moving away from the dock and they were on their way down river! It was still dark, but there were lanterns in the front and rear of the barge that were lit. James got up and moved toward the front of the barge. He wanted to see every thing that he could.

They had been on the river for about an hour when the sun started coming up, and James Jr. could see the banks on each side. They were covered with trees and even trees that were flowering. There was an aroma that smelled so sweet. The water of the river was calm and yet there was a steady movement.

Elizabeth and Madeline had breakfast ready and everyone ate to their hearts content, eggs, bacon and biscuits and Sean had honey and peach jam and fresh milk, this was a real treat.

James Jr. went back to the horses and fed them with the hay that James Sr. had brought on board and gave them each a bucket of water. He had a bucket tied with a rope and he would drop it over board and fill it up and drag it back in to the barge and then pour the water into the tubs that were in front of the horses. It took two of these for each horse. James Jr. then had the task he wasn't crazy about doing. He had to get a shovel and throw the horse manure over the side of the barge into the river. Then get a bucket of water from the river and wash down where the horses had done their thing. It actually took four buckets to get it clean enough so that there was no smell. This was a task that he would have to do several times over the next few days. Gloria and Madeline would stand off to the side and hold their noses and laugh at him while he was doing it. It never failed that when he had finished the Frenchman would come by and pat him on top of the head and say, "Nice job, mate!" This made James Jr. feel good, like someone appreciated how hard the job really was.

Captain McMurty came over to James Jr. and asked him if he would like to fish for their supper. Well naturally James Jr. said yes and the captain went into Cabin and brought out a pole with a line and float attached and a couple of the biscuits that were not eaten at breakfast. He showed James Jr. how to roll up the bread until it was dough again and put it on the hook. James Jr. went to the stern of the boat and started to fish. After a few minutes he pulled the line in and there was no bait, so he redid it and tried again, this time something took hold of it and was really pulling. He thought he had hooked on a log or something cause the pole was really bending, but he kept hold of it and slowly pulled it toward the barge. Sean saw how much the pole was bending and came over to see, just as he got there a big, big, fish jumped out of the water right behind the barge. Sean yelled at James Jr. to hold on and he went into the cabin and came out with a net on a pole. James Jr. got the fish up against the barge and Sean reached in with the net and brought it on board.

Sean said to James Jr., "Son, ye have caught ye a trophy, this here catfish must weight 20 pounds. Lad, you hold the barge record!" By that time all the men had come to see and they all marveled at how well James Jr. had done. The Frenchman took the fish and told James Jr. to come with him. They went to the front of the boat and the Frenchman took out his knife and proceeded to skin the catfish. James Jr. watched and it really looked like a hard job, but the Frenchman made it look easy and he did it real fast. After the skin was off he filleted it and James Jr. got a bucket of water and washed the two big pieces. James Jr. took them to his mother and she said she would fix them for supper.

That night there was plenty for everyone, and the deck hands all had second helpings. At supper the captain gave every one a piece of garlic and told them to chew it real good and to swallow it. He said the reason was that it would help give them some protection against the mosquitoes. By the time evening came James Jr. was so tired that he didn't think the mosquitoes would bother with him, or rather it didn't matter if they would. He slept through the night.

The next morning at breakfast the captain again passed out the garlic and everyone took a piece and chewed it because the mosquitoes were now in patches on the river that were so dense that it looked like a black cloud. It was nice when a breeze would blow up and blow the mosquitoes away. At times they were so thick they would get in your mouth and ears, but the garlic was working cause they were not biting anybody!

They came to place where two rivers merged and Captain Sean had them pole the barge into the west side. He said the East Pearl was not good for barges so now they were on the West Pearl River. On the east bank James Jr. saw a really large house. It had eight big columns and was two stories high. The grounds leading down to the river were really kept neat and there was grass and flowering bushes. It was really a pretty place, and he asked the Frenchman what it was. The Frenchman told him that was a rich plantation home. James Jr. wondered how rich a person had to be to have a big home like that?

The next morning when James Jr. awoke there was all kinds of activity on the barge. When James Jr. tried to stand up he almost fell as the barge rocked. He got to the side of the barge and he could see large waves everywhere. They had entered the Gulf of Mexico.

Captain Sean McMurty was calling to the men to raise the sail. James Jr. didn't even know there was a sail on the barge,. Then he told them to get the oars out. James Jr. didn't know their were oars on board. In just a few minutes there was a large sail that was blowing full with air and the men, four on each side, were rowing. James Jr. found James Sr. and asked if there was anything he could do. His father told him to go steady the horses and to take care of their needs.

Captain McMurty came by and told James Jr. that they would enter the mouth of the Mississippi River in a day or two and that after they had passed the strong currents of the river flowing into the Gulf that it would become easier and that they would have to do a lot of rowing against the current. If they were lucky the sail would help a lot because the wind normally blew from the Gulf toward the inland. The salt water sprayed James Jr. in the face and it stung, he sure hoped they would find the mouth of the Mississippi real quick.

Dark came and everyone had supper, the barge was traveling along well with just the one big sail. James Jr. fed the horses and gave them water from a barrel on board the barge. The horses didn't seem to like this rolling motion of the barge, they kept shifting their weight from one side to the other. One kept snickering like she didn't like this at all. James Jr. asked his father if they shouldn't try to get the horses to lay down, but his father said they were better standing, if they laid down they might get sick and not be able to get up.

James Jr. didn't sleep well that night. He actually felt afraid, being out on a barge on the water so far from land they couldn't even see it. When he finally fell asleep it was only because he was lulled to sleep by looking at so many stars and the rolling of the barge. Next morning James Jr. awoke to sounds of oars in the water and the stroke commands of Captain Sean as he urged his men to pull heavy on the oars. They were entering the Mississippi and the current was not swift, but the flow was more than just the sail could propel them up the river, so the men were now really earning their keep! Two men on each side would rest for a few minutes and then they would row and the other two would rest.

When the sun broke in the east they had reached a point where the flow seemed slower and the sail was carrying the barge up stream. The men still had to paddle, but not as hard and mainly to keep the boat on course.

Elizabeth Willard and Madeline fixed a really big breakfast for everyone. She said it seemed to her that "All these find hands would need all their strength!" Captain Sean agreed with her and thanked her for her observance of their needs. After breakfast Madeline and Gloria did the dishes so that the men could stay on the oars.

They passed several boats and ships that were going down river and people on each hailed a hello. They passed a few small settlements along the river but the Captain was not pulling into any of them. Then James Jr. spotted a Fort on west bank of river, Captain Sean told him that it was Fort Jackson and that the Confederates had captured it from the Yanks a few months back. Then there was a Fort on the east bank and Captain Sean told him that it was Fort Saint Phillip and the Confederates had also captured it. That the two Forts were guarding New Orleans for the south so that they would have a port city. According to Captain Sean this was very important, because the south needed to have ports where they could bring guns and ammunition and supplies for troops and for the civilians. Captain Sean told James Jr. that New Orleans was a very important city. That it received goods from up river all the way to Illinois and then through the Gulf of Mexico from all over the world.

Late in the afternoon they reached a settlement called West Pointe a la Hache. James Jr. thought that this was a pretty fun name. Captain Sean told them that after supper if they wanted to they could go on shore and stretch their legs and feel some "almost solid ground!" With this he really laughed, but he warned be careful, there are lots of snakes in the area. At supper they all had their daily dose of garlic. The family went together as a whole just at dusk, but really there wasn't anything to see, a few shacks, a large stable of horses and a very small store. They only walked around for about an hour and then headed back to the barge. James Jr. awoke to the sounds of horses the next morning. His first thought was something was wrong with their own horses, but then he realized that the sounds were coming from the river bank. Dawn was breaking and he could make out two teams of two horse and some black men driving them. They were hooking them to the barge with long ropes, this amazed James Jr.

Captain Sean was up at the front of the boat and James Jr. went to see what they were doing and why. Captain Sean told him that the horse teams would pull them up the river into New Orleans, that the current would be too strong for the sails or the men to get the barge up the river. At this point is when it dawned on James Jr. just how many men it took to transport goods from one point to another.

He asked the Captain how long it would be until they reached New Orleans. The Captain answered that if they were lucky, they would be there about four or five in the afternoon. This news really made James Jr. happy, he went into the cabin where Madeline and his mother were cooking breakfast and told them. They both really thought that was great, that if they were lucky, tonight they could bathe and sleep in a good bed. He hugged his mother and slapped Madeline on the back and told her, "Wow, that was a bigun!" He laughed and ran out of the cabin.

After hearing the good news that their journey was almost finished. James Jr. took delight in feeding and cleaning up after the horses, it didn't seem like a chore but something he enjoyed.

During the day as they moved further up stream more and more buildings came into sight along the shore. They were passing more boats that were headed down- stream. James Jr. perched himself up on the top of the wagon where he could see everything. He didn't want to miss any of the sights. After a little bit, Gloria joined him. She made him giggle because she would keep saying, "Wow, look at that!"

She must have said it at least a hundred times.

The horse teams kept pulling the barge, at one point they changed teams. It was amazing that they changed them so quickly. The horses that were now pulling them upstream were not the same ones that had started early that morning.

At about 3 p.m. the horses unhooked and the men went back to the oars. Captain Sean asked James Jr. to carry bucket of water to the men and give them a drink when they wanted it. He did this gladly. When one of the men stopped to drink, James Jr. asked him if he could row. Sure said the man. Well, James Jr. took the handle of the oar and stuck it in the water. When it hit the water it literally lifted him up completely off the seat and he was suspended in mid air holding the handle! Everyone laughed so hard they were not able to row for a few minutes and James Jr. was just up in the air with his feet dangling. He let himself down and he too was laughing.

He did gain great respect for these men and the job they had to do and how strong they really were.

At 4 p.m. they docked at what Frenchman told him was the "Vieux Carre," the old French part of the city. No sooner had they tied to the dock than three Confederate soldiers came on board, two were carrying rifles and one apparently was an officer who had a pistol at his side. The Officer talked to Captain Sean. The other two men looked through everything, they opened the back of the wagon and checked inside. They inspected every one of the boxes that were in the front of the barge. They apparently were satisfied and left.

Now the work really began, they untied the wagon and all the men helping they turned it around and rolled it onto the dock. James Jr. already had the horses on the dock and as soon as the wagon was up on the dock he hitched the horses to it. James Sr. thanked Captain Sean and shook hands with each of the men. Elizabeth Willard was hugged by Captain Sean and so were Madeline and Gloria. He shook James Jr.'s hand and thanked him for all his work in keeping the barge clean of the horse manure and catching the big catfish.

James Sr. took the reins and they started up St. Peters street. They only went two blocks and turned down a narrow street. On each side were brick buildings that were two and three stories high. James Sr. told James Jr. that this was The French Quarter. After two blocks they came to a square and this was a farmers market. They found a place to park the wagon and Elizabeth and the girls went to buy some fresh produce. They were going to James Sr. brother's house but they wanted to bring some food. While they were shopping, James Jr. went exploring.

Everywhere were soldiers all in gray. His ears heard so many different languages that he didn't know what he was hearing. He saw white people, brown people, half brown people, black people, but yet there was an air of festivities everywhere. People were laughing and talking and it seemed they were all enjoying life. Many of the buildings had gates and thru them you could see small gardens with fountains and all kinds of iron work scrolls. Ivy grew on the walls and in some there were large trees that had big white flowers, James Jr. pulled one of the flowers down and smelled it, it had a wonderful sweet aroma.

When he returned to the wagon the ladies were already back and they immediately headed out to the Irish sector of New Orleans. When they entered this sector James Jr. was disappointed. It was what appeared to be run down and small wooden frame houses. Finally they came to a house that was wooden but two stories and it set on a really big lot with a stable behind it, this was their destination.

Chapter 2

Life in New Orleans

No sooner had they entered the driveway to this house than people started to pour out of it! A man that looked a lot like James, Jr.'s dad but older, a woman who was on the plump side, a boy in his teens, and two girls, one about Madeline's age and one about James Jr.'s age.

Mother Elizabeth was out of the wagon and hugging the plump woman and they were laughing and dancing and James Sr., as soon as he had the wagon stopped, was down and hugging and dancing with the man. All the kids just stayed where they were and waited for the commotion to die down, which it finally did. James Sr. and Elizabeth brought the two adults over to the children who had gotten out of the wagon and were just standing there.

James Sr. said, "Children this is my brother Patrick Willard and his wife Mary. This is their children, their son Niall and daughters Melinda and Mary Jane. To the others he said and these are our children, Madeline, James Jr. and Gloria." The children exchanged handshakes all around.

Niall asked James Jr. if he wanted help stabling the horses and James Jr. said, "You bet." So they pulled the wagon around back and unhitched the horses. They then led each horse to a separate stable. Then they put hay and water in the stalls for them. Niall told James Jr. that he was fourteen and that he was going to a school, but that as soon as Louisiana seceded from the union the school had closed. He told James Jr. that Melinda was twelve and that Mary Jane was eight almost nine.

Niall took James Jr. into the house and up the stairs and showed him to a bedroom and told him that this would be his bedroom while they were here. It was a really nice bedroom and there was actually built in bathroom just down the hall with a real bathtub. James Jr. was amazed! He asked Niall what his daddy did to be able to afford a big house like this. Niall answered that his dad was a superintendent for the railroad. He was in charge of making sure the rail lines were in good shape for all the roads between New Orleans and Gulfport, Mississippi and then west to some place halfway to Texas.

James Jr. went down to the wagon and got his clothes out and took them upstairs to the room Niall had told him was his. Madeline and Gloria were in rooms with the other girls. Madeline was with Melinda and Gloria was with Mary Jane. James felt privileged that he had his own room all by himself! Elizabeth and Mary were already fixing supper. Since the bathroom was empty, James Jr. took a bath. The water wasn't hot, but it was warm and James Jr. wondered how it got warm. It really felt good after being on that barge for so many days to actually have soap and warm water to bathe in. The girls started pounding on the door wanting to bathe, so as much as he didn't want to, he got out and dressed and allowed them to take a bath.

Supper was very special. They all sat at this large table in the dining room and they had chicken and mashed potatoes and lots of vegetables that they had picked up at the farmers market. The adults had wine and all the children drank lemonade. Melinda was a real talker, James Jr. didn't think she took a breath during the whole meal. He had to laugh because her and Madeline were both talking to each other and they were talking at the same time and yet they knew what each other was saying, James Jr. and Niall both laughed about it. Gloria and Mary Jane neither said anything, they just listened to the others. Elizabeth and Mary were talking quietly to each other and from what James Jr. could tell they were talking about other relatives in the area. James Sr. and Patrick seemed to be also talking about maybe sisters that were in the area. Then Mary went into the kitchen and brought out cake covered with whipped cream and strawberries. James Jr. was sorry he had eaten so much of the other food, but, he made room for a big piece. It was delicious!

Sleeping that night was wonderful for the whole family. No rolling as on the barge and no sounds of the wagon wheels as they ground their way over the dirt roads.

Monday morning came and James Jr. was up early and completely rested, he felt wonderful. The first thing he did was go out and feed and water the horses.

The horses seemed like they were happy not to have to pull the wagon any where today. They made noises as if to say hello to him. He went into the house and his aunt had a big breakfast ready, his dad and uncle were already at the table and almost finished. James Sr. was going with his brother Patrick to the train depot. They were going to see if there was any job open that James Sr. could take.

James Jr.'s mother and aunt were in the kitchen and seemed to be chatting about all sorts of things. He had no idea where the girls were, so he asked and was told they were still asleep. He was so tempted to go tease them awake, but not knowing his cousins well enough, he thought better of it.

Niall came in and sat down and James Jr. asked him what he was going to do today. Niall said that he was going to go look for a job he felt that his other cousin might have one down at the docks. James Jr. sort of felt left out, because he was only nine (almost ten) and he knew no one would hire him to work, but he was also glad because this would leave him free to explore the city.

James Sr. and his brother Patrick left right after they finished breakfast. James Jr. noticed that his dad was a little apprehensive about having a job that would require him to be somewhere at a certain time, after all for the last two years they had made good money selling the elixir. His father really enjoyed this, putting on a show for the people, which normally only lasted 15 or 20 minutes, not really work, more like fun! One of the things that James Jr. had been doing was practicing doing some of the magic his father did and even though he was only nine (almost ten), he had gotten pretty good at some of the sleight of hand tricks! He always carried a couple of coins and a deck of cards in his pockets just in case he got the chance to show other kids. James Jr. asked his mother if it was alright for him to go look around and she said it was as long as he was back about 12 noon. His aunt Mary told him about a plantation that was only about half mile south of them that was interesting, so that is the way he headed.

After he had gone about two blocks he saw some kids playing in the fields and went over to see if he could join in. There were three boys and six girls, they actually were just kicking a ball around and told him they would love for him to play with them.

Every one introduced themselves, but even though he remembered one of the boys names, that was Sean and one of the girls, her name was Gale. She had long black hair and olive complexion like Spanish. The girl that really stuck in his mind was a girl named Amber. Amber was eight and said she was Irish and that they had come to New Orleans from Knoxville, Kentucky. She had blond hair and large blue eyes that danced the way his mother's did. James Jr. and Amber after kicking the ball for a few minutes, went over and sat under a tree and watched the other kids. James Jr. had never really had a conversation with a girl before. This was a new experience for him and he was really enjoying listening to her. When she talked her eyes danced and her head sort of flipped from side to side. She told him her dad was a supervisor for a freight company that shipped stuff by the railroad and that he had been transferred down here to New Orleans. She liked New Orleans because it didn't get as cold as Knoxville. Now that there was no school, her mother was teaching her at home. Time flew by for James Jr. and all of a sudden he realized that it was near noon, so he told Amber he had enjoyed talking to her. Actually, he had done little talking but a lot of listening and he asked her what her full name was. She said, "Amber Marie O'Brien." James Jr. told her he hoped that they could talk again and she said she hoped so too and back to his aunt and uncle's he went.

Entering the kitchen from the back door he saw that all four girls were already there and sitting at the table and that there was lots of food on it. His mother told him to go wash up and come to lunch. This he did, because playing ball and listening to Amber had really made him hungry.

Aunt Mary asked James Jr. after lunch if he could drive a buggy. He said, "Yes Ma'am." She asked him to hook a horse up to the buggy so they could all go to the market place. James went out to the stalls and found a horse that looked like it was used to pulling a buggy and hitched it to the buggy. It was really a fine looking buggy. It was a carriage because it had two seats facing each other and six adults could sit in it very comfortably. This made for plenty of room for the two ladies and four girls.

James Jr. drove it to the front of the house. When the ladies came out, they all looked very pretty. Madeline was in a frilly green satin dress, Gloria was in her bright pink dress, Melinda was in a blue dress. Mary Jane was in a white dress both mothers were in white dresses. James Jr. gave a wolf whistle at all the ladies and everyone laughed! Elizabeth Willard popped James Jr. on the head with her fan and said, "Young man, show respect to the ladies!" Everyone laughed! James Jr. drove them to the market and needless to say they really drew a lot of looks from people on the streets. James Jr. did have one big laugh, because a young man about eighteen turned to look at them and stepped right into the middle of a mud puddle. All the girls saw it and again everyone had a big laugh. Needless to say the young man was quite embarrassed. The ladies spent a little over an hour shopping. James Jr. stayed with the horse, since he wasn't sure about this horse. Also he wasn't he sure about thieves in New Orleans and he sure didn't want to lose such a fine carriage.

On the way back to his aunt and uncle's they passed a house that was real nice and he saw Amber Marie out in the front yard. He waved and she waved back, he didn't know why, but her wave just sent a real warm feeling through him. Madeline saw it and she immediately started with, "James has a girlfriend, James has a girlfriend!"

Aunt Mary tuned in and said, "James Jr. have you already met that young lady?" He answered her "Yes Ma'am!" Aunt Mary then said, well she is a nice young girl, her father does a lot of business with the railroad, he ships lots of cargo that comes in by boat to other places. Besides they were all Irish Catholics. James Jr. was sure glad to pull the carriage up in front of their house so that this conversation would end. He was so embarrassed that he wasn't sure he would wave the next time, he could feel that his ears were red!

None of the other men got home till after 6 p.m. Niall came in about 6:15 and he was covered with dirt from head to toe. He immediately went up and took a bath and changed clothes. James Sr. and Uncle Patrick came in at 6:30 with good news, well James Jr. thought that it was good news, he was sure his dad was glad. James Sr. had been hired as a foreman for a road crew that went out and checked and fixed the tracks.

He was to start work the next day and he would be getting a good salary. Elizabeth said that she was glad he had two pair of clean overalls and some good work shoes. Niall came down and was all washed up and clean clothed. He said that his cousin had gotten him a job unloading ships at the dock, but boy it sure was hard work. The pay was decent and he was glad that he had a cousin with connections. James Sr. asked him which cousin and he told him that it was the son of James Sr.'s sister, Rebecca O'Malley and John

O'Malley, that the boys name was Eoin and that he was 20. He had been working on the docks for several years and was now a checker, a person that checked the manifest to make sure everything arrived as it was supposed to.

Niall told his father Patrick that Eoin was actually thinking about shipping out on one of the sea going cargo ships because he didn't want to join the Confederate army. Patrick told Niall to tell Eoin not to do it too fast because he felt that there probably wouldn't be a real war, that the north would quit trying to make the states stay part of the union, after all they were all free independent states and had joined the union on their own. So there was no reason why they had to stay. James Sr. told Patrick that he wasn't really sure about that, from what they had seen on the trip, people on both sides seemed to have very strong feelings about this whole mess. James Sr. and Patrick both agreed that in many ways it was really stupid. That if a war came, it would be a real bad one. Niall said that was what Eoin had said he was afraid of because of what he had heard the soldiers talking about!

Aunt Mary told Niall to tell Eoin that they were all invited to Sunday dinner and to please come, that they were also inviting the other two sisters and husbands and their children so it should be quite a reunion. James Jr. hoped there would be at least one other boy his age. James Jr. had to admit that actually he really looked forward to meeting all his relatives, especially if they were as nice as these were.

Sunday came and the house filled with relatives. James Jr. didn't know there were so many people related to him. In Brooklyn they only had a couple of his father's first cousins who where kin. Here in New Orleans there was his fathers brother and his two sisters with their husbands and kids. He counted and there were 14 kids all together that were his first cousins, thankful there were two other boys his age, Arthur O'Malley and Bubba Burke. That Sunday James Jr. got acquainted with both of them. Arthur preferred to be called Art and was redheaded and had lots of freckles. There was no way James Jr. could remember all the other names. He was sure that in the future when he visited with them he would learn them.

On Monday he had pretty much settled in to his routine of waking up, feeding and watering the horses and then eating breakfast. Today he was continuing to explore the area around them. He wanted to see it all and wanted to find the things that were fun.

He left with full intentions of finally going to the plantation that was near, but when he got to the field where he had met Amber, well there she was sitting under the tree. He went over and sat down beside her and she asked what he was doing. He told her he wanted to go see the plantation, she got up and said, "Well lets go!"

What a day they had. It seemed that almost anything James Jr. said Amber thought was funny and her bubbling laugh just kept him going. He never dreamed he could have so much fun with a girl! Amber convinced him to cut a stalk of sugar cane and showed him how to peel it with his knife. They chewed on it and it was sweet. After the sugar was gone they would spit out the bulk and take another bite.

There were fields and fields of cotton, but it was still in the bulb stage and hadn't bloomed into cotton yet and there were also fields and fields of sugar cane. In all the fields there were Negroes working. In several places they saw men on horses. In one field there were about 30 people working and they were singing a song. Amber and James sat down on the road and listened to them, they were too far away for them to hear the words, but they could sure hear the harmony and they totally enjoyed it. About 4 p.m. they started back and James Jr. walked Amber all the way to her house. When she got inside her gate he thanked her for spending the day with him. She told him that it was really fun.

When he got back to his aunt and uncle's their black housekeeper was there and she sort of kidded him about where he had been all day. They called her Aunt G, she was a free black that worked for them for wages. She was a large woman and had a strange voice. She spoke with a funny dialect, but she was a good woman.

She lived with a free black man who worked on the docks and they had seven children. She was always happy person and liked to kid, especially James Jr. She had taken a liking to him and would tell him that she was going to take him home with her and marry him to her daughter. Then she would laugh and laugh! This was pretty risky kidding in the 1860s but Aunt G wasn't a lady to be "proper"! James Jr. and Amber had a lot of adventures together that summer.

The summer flew by for James Jr. much too fast, for he enjoyed everyday with Amber. September 1st the Ursline Nuns opened a school. It was for all kids that were Catholic and from the ages of six to twelve. Well, Amber and James Jr., Madeline, Gloria and several other kids in the family had to go, this included his two cousins Art and Bryan and most of their sisters.

This was truly a new experience for all the children, because the sisters were real hard and they demanded that the children learn. If you got out of hand or made a joke about something, the sister would rap you across the knuckles with a ruler.

There was no cutting up in these classes. The classes were arithmetic, geography, English and Latin. James Jr. Art and Bryan had a hard time with the Latin but the girls seemed to catch on to it real easy. The girls had a hard time with the arithmetic, the boys caught on to it real easy. None of the children knew what to expect from this schooling, but their parents made them all go. There was one sister that did have a sense of humor and she was Sister Magdalene and she taught geography.

She had an amazing way of acting out what the people in each of the countries that they studied wore and talked. Apparently Sister Magdalene spoke a bunch of languages. She spoke French, English, Gaelic, German and Latin or Italian. James Jr. could never tell the difference between Latin and Italian. They all attended school without any breaks until Christmas. Dec. 20, 1861 the nuns told them that the school would be closed until January 5th, 1862. There was a large cheer from the kids, they were all ready for a break. They felt like their heads were so full of new things they thought they would pop! They all looked forward to having a good Christmas.

Some food items were becoming hard to get and some people were not getting all the food they needed. The north had ships in the Gulf of Mexico and were stopping a lot of the cargo ships. Sister Magdalene had told them this was called a blockade. Because of the blockade Niall and Eoin had not been working a lot because there were few ships to unload. The ships that did run the blockade were charging more for the products they brought, but so much of it was guns that immediately went to the railroad and were shipped east.

News of the war was not good for the South, it seems that they were losing every battle that they were in. When word reached New Orleans it seemed to cause a lot of gloom with the people there. The Willards were really a neutral family, being Irish they had so many friends on both sides. They were actually against slavery but they also felt that the independent states had the right to be what they wanted. In that way they had feelings for the South. James Jr. had made many friends among the local people and some of them were down right fanatical about their belief that the South was right. James Jr. agreed with them, but he wasn't real sure.

Patrick Willard had insisted that his brother and family stay with them because of the war. James Sr. agreed because of the uncertain situation. They both felt that the families were better off all being together. This decision would prove to be great planning with developments that were to happen in the future.

On Christmas day, 1861 all the sisters and their families came and it was quite a feast day. James Jr., Bryan and Art enjoyed the day. They went over to Amber's house and got her and they all went walking to the plantation. The plantation was also having a feast. There were tables out under the big trees and they could see all the black people sitting around and eating. James Jr. noticed that these people were really dressed well, unlike some he had seen in Mississippi.

The owner of the plantation saw the kids and sent one of the blacks over to get them, this scared them because they were afraid they were in trouble for being on his land. He was a Frenchman and spoke with a heavy accent, but he was a warm person who made them feel at home. He introduced them to his wife and two daughters who were in their middle teens and very pretty. One of the girls was Gale that James Jr. had seen in the field that first day. She was older than he had thought and now in her finest dress you could tell she was at least sixteen and really a very pretty girl, long black hair and very pretty dark eyes. They were offered food, but all declined because they had eaten so much at dinner. They all did take a glass of lemonade.

The black people started singing and everyone seemed so happy. There was no way from the way these people acted that you could tell that they were slaves. Actually James Jr. thought that the Frenchman's wife was maybe not all white. Her coloring was sort of tan, maybe you would say yellow, both daughters were lighter skinned than she was. Both girls had really black hair. When the wife spoke she had a mellow voice that had a lilt to it with a French accent. James Jr. loved to hear her speak and when she sang she sang beautifully.

They had felt so welcomed by the entire group of people that they really hated to leave. It was starting to get dark and so they all thanked everyone for their hospitality and headed back to their uncle's house. As they were leaving the Frenchman told Amber she had one of the prettiest smiles he had seen in a long time. This really made her happy. James Jr. walked her all the way home. After Bryan and Art stopped at the uncle's he continued with Amber alone.

When they were about half way to her house she surprised him by taking hold of his hand and holding it while they walked. When they got to her gate, she reached up and kissed him on the cheek. He immediately turned red and she ran into the house.

This would truly be a Christmas day that James Jr. would remember all his life!

School resumed in January but it had a very different feeling! James Jr. felt a lot of tension from the nuns. It was a feeling of impending doom! Being almost ten he did not understand the feelings he was having or was receiving from the nuns. There was a lot of talk in the classes about the war and how it was proceeding. By March 1862 food was starting to get hard to buy. It seemed that the northerners were now blocking the Mississippi up river and down river and ships and barges were not getting through.

Also the train traffic was becoming very limited, only trains from the west or from Birmingham were making it, and a lot of times union soldiers would even stop the trains from Birmingham. Every train now had details of Confederate soldiers assigned to it and when the trains from the east arrived they would have bullet holes in the cars where union soldiers had shot at them. On Easter Sunday, April 1862 word came that Flag Officer David Farragut had attacked Fort Jackson and Fort St. Phillip.

The whole family had gathered at Uncle Patrick's house for Easter Sunday dinner and there was a lot of conversation as to what was going to happen! No one really knew what the outcome would be or how it would affect them. One thing James Jr. could sense was that there was a lot of fear. It would not take long for them to all find out. On April 24th General Mansfield Lovell left New Orleans with his 4000 Confederate soldiers, leaving the city defenseless.

That night New Orleans became a hellhole! Mobs were everywhere stealing what they could. James Sr. and Patrick set up a barricade at the front of the house and when a mob started toward the house they fired rifle shots over the mobs heads. This worked and the mob left. All the Irishmen got their rifles and set a barricade at entrance to the Irish sector. When another mob started that way, they fired shots over their heads and immediately the mob headed in a different direction.

The ladies and children went to the carriage house and blocked the door. Both women had pistols and told the children to all be quiet. The carriage house was at the back of the property, so if a mob did break thru they would be behind the house and the men would have time to get back there and try to help. Needless to say,

James Jr. and all the kids were afraid. It was really a frightening night and they were all glad when the sun came up. The mobs seemed to become quiet when the sun came up. James Jr. figured they had tired themselves out. The ladies went to the kitchen of the house and made lots of coffee and a really big breakfast so that anyone who came could eat.

Uncle Patrick had all the Irishmen come to his house and they organized a patrol that would guard the Irish sector of the city. Since the Irish sector was the last part of the city before the plantation, the Frenchman came and brought some of his black men with rifles to help out. They worked with the Irish so that the area would be safe for all the women and children. James Jr. thought that there was something funny about seeing the black men with rifles. According to the Union these men were suppose to be slaves. Well, it sure didn't look like it! Of course he knew that the Frenchman treated his people different than most slave owners and that these men would do anything that the Frenchman asked.

Four days later the mayor of New Orleans officially turned over the city to the Federal forces. Now New Orleans belongs to the United States again, but by no means does the state of Louisiana. There will be many battles to come in Louisiana before the war is over. In just a few short days life in New Orleans will change for the worse and it will affect the lives of all the Irish for many years to come. Actually it affects every person that lives in New Orleans for years to come.

Chapter 3

Move to Houma, Louisiana

On April 29, 1862 General Benjamin Butler arrives in New Orleans to take control. He post the American flag on the custom house and on the City Hall. This angers many of the southern citizens and causes a lot of sorrow. But Gen. Butler and his troops are not people to be messed with. Over the next few days Butler's troops shoot several men and hang a few others. Butler wrote that the city was basically being ruled by mobs and it was his duty to restore law and order.

James Jr. and his friends now were afraid to do very many things. As children they could go places that a lot of adults would have a hard time going. Union soldiers were totally different from the southern soldiers. The northern soldiers under General Butler did about anything they pleased. Actually the northern soldiers were little more than thieves in uniform. They looted many of the southern homes. James Jr., Bryan and Art saw a group of them looting a fine home. They had a wagon and were carrying all the paintings and silverware and dishes out of the home. They did this to any home where the owners had left. Many fine paintings ended up in northern homes that were stolen from New Orleans homes. Ladies were no longer safe to walk the streets in New Orleans. Gen Butler's men treated them all as if they were all ladies of the evening and would not allow them to pass on the side walk. To get around them the ladies would have to go into the street which many times was so muddy it was hard to walk . James Jr.'s mother, sisters and aunts no longer went to the market. This job was now the men's job and the women all stayed at the house.

Soldiers took over the Frenchman's plantation and used it as a barracks. He was arrested and put in prison. His wife and daughters were moved into one of the slave houses. If this war was really about freeing the slaves it didn't happen on the Frenchman's plantation. The soldiers made the slaves wait on them hand and foot. Even made them shine their boots, several of the black women were made to be "women" for the soldiers! Gale told Madeline that the only thing protecting her was that one of the slave women told the solders that she had a disease, so they were leaving her and her sister alone, because the solders were afraid they would catch it.

Gen. Butler called James Jr.'s uncle Patrick to see him about the railroad. There was going to be very little that the railroad could do for some time to come, because most of the lines were in southern hands. There were to be no trains going east from New Orleans, only west and those would be restricted. This meant that James Sr. was going to have to make a choice. There was no work for him or his crew out of New Orleans, but they could move to Houma, Louisiana and there work on the railroad from Houma to Kinder, Louisiana.

Uncle Patrick made the arrangements and James Sr. took Patrick's wife, Mary and children with them to Houma. They actually loaded the wagon on to a flat car and the horses and they all went by train to Houma.

Leaving New Orleans was hard on James Jr., Madeline and Gloria, as they all had grown to love this city and the church and school. But the hardest of all for James Jr. was saying good bye to

Amber. She had been a lot more to him than a friend. It would be the last time he would see her. She told him her father was actually going to leave and go back to Kentucky in the next few days. She grabbed James Jr. and held him tight, then she ran into her house crying. James Jr. would remember that hug the rest of his life and the sight of her blond hair bouncing as she ran into the house. He had never felt so sad about leaving someone in his whole life. He wondered if he would ever meet a girl like her again?

Houma, Louisiana was totally different from New Orleans. It was a fishing village and the people there were mostly French, except for the priest and nuns, who were all Irish. They went out of their way to make the Willards feel like this was home. There were only 30 union soldiers there and the captain that was in command was a very nice person. He kept all his men very well behaved. The soldiers only concern was keeping the railroad there running and they did not try to put any pressure on the civilians in any way. When the train would leave for Kinder, Louisiana, ten of the solders would ride along to make sure that it made it okay.

Occasionally some Confederate soldiers would attack the train, but they were mainly looking for food or ammunition and really did not want to hurt anyone.

James Sr. and Niall Willard and Eoin O'Malley went each day to check the tracks to make sure they were in working order. Niall and Eoin had come with them to Houma and James Sr. and put them on his crew. Several men had left when the Yankees came so he needed them and they needed to be away from New Orleans. Mary Willard and daughters Melinda and Mary Jane had also come with them as Uncle Patrick did not want them in New Orleans.

Patrick Willard would come over to Houma on the weekends then go back on Sunday night. He brought stories of how bad it really was in New Orleans, but he was safe because of his railroad job. This was pretty much the life of the Willards for the next three years. All the kids went to school with the nuns and daily life was pretty normal.

James Jr. made friends with some of the kids there and would for the rest of his life feel that this was sort of home to him. His friends all spoke with accents and he started to learn Cajun. He actually became so fluent that most thought he was a Cajun and he was treated as one of them.

One of his friends, Norb Newton, who was Cajun, James had no idea where the name came from. Norb's father owned a fishing boat, when James Jr. was 12 he went with Norb and his father shrimping! At the end of the day, James Jr. had a real appreciation for the work this involved! They brought back about a ton of shrimp and his hands were blistered and his back ached! But then the Newton's invited the whole family over for shrimp and boy did they all eat a lot.

Norb's father had this really big black kettle, he had it over a big fire and they would drop in a big basket of shrimp. In just a couple of minutes the shrimp would float to the top all pink and ready to peel and eat. Aunt Mary and James' Jr.'s mother made Irish potato salad and brought it and one of the other ladies brought a big pot of "dirty" rice and boy was it all good! James Jr. really liked the "dirty" rice. It is boiled rice, with spices and sausage added, and boy you can make a meal out of just that. It is so good! No one can eat as much as two twelve year old boys and Norb and James Jr. really piled it in that night! These two boys would be friends for the rest of their lives. Norb and all the other boys in Houma called James Jr. "J.J." and that would pretty much stick with him from there on. Madeline and Gloria picked up on it and they also called him "J.J." his mother also liked it and she called him that except when she was mad at him. Then she would scream his full name, but lucky for him she wasn't the type to be mad very often and he usually had done something wrong when she was.

James Sr. and Elizabeth were doing something that sort of surprised the kids. They were learning more magic and practicing it. James Jr.'s aunt Mary had taught them a trick that she had learned from her grandmother. It was called the "Spirit Cabinet" or the

"Ghost Cabinet". This was a fun act and James Sr. said that when the war was over that they were not going to do manual labor any longer. They were going back to having fun in life!

One Saturday night they invited a bunch of their Houma friends to the church hall and to the surprise of all present James Sr. and Elizabeth Willard put a magic show on for them. The captain of the army came and a bunch of his soldiers came and they all really enjoyed it. James Jr. was astounded at how much magic his father could now do! They went non-stop for an hour and a half and closed the show with the "spirit cabinet". It was the first time they had performed this in public. Aunt Mary assisted with the show and she was sort of out of her element, even though she had taught the cabinet to them, her weight was a little awkward on the stage. Her good sense of humor made a lot of people laugh and she did enjoy it and James Sr. would poke a little fun at her.

That night when they had all got back home another surprising thing happened! James Sr. came to J.J. and asked him if he thought that his mother and him were good enough to go on the stage or to perform on a riverboat when the war was over. This caught J.J. by surprise, because his father was actually asking him if he thought they were good enough. James Jr. told his father that they certainly were and he hoped they all could leave and start acting soon. He also asked his father if he would teach him all the magic. James Sr. told him that he wanted to teach him, Madeline and Gloria all that they knew so if something happened they could fill in for them! From then on all three kids would start learning the different acts and even practicing with their mom and dad. James Jr. without telling anyone would practice sometimes for hours doing certain tricks with cards or coins in front of a mirror. He became quite proficient at it by the time he was fourteen; he, Madeline and Gloria even put together their own magic act, which was really just playing, but even at that they all worked out some routines that their mother and father knew nothing about. Sometime in the future they would surprise their parents with their own show!

Chapter 4

Return to New Orleans

Some things happened in the year 1863 that both affected the Willard families and the outcome of the Civil War! In August word came that two of the first cousins of James Sr. and Patrick had been killed in the riots of New York over the draft. Many Irish had rioted over the unfairness of the act and that Yankee soldiers had fired on them, killing the two cousins. Rioting continued for several days and Boss Tweed stepped in an offered a compromise that had the effect of stopping the riots. It took several months but his proposal got approval and every person that was drafted from New York City received $777.00. This in most cases was at least 3 years salary. The other part of this was a lot closer to the Willards—Eoin O'Malley, J.J.'s first cousin left in April to become a sailor with a private ship which was a cargo ship flying under the U.S. flag. The captain of this ship had known Eoin when he was the freight checker in New Orleans and offered him a job. This would keep Eoin from being drafted! They would never see Eoin again.

During 1863 and 1864 the north was not making many friends

of the American people. In Kansas a misguided Federal commander at Kansas City ordered civilians out of their homes and burned the homes and the crops leaving thousands of people homeless. This action caused bad feelings that lasted for years. The northern soldiers also burned Jefferson Davis's plantation to the ground. This action even made many who supported the north mad, as it was seen as a revengeful action against a great man. On top of all that grief Jefferson Davis's young son died from a fall at the capital. It seemed more grief than one man should have to bear.

In the early part of 1865 most of the Confederates were cleared out of Louisiana and the State was in away getting back to normal! President Lincoln was giving pardons to all that signed a paper of allegiance to the union. Uncle Patrick came and took ever one back on the train to New Orleans. He said it was now safe and that General Butler had been assigned to the eastern front. He was such a stupid man that he should never have been made a general or put in charge of anything more than a stable! The harm he caused in New Orleans would last for years!

J.J. hated moving back to New Orleans and leaving all the friends that he had made in Houma, but what is a 14 year old to do? When he told Norm and all the others goodbye he knew they would be friends for life! He had developed a love for Houma that would last all his life. Little did he know how much learning to speak Cajun would help him in the years ahead.

New Orleans was certainly not the city they had left! Yankee soldiers still patrolled the city. There were fewer people here than there had been and worst thing of all Amber wasn't here and the Frenchman's plantation had been totally burned down! One of his friends told him that the Frenchman and his wife and daughters had escaped to the islands in the Caribbean and were safe! J.J. was glad but he wondered what had happened to the black people that lived there, so he went to check. He found their quarters untouched and several of them living there. They were doing okay, and were raising food. They had also hidden some cattle and hogs from the union soldiers. Everyone of them told J.J. that they really hoped that the Frenchman would return! One told him that the swamp was a place that most of the union solders didn't go and that there were a lot of people hiding out there. James M. Willard Sr. and Patrick S. Willard were still working on the railroad but now Patrick was in charge of the entire "working" part of the railroad and he put James Sr. in charge of coordinating all freight shipments.

Two weeks after they had returned James Sr. came home just bursting with excitement, he had gone to one of the theaters in New Orleans and they had hired him and Elizabeth to do shows at night. They were to start Friday night and if the people liked their show they would work every Friday, Saturday and sometimes on Sundays doing one show a night! This would be a big boost in the family income and would also help out Uncle Patrick. The two brothers had also been helping all the other Irish that they could, either with money or food. The Irish community had pretty much stayed together helping each other.

Elizabeth and Aunt Mary immediately started making costumes and at night they would rehearse. It was decided that Madeline would help on stage as she was now actually becoming a very attractive young lady. James Sr. would also leave early from work and go post flyers about them appearing at the theater. He always left with ten of them and a hammer and tacks to stick them where ever he could. James Sr. had made a deal with the theater that he would make 40% of the ticket sales and the theater would make 60% and that he would do most of the adverting. J.J. and Gloria sort of felt left out but, they both knew that this would really help the family.

Opening night came and the family was sort of disappointed because there were only about 50 people in the audience, at 25 cents per person that wasn't much money, only $5.00 for the Willards. James Sr. was excited because those that were there came and told him how much they enjoyed the show. They said they were going to tell all their friends how good it was! This excited James Sr. to no end. He knew that it takes time for audiences to develop, not like selling the magic elixir where the drums would bring a crowd. Well not always, but when they started playing the mandolin and violin then the crowds came. Gloria had been learning the violin, but, honestly, she wasn't too good at it yet, but hey she was only ten.

Saturday night was much better, there were at least 100 people in the audience and even several soldiers. This surprised them, for the soldiers were not allowed to go a lot of places. The Sunday show was about like Friday but James Sr. was happy that they had made a whole $14.50 for the three shows and he was happier than J.J. had seen him in years. He was performing again! During the following week James Sr., Elizabeth, Madeline and Aunt Mary worked on some new tricks. James Sr. worked in the barn for two nights very late. Thursday he brought in a box that was all painted, it looked almost like a coffin it was painted real bright reds and greens and blues with lots of gold designs. J.J. wondered where his dad got the gold paint. Thursday night they got Gloria and she worked with them and on Friday night, they introduced a new illusion. James Sr. called it "Sawing the Woman in Half"!

Now, J.J. was the only member of the family that wasn't performing. The new trick sawing the woman in half, was simple.

Gloria was already in the box under a dummy shelf and when Madeline was suppose to stick her feet out, Gloria would stick hers out. They had to do was make sure Gloria was wearing the same shoes and the same socks. It was an instant success and they would use the trick for many years to come.

✳✳✳

Saturday night was a real surprise, the theater was completely full, every seat all 350 were full and there was standing room only! James Sr. seemed to float on air, he probably did the greatest performance of his life, it was flawless. J.J. watched from the side of the stage as his family performed. People in the audience applauded every time his father did something new, at the end of the performance they stood and hollered, "More! More! More!" This

was the moment that J.J. realized that he was going to become a magician!

Sunday the show was packed again and when it was all over James Sr. and Elizabeth were so excited that they actually did an Irish jig on the stage, something that the kids had seldom seen in the last 7 years, everyone was excited as they had made over $60.00 Union. This was twice what James Sr. was making on the railroad. On the way home, James Sr. insisted that they go by the church and he gave the father $6.00 and told him that there would be more every week. No one knew about these donations except the family and James Sr. true to his word stopped by the church and gave the priest 10% of what ever they made every week.

J.J. started working harder on his magic skills, he actually never let any of the family know except for Gloria. She was his straw boss, his supervisor, his critic, she was very stern and if she caught him doing something she told him straight. He was pleased that she was so honest because it really helped him get better. J.J. went to the library every chance he got and read and reread any thing he could find that was about magic and about magic tricks. He found one book that was written by a French magician, a Mr. Houdin, that detailed many tricks. When he would leave the library he would hide the book so no one else could find it. One trick that he read and read several times, then wrote down every move. When he got home he went to the barn and started constructing the trick. Once he had it finished he did not take it into the house, not until he had practiced it at least a 1000 times and thought he was ready for Gloria to see it and tell him what she thought! What she thought was that it was the most fantastic thing she had ever seen. He went to his mother (Elizabeth) and asked her if she would make him a suit, but, that he wanted it made a certain way and that she was not to tell his father that she was doing it.

Elizabeth was a terrific mother and when James had described what he wanted, she made it in total secret; only she and he knew. Actually she was so amazed that such a young man could be so mature in having a coat and trousers made and knew exactly what he wanted. One day when they were alone and he was trying it on, she took a good look at her only son and realized that she had missed it, he actually had become a young man! He was already a good two inches taller than his father!

In 1866 on his birthday, J.J. asked his father if it would be alright if on this special night if he could perform a few tricks for the audience before the family started the performance. James Sr. was really hesitant, but Elizabeth told him to let the boy do it, he might be surprised.

J.J. was so nervous that he thought he would throw up before he went out, but Madeline and Gloria kept telling him he would be great. His mother came to him and gave him one of her special hugs that made him feel good. James Sr. even came over and told him to just relax and enjoy the moment, that this memory would last him all his life, he then gave him a big hug.

J.J. was careful when he went out not to do anything that his father was doing and that moment he stepped out and all of a sudden people started applauding he knew he was where he wanted to be. There were already 200 or so people there and the first thing he did was a card trick he had learned from his dad years ago. On one side of the stage he saw his mom and dad and the other side were his two sisters. When he looked into the audience there were his Uncle Patrick, Aunt Mary and their daughters sitting right on the front row, plus there was his fathers sisters and their husbands and kids on the next row. Well, what the heck, he had a captive audience that would love him no matter if he messed up or not. After two card tricks, two coin tricks he felt like he had them in his palm, so it was time for the big trick.

He went down into the audience and got two young ladies that he didn't know and had them come up on stage with him, he had one stand on his left and one on his right, then, all of a sudden he was holding a small bird cage in his hand. No one could figure out where it came from, not, even his father, but there it was! Like a real pro he then asked one lady to hold the top and bottom and one to hold each side, then he stopped and said, "Wait, a bird cage should have a bird!" He produced from nowhere a canary, bright yellow, and placed it in the cage! The audience was dead silent, they had never seen such a smooth young magician before, skilled far beyond his 14 years! Again he placed the ladies hands on the top, bottom and two sides of the bird cage, then with humor, he asked each of the ladies if they had another hand so they could cover the entire bird cage. The audience loved this and everyone laughed, just as they did the bird cage disappeared right before their eyes. There was a sound of everyone catching their breath at the same time! Both ladies looked totally shocked and their hands were still there holding thin air. He then asked them to look under his coat, as he opened it for them to see. There was no bird cage to be found. He then walked each lady back to her seat and from nowhere produced a rose for each. He went back up on stage and took a bow and left! The audience was standing and hollering for "More! More! More!" and the applause was like thunder.

James Michael Willard Jr. remembered that night for the rest of his life! The audience that saw it also remembered it, for they had seen the "Flying Bird Cage" for the first time ever in the Americas. He quickly removed the canary as soon as he got back stage, while the audience was still hollering more. His dad told him, "Go out and give them one more!" Into his coat he quickly loaded six doves and went back out and from white handkerchiefs right in front of the audience he produced the six white doves. The audience was silent. All you could hear was deep breaths being taken every time a new dove appeared. He was about to leave when his father came out, hugged him and took his hand and they both bowed to the audience. Then James Sr. told the audience, "This is my son and today is his 14th birthday and this was his first stage appearance but I assure you it shall not be his last! Now, the rest of James Michael Willard Jr.'s family will entertain you and we hope you enjoy the show!"

The audience applauded them off the stage, and James Sr. took

J.J. by the shoulders and looked him right in the eye and said, "Son, I am so proud of you that I think I am going to bust my buttons." After the show, the entire family went out for a bow and the audience gave them a standing ovation. It was lucky it was a Saturday night, because when he went to bed, there was no way J.J. could sleep. He kept hearing the audience and going over every single thing that went on that night, he actually heard a rooster crow before he finally fell asleep.

He finally awoke about 12:30 p.m. and when he went down stairs everyone was at the dinner table for Sunday dinner. Uncle Patrick was the first to speak. "Well, gee, look a star has appeared!" Aunt Mary then chimed in and said, "Aw, yes an entertainer that works at night and sleeps during the day, it must be a star!" Every one laughed and even J.J. laughed.

From then on, J.J. would perform before the family and he was constantly adding new tricks that he learned from the book. He had practiced and practiced and never did them until Gloria said he was ready, his timing was so good that you could set your watch by him, always exactly ten minutes, then one more for a curtain call. James Sr. started giving him 10% of what the family made, his explanation to J.J. was simple, I give the Lord 10% of what we make and you are my son and you should receive the same as I give the lord. The money helped J.J. buy things to invent new tricks. His storehouse of tricks grew and grew.

New Orleans in 1867 wasn't a really nice place! Military was still ruling and controlling the government. Many men had come to Louisiana with bags full of money to buy what they could from confiscated government lands. These men were called carpetbaggers. Shipping had returned and the railroad was running at full steam. Uncle Patrick's job was pretty hectic and he now employed both of his sister's husbands and a couple of the nephews. James Sr. was still with the railroad, but he was becoming restless and was wanting to be a magician full time. James Jr. (J.J.) was performing with the family doing his magic before the show each night.

J.J. had noticed something about Madeline, she was acting sort of funny and he noticed that she slipped out of the theater on Friday and Saturday nights before the family did and although she was always home when they got there, he sort of thought she was acting strange!

Gloria had now grown into a lovely young lady and she was helping more and more on the stage. Before when she was selling the elixir the audience seemed to love her. She now could do anything that Madeline could. Since she was such a perfectionist some things she did better.

At Sunday dinner with all the family there in May of 1867 a knock came at the door and Madeline rushed to answer it, there stood a tall blonde headed captain in the union army, Madeline had him come in and she introduced him to every one as Captain Forrest Clark Edwards from Pennsylvania. J.J. shook his hand and he immediately knew why Madeline had been leaving the theater early. Well Forrest had Sunday dinner with the entire family. After dinner James Sr. and he went out on the porch and had a long talk. James Sr. re-entered without Forrest and announced to the family that he had given his consent to the captain to court Madeline. Madeline went over and hugged her father. Elizabeth immediately went and hugged Madeline her oldest daughter and made a remark. "Well, Young Lady, are you trying to make your mother an old woman?" It was said with Elizabeth's normal Irish humor and everyone laughed.

Over the next few months J.J. got to know Forrest very well and grew to like him a lot. Forrest told him that his family had a large farm and that he planned to return there just as soon as his enlistment was over, which would be in 1868. Captain Forrest had purchased about a dozen horses from some of the Cajuns and he was taking them back to breed horses on the farm and to sell them to the army. He and J.J. spent hours in the stables and J.J. showed him some things about horses that the captain didn't know. In September Captain Forrest received new orders to go to Washington, D.C. so everything got into a rush. Madeline and Forrest were married in the Catholic church with all of the families there. J.J. was Forrest's best man and he stood there so very proud for Madeline, she looked so beautiful! The next day they left for the capital and a new life together. Washington wasn't going to be bad for Madeline because several of the Willards lived there. Forrest had arranged for a ship to carry his horses to Wilmington, Delaware and from there his father would come get them and carry them to the farm. J.J. had helped Forrest take them to the docks along with about four soldiers.

At the train station there were many tears, Elizabeth cried, Gloria cried, Madeline cried and Aunt Mary cried. J.J. knew better than to make fun of his mother's tears. He had a fun teasing Gloria, he even saw tears in James Sr.'s eyes. They all stood silently as the train pulled out and everyone just kept waving until it was out of sight. They all knew that their life had changed forever!

Aunt Mary returned to helping on the stage, but, mostly from the side of the stage and Gloria now with her mother did all the illusions. The audiences were still very good; they only would have sold out houses on Saturday nights. In October James Sr. told his brother Patrick that he was going to quit the railroad and just perform full time. Patrick hated to see his brother go because he was one that he knew he could trust. Patrick knew his brother would be happier just performing and the family now had plenty of money in reserve, plus all the family was working. January 1868 brought a brand new surprise to the Willard family and to J.J.!

The second Saturday night in January a well dressed gentleman came back stage and told J.J. that he was Captain James Reed. That he would like for J.J. to be his main performer on his boat the *Mississippi Queen* that was running between New Orleans and Evansville, Indiana. Captain James Reed was not at all what you would expect a riverboat captain to be. He was tall, about 6 feet; he was young, only in his early 30s. He explained to J.J. that he had seen his performances for 3 times and each time was totally amazed. His boat was brand new and that he had several northern backers who had financed building the boat and that they had two missions, one to carry passengers so they had put in a gambling room and a small theater. Their second task was to carry freight both ways, supplies that came into New Orleans from abroad and then to carry farm products from the northern states to be loaded on ships to be taken to France and England. The *Mississippi Queen* had 20 cabins, which in the 1860s was elaborate. Most riverboats would only have two or three sometimes four. They also had a large room for steerage passengers that could hold up to 100 people, but not very comfortably. Before leaving, Captain James Reed, told J.J., "By the Way, your Salary will be $100.00 per week and you will have top billing and have your own cabin!" James Jr. told him that he would come down and look at the boat the next day and would give the captain an answer then.

James Sr. and James Jr. had a very long conversation that night. They talked till the wee hours of the morning. James Sr. actually was very supportive of J.J. and told him that it was his decision. James Sr. pointed out to J.J. that he was just fifteen (going on sixteen) that he had already finished his higher education at the catholic school. The only other thing was for him to go to college, which, the family would certainly support him in doing so if that was what he decided. James Sr. also told him, that a $100.00 a week at fifteen was a tremendous challenge, but, he knew J.J. knew how to take care of his money. He had proven that over and over. On riverboats there were a lot of thieves and that J.J. would have to be careful. They finally went to bed about 3 a.m. J.J. went to sleep thinking about how much of a challenge it would be and appreciating his father's support. They had not said anything to his mother. At 8 a.m. J.J. awoke, took a bath and dressed and went down for breakfast, his whole body seemed to be alive, he was as rested as if he had slept for eight hours.

After breakfast, when the ladies had finished with the dishes, J.J. got his mother and asked her to go with him for a ride in the carriage, he also asked Gloria to come along with them. Elizabeth asked J.J. were they were going and he just said, "Mother, you will see!" Gloria said, "Well, are we not being a mysterious person this morning!" Then her and her mother both laughed with that wonderful sound, hearing their laughter J.J. knew that was something he was truly going to miss. Then Gloria said, "Mother do you think J.J. is going to surprise us with a new girlfriend, like Madeline did when she brought Forrest home?" They both laughed again. When the carriage pulled up by the *Mississippi Queen* both of the women looked at each other with curiosity in their eyes. He helped them down and said, lets go on board and see this boat. Just as they crossed the gang plank to the boat Captain James Reed appeared and bowed to the ladies and said, "James, I am so glad that you came and brought your sister and mother!" He then kissed both ladies hands like a real southern gentleman. They both giggled. "Come let me show you my boat!" During the tour, J.J. pulled the captain aside and asked him not to indicate anything about him performing on the boat, Captain Reed agreed.

When he took them into the theater he told them that this was the dining room and the show room and that they had a band that played on the stage, there were about 30 tables and each had seating for four and maybe a couple that would seat eight to ten. The captain then took them to a very nice cabin and told them that the cabin was for the featured performer. J.J. looked at the cabin and realized that it was bigger than the room he had at his Uncle Patrick's.

Captain Reed then asked if they would like to see the wheelhouse and Gloria was ready. Elizabeth said she would just like to rest a few minutes. J.J. took this opportunity to sit with his mother on the second deck in a couple of deck chairs. He asked her what she thought about the boat. She said it was the nicest boat she had ever seen. That is when he told her that the Captain had asked him to be his featured entertainer, her mouth fell open and she was speechless. Then he told her how much they were going to pay him and again she was speechless. She stood up, opened her arms to him and he went to her and she gave him the longest hug she had given him in many years. When they parted she was crying, but she

immediately told him they were happy tears for him.

Captain Reed and Gloria returned and J.J. stuck out his hand and said, "Sir, you now have a magician as your main performer!" The captain grabbed his hand and told him he wouldn't be sorry, then he turned to Mrs. Willard and said, "Ma'am, please do not worry, I shall watch out for James, after all, his name is James!"

Gloria's mouth popped opened and she just stood there in stunned silence. Then her face lit up like it was bursting with sunshine and she ran and grabbed J.J. and gave him a real "bear hug"!

On the drive back the conversation was continuous. Elizabeth and Gloria both talking at the same time (a Willard trait) but they both knew what each was saying.

The *Mississippi Queen* would be leaving Wednesday at noon and James Jr. had to be aboard by 9 a.m. Gloria went with him to the barn and they packed all his magic as soon as they got back. This took about five hours, so the day was gone and that night they had to perform.

J.J. did his normal before the show performance, but when he was finished his father came out. Then James Sr. with his heavy Irish brogue announced to the audience that, "This har is me son, James Michael Willard, his mother and I are proud to announce to you har tonight, that he shall be the featured performer on the boat 'The Mississippi Queen' starting this week. From this night forward, he shall be referred to as "James Willard the Magician"! Everyone stood and gave J.J. a standing ovation. He bowed and left the stage knowing that he would probably never perform on this stage with his family again, it actually made him sad! Yet he knew that his life's adventure was really about to begin. He looked forward to all the people that he would meet and know and all the places in his life that he would go. Of course, he also knew he would be back in New Orleans about every 3 weeks.

Chapter 5

Performing on the Mississippi Queen

The *Mississippi Queen* slowly pulled away from the dock, J.J. stood on the second deck on the port side and waved to his mother, father, Gloria and several aunts, uncles, cousins and friends. The boat band was playing and it was such a festive time since this was the boats very first trip!

Both decks were filled with people, the *Mississippi Queen* had completely sold out for this trip. Every cabin was full and there were at least 80 people in the steerage class. J.J. worked his way to the stern so that he could watch as they left New Orleans and he could see it all. Knowing that he had to perform tonight he then headed to his cabin. He sat down and made a list of the tricks he would perform tonight, then the ones for the next night and the next. He was careful to make sure that he did not repeat any of the tricks. Over the last two years J.J. had built quite a collection of different things that he could do alone, but for the first time, he wished that Gloria was with him so that he could do some different illusions. He thought to himself that maybe his father would consent for her to come along on one trip.

By 6 p.m. the boat was in Baton Rouge and docked and some passengers were getting off and some others were getting on. The crew was also loading some additional cargo to take north. J.J. went to the dining room and sat at the table that would be his for the entire time that he was aboard the boat. His waiter was a young black man by the name of George. He and George would become friends. This first night George did not know what J.J. wanted to eat. As time progressed, George wouldn't even ask J.J., he would just bring him his food.

George was in his thirties and had been a slave in Alabama. When the war ended George had left the plantation and headed west. He soon realized that there really wasn't much that he knew about except farming and he really didn't like the work of farming. He found a job washing dishes in a restaurant in New Orleans, but he didn't like that either.

George met this cook named Jon Boudreaux at the restaurant and when Captain Reed offered Jon Boudreaux the job of being cook on the *Mississippi Queen*, Jon asked George if he would like to be a waiter. George said yes immediately and that is how he became a waiter on the boat. Waiters on these boats were not just waiters. They did lots of things, cleaned and mopped the dining room, helped the cook peel potatoes and other things. One thing was certain about the *Mississippi Queen*, it was always cleaned in every nook and corner. Jon Boudreaux was not only a premier chef, he was a man that wanted every thing spotless and he made sure that it was. After the tables were set, Jon would go to every table and check the silverware to make sure that there was not a single spot on it or on any of the glasses. He also made sure that each table's linen was clean. If he founed one tiny spot on a red tablecloth, he would say, "Ahhh Haaaa!" The waiter of that table knew immediately to bring a new cloth, glass or silverware.

At 8 p.m. J.J. was ready to perform. He was backstage and

had everything in his mind as to what he was going to do and had all his props lined up. On this night, it was special because the Captain was to make the introduction. J.J. heard the band stop and the crowd get silent. The theater was full with at least 100 people. He had enough tricks lined up to perform for about 45 minutes, with his chatter. The captain introduced him by saying, "Ladies and Gentlemen, The *Mississippi Queen* and her entire crew are pleased to bring you the most amazing young man you have ever seen, (pause) James Willard the Magician!!!" The drummer did a military roll and the curtains rolled open! J.J. was now and would forever be a magician! His first trick was a card trick, for his second card trick he brought three men from the audience and asked them if they were gamblers, amazingly, two were! He sat them all down and proceeded to have each one cut the cards. He asked the one that wasn't a gambler if he would reshuffle the cards. He took the cards from the gentleman and held them high and dealt a hand to all of them, including himself. He asked the first man to hold up his hand so the audience could see, well, this man had a little straight, 4, 5, 6, 7, 8. The next man had a heart flush, all hearts and then the third man had a full house, jacks and 10s. Then J.J. showed his cards, he had four aces.

One of the men, said, "Sir, I do not ever wish to see you at my table!" Everyone laughed, and J.J. thanked them. He then brought a young lady from the audience and had her hold a basket, which he filled with flowers from an empty cone. When he took her back to her seat, he bowed and produced a real rose for her!

The night went really well and J.J. could see Captain Reed at the back, and he had a real big smile on his face and applauded eagerly after each trick. As J.J. finished and took his bow, the whole audience gave him a standing ovation with lots of whistles. After that night J.J. could not go anywhere that the people didn't sake his hand and tell him how great he was. Young ladies were constantly wanting him to walk with them on the deck. Most of the time he would be more than obliging but on some occasions he would simply say he was sorry that he had something to do. He soon learned ways of getting around the boat in order to avoid the ladies.

One of the things that he really enjoyed doing on the boat was going to the wheelhouse and watching as they went up or down the river. There were always two sailors in the wheelhouse, one did the steering and watched the left bank and the water passage and the other watched the right bank and the water passage. This way there were four eyes always looking for something in the water that might harm the boat and watching the banks. Even though the boat was made of steel and wood a log could damage the power wheel or the rudder and this could be disastrous.

Captain Reed was on duty in the wheelhouse on a rotating schedule as were the other four men. Each man was only on duty for four hours. With Captain Reed that would allow one of them a full eight hours off every so many shifts, except for the Captain the other men usually used that time to sleep.

One of the pilots was named John Thibodaux, he was in his 60s and told J.J. that he had been a pilot on the river for over 20 years and knew every sandbar and shallow in the river. He told J.J. that you had to be careful in the Mississippi because new sandbars could jump up at any time. Some were like islands that they moved almost as if they were trying to hang boats up. Every time J.J. was in the wheelhouse with John Thibodaux, John would show him something new, J.J. actually became good at spotting sandbars, floating logs and shallows.

Natchez, Mississippi and Vicksburg, Mississippi were shocks to J.J. There was so much destruction that had been caused by the bombardment of these two towns that it was hard for J.J. to imagine. He took the time to go off the boat at each of these two places to see the towns. He was totally sick to his stomach at the destruction that had been cause by the cannons and could only imagine how bad it was while it was going on. He realized how lucky he and his family had been by living in Houma and New Orleans.

Memphis, Tenn. the weather turned cold. At Memphis

many of the passengers got off and a few got on. From there to St. Louis they did not have a full boat. One day outside of Memphis it started to snow, it had been years since J.J. had seen snow. The snow changed the banks of the river. Trees were covered with ice and no one except J.J. and the crew were outside on the decks. You had to be very careful because the decks were very slippery, a false step could send you into the icy waters and you would not survive long in that water. Actually it was so cold that you could only stay out on deck for ten or fifteen minutes and the wind was really blowing, there was even some ice in the water, but thank goodness it wasn't very thick.

At St. Louis, Captain Reed decided to only stay long enough for the passengers to get on and off and for them to load any freight that was going to Quincy, Illinois. Captain was afraid the river was going to freeze and they wouldn't be able to get to Quincy and unload and load and head back.

When they reached Quincy the Captain called the entire crew into the dining room and told them that it was very important for them to unload and load as soon as possible. He wanted to be headed back south as soon as they could. He was sure that none of them wished to spend the next two or three months in Quincy. You never saw men work so hard unloading and loading a boat. J.J. helped because he certainly wanted to make sure they were on their way as soon as possible. Six hours after they had docked, the boat was headed south, with new passengers, though not many. They had a full load that was completely for New Orleans, which meant that they would not have to do any loading or unloading at the stops south. Of course they would have to stop and pickup passengers and fuel and food, but that never took long. When they reached St. Louis they learned from the telegraph that the Mississippi river was frozen solid at Quincy, they had made it out just in time.

Captain Reed wasted no time in St. Louis, as soon as the passengers, fuel and food were loaded they were off again.

At St. Louis they had loaded a full load of passengers, even the steerage was almost full, about 90 people and every cabin was taken. For the next two nights J.J. had full houses for his performances and as usual, he totally amazed them. The flying bird cage was his closing trick and then for an encore he would either produce flowers or doves. He tried to use the doves only once during a trip, because sometimes they would fly up into the rafters and Jon Boudreaux was never too happy about that! A feather floating down from his ceiling would send him into a real fit! He would tell J.J., "One of these days, them birds going to be in my frying pan!" Then he would laugh. J.J. would tell him, "Jon, my birds end up in your frying pan and I know one cook that a certain magician will make disappear!"

Jon and all the waiters would laugh at this remark. This banter between Jon Boudreaux and J.J. would go on for the two years. Jon was always saying, "Hey, there Mr. Magician where them thar birds?" J.J. would always answer, "Man them thar birds is vanished into thin air!" Jon would answer, "Well, Mr. Magician, when them thar birds come back, they may get scorched in my pan!" Then he would let out a big laugh.

J.J. had gotten into a routine during the trip, after he did his show at night, he would put up all the magic in his trunks, then lock them. He locked them because one thing he didn't need was someone stealing his tricks, or for that matter just looking at them to see if they could figure out how he did them. He would also check and see that he had everything ready for the next night's performance. With the loading and unloading of passengers he now just about knew what and when to repeat tricks. He would then water and feed his doves and his rabbit. That was enough animals to care for. He seldom used the rabbit unless there were children on board. He had about four different tricks he used the rabbit in. Children loved that rabbit—his name was "Bouncey"!

Jon Boudreaux would pat Bouncey on the head and say, "Aww, Bouncey, ya gonna be just fine yes sar, 'Boudreaux's Rare Rabbit in Wine Sauce' with nice green beans and new potatoes!" J.J. would always tell Jon the same thing, "Bouncey poops on me one more time and that 'Rare Rabbit in Wine Sauce' gonna taste real good!" Jon would always let out with a big laugh.

When they arrived back in New Orleans it had been three weeks short one day. Captain Reed went on shore and when he came back he told J.J. that they would not be going back north for at lease three days. He paid J.J. and told him that he was really proud of him! Captain Reed also said that their next trip would be shorter because they couldn't go as far north because of the ice, but that they would probably go as far north as Memphis.

Before leaving the boat J.J. found George and asked him if he was going to stay on board. George told him that more than likely he would, except maybe for a few hours each night that he would spend with the "ladies"! J.J. asked him to water and feed the doves and Bouncey. George said that he would. J.J. told him that he would pay him five dollars to do so. George told him that was okay and they shook hands. Just as he was about to go, J.J. told George, "George, don't ya let that crazy Frenchman anywhere near my birds or rabbit!" Then he and George laughed.

First thing that J.J. did in New Orleans was go to the bank and deposit $200.00, then he went and bought a real nice table cloth for his aunt Mary and a white parasol for Gloria and a real nice shawl for his mother. He also bought things for each of his cousins and cigars for his father and uncle Patrick. When he got to the house everyone was anxious to hear all about his trip. J.J. had one of the Irish traits of the Willards and that was the gift of gab. He went into details telling them about the crew, George, Jon Boudreaux, John Thibodaux and all the others. Since they had arrived back on a Tuesday the family was not performing until Friday. He had plenty of time to spend with everyone. James Sr. wanted to know about how the act went and how he enjoyed it. Gloria wanted to know about the towns and what he had seen, but of course Gloria was in school during the day so they only visited at night. One of his girl cousins wanted to know about the men that were passengers. Melinda Willard, uncle Patrick's and aunt Mary's oldest daughter had a very curious side about her, she was more interested in the men that were gamblers, but, she was 17 and was really thinking about a husband more than anything else. J.J. figured she wanted to know about them because she was looking for a rich husband! This was something J.J. assured her that most of the gamblers were not rich. The ones that had been on the trip that he seen anyway. Mary Jane the youngest, just turning 14 wanted to know about the ladies that were on the trip, how were they dressed, how did they act, were they ladies or were they "ladies of the evening?" J.J. assured her that all the ladies that he saw on the boat were "ladies" and he described how they dressed in detail. J.J.'s attention to details was because he was a magician also made him a good watcher and observer of people.

Friday came much too fast for J.J., but, he was back on board the *Mississippi Queen* by noon. The first thing he did was check his birds and rabbit and they were okay. He found George and paid him the five dollars. The boat was on it's way by 2 p.m. and she had a good load of passengers, all the cabins were booked all the way to Memphis so J.J. laid out his performance plans for a week. He then went and found Captain Reed and they talked for a few minutes, then he went to the wheelhouse to tell everyone hello, he stayed there watching the river and the river banks until 5 p.m. The Mississippi was very low and the crew was having to watch it very close.

Chapter 6

New Entertainers on the Mississippi Queen

Having made seven trips on the *Mississippi Queen*, J.J. had become very aware of all the pitfalls of the Mississippi. He had learned that no matter how much you thought you knew about the river. She always had some surprises that she held back to spring on you when you least expected it. In mid-May the river was running rapidly when all of a sudden the boat became hung up on a sandbar right in the middle of the channel! It was night and no one had seen it, thank goodness that Captain Reed was the one at the wheel when it happened! The next day the Captain had to take one of the boats ashore and find some mules to pull them off the sandbar. This took the better part of the day, it was about 4 p.m. when they finally were on their way again!

Captain Reed came to J.J. one evening and said he wanted to talk to him. He and J.J. went aft on the boat and sat on some benches where they could watch the river. The Captain asked J.J. what he thought about adding some other entertainers. J.J. asked him what he had in mind? Captain Reed said that he felt they needed just a little more entertainment, that J.J. was fantastic, but, maybe they should have something else that was different, something to stretch the evening a little longer. He asked J.J. if he would mind going into the different towns when they stopped and seeing if he could find some entertainers that would be happy on the boat and that would add to their evenings. His reasoning was simple, if the people stayed in the theater a little longer they would buy more drinks and there was good profit in the drinks. J.J. asked him what he wanted to spend for this entertainment and the Captain told him no more than $50.00 a week. "James," the Captain said, "you are my featured entertainer and I am really pleased at how you have taken to the river and how you entertain the customers, I have had people come up to me and say that it is their third or fourth time on my boat and that they wait for the *Mississippi Queen* just to watch you perform!" J.J. thanked the Captain for the compliment and told him that he would start going ashore to see what he could find. The Captain told him there was no hurry, to look for something that would make their boat different and make the trips easier for the passengers.

J.J. made a point of going ashore at every stop and looking for theaters and places where there might be entertainers. On the way back down the river they had an over night stay at St. Louis and so J.J. spent the evening looking, he went to the two theaters, but, didn't really find anything that struck his fancy or that he felt like would be an addition to the boat. He decided to stop and have a late supper, it was 9 p.m. and for J.J. that was late. He asked around and several people told him about an Italian restaurant that had excellent food so he headed there.

When he entered he noticed immediately that there were three violin players and that they were playing some beautiful music. J.J. sat where he could watch the players. The waiter told him that their specialty was a pasta dish with meat, so that is what he ordered and to say the least, it was delicious. There were about 30 people in the restaurant and all of a sudden the violins started playing a fast song and two dancers appeared, a young man, J.J. guessed in his 20s and a young woman with dark hair, olive complexion and very pretty and J.J. guessed her to be in her teens.

This young couple danced like J.J. had never seen and the audience applause was very loud when they finished a dance! With the girl's beauty, J.J. had not paid much attention to the young man, so when the applause was going on, J.J. looked at him closely. The man had very dark hair, silky black and his eyes were also a very dark color, J.J. couldn't decide if they were black or just really a dark brown. He had a chiseled face, sharp features and was also olive skinned. The couple danced for about 30 minutes and they had the audience spellbound for the whole time. J.J. asked the waiter to have them join him for a drink when they finished.

The girl did not come, but, the young man came and J.J. stood up and shook his hand and introduced himself. The young man said his name was Mario Misuraca and that the girl dancing with him was his sister, Patricia Ann. J.J. asked him if they would be interested in performing on a riverboat. Mario, said very matter-of-factly that they would be interested but how much was the pay? J.J. very smartly asked him, "Sir, what would you want?" Mario thought for a few minutes and finally said, "Sir we would need $20.00 a week for each of us!"

Then as a second thought, Mario said, "But you must understand that we would have to discuss this with our father, first!" J.J. told him that he understood and that he also would have to discuss it with the Captain of the *Mississippi Queen*. He wasn't sure if they would have two cabins available. Mario told him they didn't need two cabins since they had been sleeping in the same room since they were children. They would appreciate having two beds. Since J.J. knew every cabin on the boat, he knew they had this type of facility and he also knew that unless they had rented it tonight, that it was available.

J.J. told him that he was sure this could be arranged and asked how long it would take them to check with their father. Mario, excused himself, by this time the restaurant was almost empty. Just one other couple and they were so engrossed in each other. Holding hands over the table with the candle flickering in their faces that no one else in the room mattered. Mario came back with an older gentleman. He also was dark skinned and had the same dark eyes as Mario, except he had very gray hair and gray eye brows. Mario said, "Mr. Willard, this is my papa, his name is Anthony Misuraca and he does not speak any English, but I have told him about your offer, he just wanted to meet you!"

J.J. stood and took the elderly man's hand and looked him directly in the eyes, Mr. Misuraca held his hand and spoke to Mario in Italian. Mario said, "Mr. Willard, he is not concerned about me, but, he is worried about Patricia!" J.J. assured him that the crew of the boat would watch out for her and take care of her and protect her.

This seemed to satisfy Mr. Misuraca, he said something to Mario, squeezed J.J. 's hand and headed back to where he had come from. J.J. asked Mario if they could be at the boat the next morning by 8 a.m. Mario said they would be there.

J.J. headed back to the boat and told the Captain all about it and Captain Reed told him that he had done good, then the Captain told the cabin steward to have the cabin ready.

Mario and Patricia were there at 7:45 a.m. the next morning and J.J. showed them to their cabin. He then asked them if they could do a rehearsal with band that afternoon about 2 p.m. They agreed that would be fine. All J.J. had to do was convince the band to stay after the lunch hour.

The band normally played from 11:30 a.m. till 1:30 p.m. for the lunch period. He wasn't too sure, how they were going to take this. It turned out, a couple had seen Patricia and they were more than willing to practice with them. J.J. laughed, it seems that band members always have the same thing on their minds. He then told them about Mario and Patricia's father. How the Italian had told him that if anything happened to his a little girl, he would make a sure that the man responsible would no longer be a man! Of course he hadn't told J.J. that, but, laughing under his breath, J.J. had shown how the old man had waved his knife and pretended to cut the air! The drum player did a roll and said, "Ouch!" Everyone laughed!

That night, Captain Reed introduced them to the audience, as Mario and Patricia Dancers "extraordinaire", apparently a word that he made up! J.J. watched and they really were fantastic, considering they had only had one rehearsal with the band.

J.J. watched the Captain and from the applause and big smiles and also how the audience was accepting them, J.J. knew that he had done good! They danced for twenty minutes and then ended with a comedy routine that had the audience standing and applauding.

J.J. found that to follow them made his performance better and easier, the audience was already warmed up and ready for him to amaze them. Which he always did!

Over the next few months, J.J. really got to know Patricia and Mario. They really were quite a pair. Patricia had a way of looking into your eyes like she knew just what you were thinking, plus she did something that unnerved the band and J.J. She would sneak up very quietly behind you and pinch you on the butt. None of the men were used to any woman doing this to them and their reactions were always so very funny! This reaction was what made Patricia happy, she would then laugh with such gusto that you would think she had been told the funniest joke. The funny thing was that she even laughed with an accent! J.J. found out she was only 15 and that she was one of five sisters and she was not the youngest. She and J.J. became friends. There was never any romance between them, he actually sort of regarded her as a little sister.

Mario, well, he was truly an Italian! The women went crazy over him, he was 22 and he took great pleasure in as he called it, "Servicing the Ladies!" Mario, also had a weakness for gambling, but, on the *Mississippi Queen* it was always table stakes and the Captain made sure that Mario never got his hands on any of Patricia's money.

Captain Reed was very smart about how people handled their money, he always paid you when the boat was in your home town. After the first trip when they returned to St. Louis, Captain Reed took Patricia with him and they went to the St. Louis First National Bank, there he opened an account with her name and her fathers name and had her put the $60.00 in the account. From then on, he would give her $10 and deposit the rest into her account. She would save her money for two or three trips then in New Orleans she would buy things for her sisters and mother. Her mother Rose was appreciative of the things that Patricia did for her.

Every gambler has his day, and one night Mario had his, he could do no wrong and the cards just seemed to be attracted to him, at the end of the evening Mario had won over $1,000.00. He couldn't believe it. J.J. pulled him up on deck and had a long talk with him. He convinced Mario to give $950.00 to the Captain and tell the Captain not to give it to him until they were back in St. Louis. It took some persuading but Mario finally agreed and they both walked to the Captain's cabin. Mario turned the money over to the Captain. When they got to St. Louis the Captain and Mario went to the bank and opened an account for him. Several things came out of this, number one, Mario nursed that $50.00 that he kept and actually became a much better poker player. He seldom lost and always left the table with more money than he started with.

J.J. didn't know for many years that something he said had really hit home with Mario. It became a challenge to Mario to give the Captain money. Every time they docked in St. Louis the Captain would deposit the extra money along with Mario's pay at the same time he was depositing Patricia's.

Mario and Patricia were very careful to go see their mother and father every time the boat docked in St. Louis. On several occasions they would have the Captain and J.J. come for supper. The Misuraca's never allowed either the Captain or J.J. to pay for a meal and they always prepared something very special for them. Several times J.J. performed for their customers and both Momma and Papa Misuraca were totally amazed at his skill. One evening he brought his special coat and his flying bird cage and did this trick. The house was full with about 50 people and many did not speak English, but from their actions J.J. knew that they all enjoyed it. Italians are so animated, they would hold their hands out in front of them and then make a sound like, "swoosh", and drop their hands and then they would look left and right and say "swoosh" again and then laugh. J.J. remembered the Italians of Brooklyn and thought about how different these people were. These were fun loving people that were warm and giving, not at all like the hard fighting Italians of New York.

Of course J.J. knew that he was only a kid in Brooklyn and really didn't remember how the adults acted. J.J. always hated leaving the restaurant, it was sort of like leaving his family. He had become very close to all the Misuraca family.

The trips on the river now became routine and boring, one day seemed like the previous and one show seemed like the last show. The people that were the travelers started to seem like all the others. Mario and Patricia did help J.J. by having him go with them on excursions into the towns and the countryside when the time permitted. More and more J.J. felt like they were actually his brother and sister.

In December J.J. had gone ashore sometimes with Patricia and Mario and sometimes alone to shop in every town for gifts for the entire family. Patricia helped him with all the gifts for his female relatives and Mario helped him with some of the men's gifts. When they docked in New Orleans for Christmas layover, J.J. had gifts for the entire clan, right down to every single cousin. Mario and Patricia had left the boat in St. Louis to stay with their family during Christmas.

December was really an exciting time in New Orleans. This year was especially one of happiness for the city. The markets for the first time after the war were full of food supplies. Most of the people were working and making a decent wage. The merchants were happy that a lot of buying went on and the families for the most part had reached the stage of forgiveness. This was a necessary thing to have peace after such an awful and tragic war. Don't get it wrong, there were still prisoners in the prisons, solders that the north had deemed unfit to return to civilian life yet because of their war crimes.

On Christmas Eve the entire Willard family, all the brothers and sisters and their kids all attended Mass at the Catholic church. The priest and the nuns were all happy to see them. Several told J.J. that they were really proud of how grown up he was and were so happy for his success. One of the nuns pulled J.J. aside and asked him if he would come the next day and entertain the orphans? She said the children needed to get their minds off being so alone. He told her he would and promised to come at 3 p.m. the next day.

J.J.'s mother and Aunt Mary really out did themselves the next day. J.J. could not remember every having such a meal. There was turkey roasted perfectly, there was cured ham, sweet potatoes, green peas, then pumpkin pies, cherry pies, a large chocolate cake. Dressing from the turkey, it was just a fantastic meal and every one ate so much that it only seemed normal to need to take a nap!

J.J. enlisted Gloria to go with him to the church and entertain. They borrowed some of his father's magic and as promised they were there at 3 p.m. There were about 75 kids and for the next hour, J.J. and Gloria performed different magic tricks. Gloria did some special tricks that she had practiced and J.J. was amazed at how skilled she had become. The girls that were there loved seeing another girl perform. As cute as Gloria was, she held the boys spell bound. J.J. noticed some of the boys with their mouths hanging open! He laughed to himself and wondered what the future held for his little sister. One thing that he was sure of, if she decided to become a full time entertainer, he felt she would be a success.

The next day after Christmas James Sr. asked J.J. to go with him for a walk. This caught J.J. by surprise because his father seldom went for walks. For him to ask J.J. to go with him, J.J. knew that something was in the wind.

They walked thru the entire Irish sector and even down as far as the market with James Sr. not really saying anything. If one stood and looked at the two of them walking, you would have to laugh. J.J. was now at least 6 feet tall and his father was so much shorter that you would think from a distance that it was father and son but that James Sr. was the son. Because of being entertainers everywhere they went the men would come over and shake hands and the ladies would curtsy to them. Both being Irish gentlemen they always shook hands and they both took their hats off and tipped them to all the ladies. Finally on the way back toward home James Sr. said, "James, your mother and Gloria and I are leaving New Orleans!" This really caught J.J. by surprise. "Where are you going he wanted to know and what will you do?" He had not given any thought that his family would leave New Orleans. Oh, he figured that Gloria might as she would probably meet someone and marry him, but his mother and father this had never entered his mind.

James Sr. explained that he had contacted several theaters in the east. Starting with a theater in Atlanta and that they were going to play theaters along the east for a few months. Then James Sr. dropped the real bomb on J.J. James Sr. "You see James, you are going to become an uncle, Madeline has written that she is with child and that your mother wants to be there when the blessed event happens!" J.J. was so excited that Madeline was going to have a baby! Then sadness set in, because he was committed to Captain Reed and would not be able to be there. He asked when the baby was due and James Sr. told him that it would be around June or the last of May, they were not sure.

James Sr. had arranged their schedule so that they would be in Washington D.C. and stay with his first cousin who had a large hotel there. Then they would travel to Baltimore and perform until the middle of May. Then go to Madeline's and be there to help her when the baby arrives. He told J.J. that he planned to stay in the east and to perform there and maybe buy some property near Madeline and Forrest.

Somewhere that would be central for them to take the train where ever they were to put shows on. The two of them became so engrossed in the conversation that they actually walked past Uncle Patrick's house and were almost to the ole Plantation before they realized it. They had a good laugh over this. December 29th the entire Willard Irish clan took James Sr., Elizabeth and Gloria to the train station. There were so many trunks that if the station manager had not been friends with them, it would have cost a fortune to load all of them. After they had performed in Atlanta, J.J.'s mother, Elizabeth, wrote James Jr. that it had cost them twice as much for the trunks as it did for their tickets. J.J. was so very sad at the station, his eyes filled with tears and he held his mother for the longest time and then he hugged Gloria and finally his father. He had true affection for his family and he was afraid that this maybe the last time he would ever see them. He stood on the platform and waved until the train was out of sight!

Even though he was a man of 6 feet, inside with his mother and his father he was still a little boy and he felt really alone for the first time. His Aunt Mary came over and put her arms around him and they walked back to the carriage arm in arm. That night in the familiar surroundings of his own bedroom at Uncle Patrick's he wondered where life was going to take him. He had no idea of the adventures that he was destined to have. The next morning he awoke with a more positive feeling and was ready to face the challenges of life. Since he had three more days before the boat would leave, he decided to catch the train to Houma and see what his friends there were doing. While there he even went with Norm and Norm's father shrimping and laughter returned because you could not be around those two Cajuns without laughing, to them, life was one laugh after another.

January 3rd the boat left and J.J.'s life was back to normal.

Chapter 7

The Robbery

May 15th was a day that few people on the *Mississippi Queen* would ever forget. It was dark and raining and the river was running very fast. They were just north of Natchez, Mississippi and the Captain was at the wheel. With the rain coming down so hard there were two lookouts in the wheelhouse. Captain Reed was thinking about putting in for the night. They did a lot of this during the spring of the year because the Mississippi River had a way of becoming very mean during this period. J.J. had finished his performance and was watching Mario play poker, when all of a sudden, armed men with masks entered the room!

These men, J.J. could tell, were men from the war that had gone bad or desperate because they were unable to adapt to life after the war. So they had become robbers. These were not men that anyone wanted to mess with, because they would just as soon kill you or hit you across the face with a pistol.

One of them got on the stage and said, "Now, gentlemen, if you would be so kind as to put all your money and watches and valuables into the bags we are passing around!" J.J. noticed that this man spoke with a northeastern accent. It was one he had heard before and that this man seemed to be more refined than the others. No one put up any resistance, J.J. was glad about this. Mario was very quite and put his money into their bag. J.J. could tell that his Italian blood was boiling. Mario handed over almost $200.00, and this he did with sort of a flare. Counting the money as he put it into the bag, the robber punched him in the ribs with his pistol and asked if he wanted to continue being a funny man?

J.J. was thankful that he had put all his coins that he used in his tricks in the trunks and when the bag came to him he put in all he had, which was only $22.00. He was also glad that he had already changed and looked just like a passenger. One of the robbers found his trunks back stage and asked the one who had talked if he should open them, the leader told him to forget it. All the robbers except for two left and those two had everyone sit down.

Ten to twenty minutes later they heard the boat whistle and the two men left, but they warned everyone to stay seated for the next ten minutes. Every one did this except for one of the men. The robbers had taken all the weapons. This man reached down and pulled two small pistols out of his boots and got up and went on deck, everyone heard two shots almost immediately. Mario when he heard the shots went out on deck, he then came back to the door and told everyone that they were gone.

J.J. went to the wheelhouse to make sure everyone was okay. Captain Reed was turning the boat around. Not an easy thing to do with the waters running as fast as they were. He told J.J. to go tell the passengers that they were going back to Natchez to talk to the military commander that was there. J.J. immediately went and informed everyone of what was happening.

When the boat was about a mile from Natchez the captain started blowing the whistle continuously, when they docked there were already soldiers on the dock with guns and a captain came aboard. Captain Oliver Lynn Farr and Captain Reed talked for a few minutes, then the captain motioned for a couple other soldiers to come on board—a lieutenant William Kennedy and a sergeant Jack Courtney. They started asking all the passengers to remember everything they saw. Well when everything came out there were apparently seven robbers. Four had come into the theater. Three had gone to the wheelhouse and held the Captain hostage while the others held up everyone.

When the two had left the theater one had left the wheelhouse. The three of them had gone from cabin to cabin to see what they could find. These men were very efficient and had taken anything and everything that was of any value. There was an exception for one thing, these robbers did not know that the Captain had a hidden safe in his cabin and they missed it. Every one was thankful for that, because most passengers that had money, would give most of it to the captain for safe keeping while they traveled.
One of the passengers, a gambler, was sorry that he had not, because he lost all he had. The reason they had not even looked for it, was the captain also had a small safe in the wheelhouse. He kept $200.00 in that, this made the robbers think that was the ships money, which it was, but there was a lot more in the other safe.

After 30 minutes Captain Farr and his men had talked to almost everyone and gotten as good a description of the robbers as possible.

One thing that they felt was the most important, the gambler that had gone out on deck and fired, was sure that he had hit one of the robbers. He said they were in two rowboats and that when he fired one of them had slumped over, this gambler was named Beverly Bergeron. J.J. had seen him on the boat several times over the last year. Apparently he would take the *Mississippi Queen* to Memphis and then there he would take one of the other boats and head south.

Captain Reed decided that they were going to spend the night docked at Natchez and then start back up river when it turned light. This was not the first time a riverboat had been held up, but for

Captain Reed it was the last time that his boat was going to be held up. Before leaving Natchez he went ashore and hired four men and bought new rifles for them, from then on there would be two of them on duty at all times from dusk till dawn. These men were crack shots. Captain Reed made a point of having them put on shooting exhibitions in each of the river ports that they stopped at. They would also entertain the passengers with shooting shows from the stern of the boat every few days. No robber in his right mind would try to rob a boat that had men that could shoot like these men could. Especially since they had repeating rifles that could shoot up to eight times before reloading.

J.J. was amazed at the rest of the trip. Every time they pulled into a port and new passengers came aboard they would ask about the robbery. Also they all new that Beverly Bergeron had shot one and all the men would shake his hand, until Memphis he was a hero. He told J.J. that he was sorry his name had been connected to the shooting, that it was going to make it hard for him to play poker for awhile, everyone would know he had the guns in his boots and would be leery of playing with him.

When they reached St. Louis the captain decided to spend the night and they all went to the Misuraca's for supper. Rose Misuraca held her daughter for a long time and they all wanted the Captain to tell about the awful robbery. Instead, Mario told the story in Italian with lots of acting! Captain Reed and J.J. sat and laughed at how Mario was telling the story. His animations were so obvious, a mask on his face, his hands acting like they had pistols in them. He even acted out how he had counted his money into the sack and how the robber had punched him in the ribs.

When he did that Rose ran over and grabbed him and said, "Aw, my poor, poor Bambino!" Every single person in the restaurant laughed. Mario turned red! He realized that he had gone from being a man to being his Momma's baby!! Not at all the affect that he had wanted, but Mario soon recovered. On the way back to the *Mississippi Queen*, Captain Reed told J.J. that he had made arrangements that on their next trip after this one that they would start going all the way to Chicago by way of the Illinois river and the Illinois-Michigan canal. This would add a week to their travel time, but that he felt the extra passengers and the freight contract he had made would make the boat much more profitable. J.J. didn't know why, but this news made him excited. Well for one thing, he had heard a lot about lake Michigan and looked forward to seeing it.

When they finally returned to New Orleans there were several of J.J. 's cousins waiting for him on the dock. All with big Irish smiles on their faces. J.J. couldn't figure out the meaning. Except, maybe it was because of the robbery. Even Aunt Mary was there, now that was a first. She had come to watch the boat leave the first time but she had never been there when it returned. After hugging him Aunt Mary handed J.J. an engraved card, on it he read:

Mr. and Mrs. Forrest Clark Edwards proudly announce the arrival of their son, Mr. Christopher Scott Edwards as of 9 pm, June 2nd in the year of our Lord 1869.

J.J. was just astonished. Melinda came over and teased, "Gee Uncle J.J. you sure are getting old!" Then she laughed and hugged him. One of the things that surprised J.J. was that the boy had not been named James after his father, but he was sure there was a reason. While ever one else headed back to the house, J.J. took Melinda with him and they went to buy something for the baby. Not knowing what other family members had bought for the boy made it difficult, but they finally decided on a small silver spoon. J.J. had the man engrave it with Christopher's initials, C.S.E. and the date of his birth, he then paid the merchant to ship it to them and he wrote a brief note to be included in the package.

The next few days there was a lot of conversation at the Patrick Willard house about the robbery. About Madeline having a son. J.J. was sorry that he could not go to Pennsylvania to see Forrest and Madeline's newborn son. Well, maybe one of these days he could. While there, J.J. wrote his mother a long letter about all that had happened and about him being an uncle. Over the next few years he and his mother would write many letters to each other, but also he would write and receive letters from Gloria. He and his father never wrote to each other, but they knew what the other was doing by the letters and they always told each other they loved them in these letters. James Sr. would tell Elizabeth be sure and tell J.J. I think of him and J.J. would always close his letters to his mother by saying, tell Papa that I think of him often. On Thursday night Aunt Mary had Patricia and Mario come to dinner. Melinda sat with her mouth open just staring at Mario the whole evening. J.J. knew she was totally infatuated with him. Mario knew it also, so he paid a lot of attention to her. To him she was just another young lady and since she was J.J.'s cousin he was really careful not to lead her on.

Patricia had a lot of fun at J.J.'s expense. She kept calling him "Old Uncle J.J." and then when no one was looking she'd pinch him on the butt several times. One time she caught him so much by surprise that he actually hollered and everyone turned to see what was the matter. J.J. turned red and acted like he had choked!

The *Mississippi Queen* left early Friday morning for her first trip to Chicago. Some thoughts had been going thru J.J.'s mind and he sat on the deck with Mario and talked about them. He asked Mario if he would mind moving in with him so that a girl could share the cabin with Patricia. Mario wanted to know if he had anyone in mind for this and J.J. told him that he really didn't but that he had been thinking about adding an assistant to his show. This would enable him to do some other things and he felt like he could make his show more interesting. Mario, told him that he had no problems with moving into his cabin with him. Besides, he felt another girl would make it more fun for Patricia. Well with this hurdle over with, he only had one more and that was Captain Reed.

The next day he asked the Captain if he could talk to him. He and the Captain went to the stern of the boat and J.J. told him his plan and asked if there could be an increase in salary to add the other person. J.J. explained that with the boat being out an additional week that passengers from Chicago to New Orleans would expect to see different shows that he felt with an assistant that he could add many more things to his performances. Also it would make them smoother on stage. The Captain said he wasn't sure if he could spare another cabin, then J.J. explained that he and Mario would bunk together and that his assistant could bunk with Patricia.

With that the Captain agreed and said he would pay J.J. an additional $25.00 a week. J.J. and the Captain shook hands on it and J.J. assured him that he would make his performances extra special. With all that accomplished. Now all J.J. had to do was find him an assistant.

When the *Mississippi Queen* docked in Chicago, the captain told them they had two days before they would be heading south. With this time, Mario, Patricia and J.J. set out to see the great Lake Michigan and the town of Chicago.

Mario and Patricia had never even seen the Gulf of Mexico, even though they had been to New Orleans. It was a long way from New Orleans to the gulf and when they saw Lake Michigan they were both in awe. This was the largest body of water either had ever seen. When they saw the ships that sailed on the lake, this also amazed them.

They hired a carriage with driver and asked him to show them a place where they could spend the night. He took them to a boarding house that was on the waterfront, a really pretty place and the lady that ran it was very nice. They then asked the carriage driver to show them around Chicago, the man had a lot of knowledge about Chicago and he was very patient to tell them about everything. About 8 p.m. they told the driver they were hungry and wished to find a nice restaurant. The driver again headed toward the lake and took them to a restaurant called the High Hat Club. All three thought this to be a strange name, but the food was excellent.

The owner came over and his name was Glen Falkenstein and his wife's name was Frances. Like Misuraca's in St. Louis this restaurant also had a violinist but they also had a piano and the two played together beautifully. But, for J.J. there was another attraction, the waitress. She was about five feet tall, blond and she just moved with a grace. Her smile, well that smile had J.J. totally captivated. She was probably about 15 or 16, but had the air of an older lady with a lot of grace. Patricia noticed the attraction between the two and kicked J.J. under the table.

J.J. asked the girl her name and she told him her name was Satin Lyons. J.J. said that he thought the name was very pretty. He wondered why she had been named after a fabric. She said that when her daddy first held her that he said her skin was smooth as silk, but, he didn't think Silk Lyons sounded to good and the mother had suggested Satin and so that was how she was named. Then she laughed and her smile and laughter made them all laugh.

Satin wanted to know what they did and Patricia told her they were all entertainers working on a riverboat. This totally fascinated her and she sat right down and wanted to know exactly what they did. Patricia told her that her and her brother were dancers. Then Satin said, okay, who is he and what does he do? Well no sooner had Patricia told her that he was the famous James Willard the Magician than Satin jumped up and ran over to Mr. Falkenstein, she talked to him for a minute then they both came back to the table.

Mr. Falkenstein was also a magician and he did performances here in the club on weekends. When J.J. introduced himself, immediately Mr. Falkenstein told him that he had heard of him, that many of his customers had told him about this outstanding young man that was performing on the *Mississippi Queen*. J.J. was flattered that he had knowledge of him. It was almost midnight when the three of them headed back to the boarding house. It had been a wonderful evening for them. J.J. felt he had made a friend for life in Glen Falkenstein and they had so much to talk about.

At the boarding house, J.J. had a hard time falling asleep. He kept seeing Satin and the grace of her movements. 5 a.m. came and J.J. gave up on sleeping. He got up, took a nice long bath and put on clean clothes and stepped outside. To his surprise the air was very crisp and chilling. He went back inside and put on his jacket, then went for a long walk along the lake. When the sun came up the lake looked like a giant diamond, the rays of the sun sparkled across the water which was completely calm and looked like you could just walk on it.

He was back in the boarding house by 7:15 and went into the dining room and sat down and had a great breakfast. Then spent a few minutes reading the local paper. He found an article about the docking of the *Mississippi Queen*. It stated that the *Queen* would be leaving the next day at 10 a.m. and that a few cabins were still available for the trip to New Orleans. It also stated that the boat did have steerage tickets available.

At 8 a.m. Mario came down, dressed and ready to eat. J.J. asked about Patricia and Mario said that he was just going to let her sleep. They could come back and get her later in the day. After Mario had finished breakfast, the two men sat out to explore the downtown area on foot.

One of the things that they noticed as they walked along was the different nationalities that they passed. New Orleans and St. Louis both had many different races but Chicago seemed to have many more and surprisingly, a lot of Indians. By noon they had seen most of the town and they found a little restaurant and had lunch.

Mario said he felt like he should head back to the boarding house and check on Patricia. J.J. told him that he thought he would go to the stockyards and see what horses were selling for. The two men separated agreeing to meet at 7 p.m. at the High Hat Club.

J.J. was pondering a decision in his mind, all day it seemed to keep popping up. No matter what he was seeing. The stockyards had about 100 horses and very few of them were of quality. Looking at the horses made him think of his brother-in-law and sister Madeline and their little boy Christopher. Finally at 5 p.m. he had his mind made up and he headed for the High Hat Club. When he arrived there were only a few early diners there. The first person he saw was Glen Falkenstein, so he asked him to join him at his table.

J.J. explained that he had been looking for an assistant and wanted to know what Mr. Falkenstein thought about his waitress Satin. That he was considering her for the role but wanted Mr. Falkenstein's opinion before he said anything to the girl. And his approval.

Glen told him the girl was an excellent worker. She was always on time and that the customers loved her and that if she decided to go with J.J. he would not stand in her way. But that there was a condition that he must agree to before he would give J.J. permission to speak to her.

J.J. would agree to perform in his club some weekend when the *Queen* was there for a weekend layover. J.J. said that he had no problem doing that, but he did not know when the *Queen* would be there for a weekend and that he would have to talk to Captain Reed about their schedule. Glen said that would be okay and that he would pay him $50.00 a night if he had at least two weeks to promote it. The two men shook hands on the deal and Glen got up and went to Satin and told her that J.J. wanted to talk to her. When Satin got to his table J.J. stood up and asked her to sit with him, and he assured her that Glen had given him permission. She sat and her big eyes were looking holes thru J.J. It made him uneasy, which sort of amazed him. He then told her he was looking for a person to be his assistant on the *Queen* and wondered if she would be interested. Satin set there with a funny little grin on her face. She said, "Mr. Willard I am interested, but, what are the details?" J.J. explained that she would make $20.00 a week, the same as Patricia. That the money would be paid to her ever time they returned to Chicago, plus she would have all her meals paid for.

Satin, then very matter of factually asked J.J, "Sir, does this mean that I also will be required to sleep with you?" J.J. laughed and turned red. "No, you will be in a cabin with Patricia and her brother Mario will be in my cabin." With that answer Satin stuck out her hand and said, "Then sir, you have yourself an assistant, when do we leave?"

Patricia and Mario arrived and J.J. told them what he had done. They both seemed happy over his decision.

Chapter 8

Performing in Chicago at the High Hat Club

J.J. went to pick up Satin at her house at 7:30 a.m. the next morning. When he arrived there was a large trunk sitting on her porch. Satin's mother, Georgette Lyons came out and said she wanted to talk to him. J.J. and Georgette walked around the side of the house and Mrs. Lyons took J.J. by the arm and told him in no uncertain words that she wanted her girl looked after and that she was going to hold him personally responsible for her safety. J.J. assured her that Satin would be safe on the boat, and that she would be staying with Patricia who's big brother was her dance partner, this seemed to satisfy her. J.J. and the carriage driver loaded the trunk and the driver asked Satin if she had packed the family silver in the trunk, it was so heavy. She laughed and said, "No, sir only a couple of bricks!" He answered that she must have the whole fireplace in there. All the way to the boat you would think Satin was a queen, she waved at every person she saw along the way and several times even called some of them by name and they waved back and called out her name. J.J. almost felt like he was riding with a celebrity.

As the carriage pulled up to the boat Satin let out a yell. "Wow, Oh, Wow, that is a big boat!" Then she laughed and giggled like a little schoolgirl, well after all she was only 15. Patricia and Mario were waiting on deck and they waved at her. Mario came and helped J.J. carry the trunk to Patricia's cabin. Both men wondered why they hadn't paid a couple of the other men to carry that trunk. Patricia had been showing Satin around. When they got to the cabin, J.J. told Satin that they would have a rehearsal at 2 p.m. in the theater and asked her to be on time. Then he and Mario went about helping to get the boat on the way. Patricia was so excited about having a female as a roommate that was her age. She was just about bursting at her seams with excitement. She and Satin talked about themselves and learned about each other until lunch time.

J.J. was apprehensive all morning about what things he could teach Satin and would she be one that would be an addition to the show or would she be a hindrance. He mapped out in his mind just what tricks he would show her that afternoon. He was also worried that she would be on time for rehearsals and shows.

His worry was soon put aside as Satin showed up for the rehearsal at 1:45 pm—a full fifteen minutes before she had to. The first thing he showed her was how to carry certain objects onto and off the stage. She grasped this very quickly. He then told her that they would rehearse until after they had docked in St. Louis. That was a full four days of rehearsals but he also wanted her to be properly costumed. He intended to buy the costumes in St. Louis at the ladies shop that supplied theater costumes for theaters all over the country. He wanted Satin to watch his show from the audience for the next 3 nights to get the feel of the flow and rhythm. She was at every show, and she most of the time started the applause. In a way, her long blond hair and big eyes were a distraction to J.J. He overcame it and amazed the audiences with his normal great shows.

Over the next four days, J.J. was very happy with how fast Satin learned and also how very agile she was, plus that smile. She was always smiling and everyone took to her, especially the crazy band members. Just before pulling into St. Louis they held a practice with the band. Between the trumpet player, the drummer and the banjo player every time she would come out the drummer would do a roll, then the trumpet player would do a little ditty, and the banjo player would finish it off with a couple of cords. This actually should have been serious rehearsal but J.J. couldn't help but laugh every time they did it. To spice up his show, he instructed them to continue doing it, at least for the first show to see how the audience took it.

St. Louis was an overnighter so as soon as the boat docked Satin, Patricia and J.J. headed out to the costume lady. With Patricia's help, they picked out five costumes for Satin. Due to her size they all fitted perfectly. They would be easy to work all the tricks that she would be involved in. J.J. paid the lady that owned the shop $50.00 for the five costumes. Then they all headed to Patricia's mom and dad's restaurant for supper. The Misuracas were glad to see them and Momma Rose hugged Satin like she was her long lost daughter. Mario interpreted for Satin that his mother was glad that she finally had a girlfriend on that boat with all those rough men! Everyone laughed, because everyone knew Patricia could certainly take care of herself. It was the men who were in danger of having their butts pinched!

The meal was outstanding and Patricia and Mario danced for the patrons and J.J. did a few coin tricks.

They all headed back to the boat because it was going to be pulling out at 7 a.m.

The first night out of St. Louis J.J. and Satin performed together for the first time!

The band was a big hit with the little gigs they did and the audience loved it. From then on it was part of the act. Satin's smile and long blond hair and big eyes had all the men in the audience (who weren't with their wives) cheering ever time she came on stage. J.J. and Captain Reed were both very pleased. Captain Reed made a point of coming back stage after the show and telling Satin how well she had done and that he was pleased she was on board. Captain Reed then pulled J.J. to the side and told him that he really appreciated J.J. and how much Satin had added to the show.

In order to be professional and not mess up a good thing, J.J. decided that Satin was going to be like a sister to him and that he would treat her as such. He was convinced that if he did this in his mind that the other thoughts he had been having would go away, and basically they did. Every once in awhile they would sneak in —you know how your mind works as a seventeen almost eighteen year old. In his actions J.J. was more like a twenty-five year old. He was very serious about his job and his magic.

They arrived in New Orleans about two in the afternoon and Captain Reed told everyone that it was a turn around and that they would be leaving at 8 a.m. the next morning.

J.J. hired a carriage and he, Patricia, Satin and Mario went first to the bank so that he could deposit his money and then went to Aunt Mary's and Uncle Patrick's.

Aunt Mary accepted Satin immediately and so did the girls when they came home from school. When Uncle Patrick came home he kept picking at Satin saying she had to be Irish, how else could she explain how petite she was. They all had supper with J.J.'s family but then had to take a carriage back to the boat because it was leaving so early. J.J.'s cousin's started teasing him quietly about having a girlfriend, saying things like, "OK. Old Uncle J.J., when we going to have a little J.J. running around the decks of the Ole *Mississippi Queen*?" J.J. just laughed.

On the way north they stopped at Natchez, Mississippi and customers came on board. There was one couple that reminded J.J. of his parents. Later that evening he met the couple, they were Dub and Dolly Smothers, come to find out they were magicians also. Dub Smothers was about J.J.'s father's height, around 5' 6" or so and Dolly was a little taller. There was no doubt that Dub Smothers was from a southern family, he was a gentile man and very gracious.

They were going to St. Louis to perform in one of the theaters there.

Dub Smothers told J.J. that he had seen his father and mother perform at the theater in Atlanta and was so impressed about their show. He had added some of the things that James Sr. was doing to his own show, with the permission of James Sr. In those days magicians never used someone else's trick without asking permission, unless it was published in a book.

That night after the show, Dub came back stage and told J.J. that his father was a great magician but that he was far superior to his father. J.J. took this as a compliment but knew he owed his skills to his father. Dub and J.J. struck up a friendship and spent the next few days on deck just talking about different things in magic and how they did certain things. Dub showed him several things and J.J. also showed Dub, they learned from each other.

Dub and Dolly got off at St. Louis and J.J. was sorry to see them go. He promised that the next time they had time in St. Louis he would come see them at the theater. Dub and Dolly played the theater in St. Louis for six months then they moved some where in Texas and J.J. lost track of them.

When they docked in Chicago J.J. got with Captain Reed and found out when they would be there for a full weekend. It would not be until September. He then got Satin's money and he and she went to the bank in Chicago and opened her a checking account. She kept $20.00 to buy her mother and father and brother and sisters gifts. This trip was a turnaround and the *Mississippi Queen* would be pulling out the next morning at 10 a.m. Satin said she would be there by 7 a.m. and left in a carriage that J.J. paid for.

He headed to the High Hat Club to eat and talk to Glen Falkenstein. The first thing that Glen wanted to know was how was Satin working out. J.J. assured him that she was wonderful. Then J.J. told him about how the band acted when she came on and how much the audience loved this. Glen thought that this was great. J.J. told him that they could perform in Sept. and gave him the approximate dates. J.J. told him that Captain Reed had a contract for freight and he was pretty sure they would keep those dates. Passengers were great, but in the 1860s. In the 70s and 80s freight was king to the riverboats; freight was what made them profitable.

Glen said that he was going to have some posters made advertising that they would be performing on those dates. J.J. said he did have one additional requirement and that was that Satin's mother and father and family be able to come at least one night to see the show. Glen readily agreed to this. After eating J.J. headed back to the boat because of the early hour that it was leaving. He had discussed Dub and Dolly Smothers with Glen. He told him they were playing in St. Louis, if they came to Chicago he hoped that Glen would be courteous to them. Glen assured him that any magician that came to his club would always be treated with respect. J.J. told him that on the next trip he would bring one of the posters from the boat so that his artist would have something to go by.

J.J., as he road back to the *Mississippi Queen*, felt a warmness over his friendship with Glen Falkenstein and Dub Smothers. He felt that he had made friends that he could talk magic to and that understood how hard he worked to be the best magician that he could be. He would never tell Glen, but, he would have performed in his club for free, but, since Glen had offered, after all he did make his living performing magic and entertaining.

From his meeting with Glen at the High Hat the other trips were uneventful except that he and Satin got much better at working together. He drew up plans for some special illusions and asked the carpenter on the boat to build them for him. He would have built them his self, but the shop was out of bounds for all but the carpenter. The only people that ever went in there were the painters and the carpenter. One of these he called the "Doll House". This was something that he had seen in a catalog, it didn't explain how it worked but J.J. knew what he wanted to do with it. When the carpenter and the painter finished, it was beautiful! He paid the carpenter $10.00 and the painter $5.00, and he was really happy with it. The first time he and Satin rehearsed it, he was very happy with the effect. Satin was able to squeeze into the small space with no trouble. He was only going to use this trick one or two times a trip and only when there were children between the ages of 4 and 12 on board. Many trips they would not have any children and then on the next trip they would have a dozen or so. Many times the children were in steerage class and couldn't afford to eat in the theater/dining room. When J.J. saw these children he would gather them up and bring them to the show. Captain Reed had seen J.J. doing this and he had no objection. He always made sure they were gone before the gambling started, which normally was right after the show.

When they landed in Chicago on the next trip J.J. and Satin both went to the High Hat Club to see Glen. They took him a poster from the boat and Glen sent a runner to find the artist he was using. They had barely finished eating when the artist appeared. He was a small in stature but was really talented. In less than ten minutes he had made a sketch of J.J. and Satin. Satin described the costume she would wear and he got it down to the smallest detail, this really surprised them both.

When they left the High Hat Club Satin went to see her parents and J.J. headed back to the boat. Patricia and Mario had gone to see some of their relatives in Chicago.

Italians were like the Irish; there was family everywhere. J.J. knew there were probably some Irish kin there but did not know who they were. He had written his mother and told her to let him know if there were any but he had not heard back from her yet.

The boat left the next morning at 10 a.m. for the return to New Orleans. As usual it was fully loaded with cargo and would not have to stop anywhere except to take on passengers and let them off. August on the Mississippi was fairly smooth sailing. Their trips in April, May and June were a lot harder due to rains and snow run off.

J.J. and Mario enjoyed sitting on the deck and watching the riverbanks, it seemed that they always saw something new and amazing.

The small towns that they didn't stop at seemed to be growing. You could see carpenters working in every one of them. One of the things that really amazed them was that there were some very large homes being built along the river. These houses always sat up high on a hill and this was so impressive that you could see all the details. J.J. said that he hoped someday he could have a home like that somewhere he enjoyed. Mario said that he was going to have a big, big home and it was going to be on a park or as close to the park as he could get it.

They arrived back at New Orleans and Aunt Mary had three letters, one from his mother, one from Madeline and one from Gloria. Since he had two nights he had brought Satin and Patricia and Mario to his aunt and uncles and they would all spend two nights there. In the letter from his mother he found out that they were headed to New York. They would be playing a theater there for ten weeks. Then they would go back to stay with Madeline and Forrest until after the new year and then they were booked in Baltimore and then in Boston. His mother was looking forward to New York so that she could see a lot of her relatives and of course a bunch of the Willards. Of course there were a lot of the Willards also in Boston area. J.J. did not remember any of them.

From his letter from Madeline was enclosed a picture of Christopher, he was a round cheeked baby with a big grin. Madeline said that he had learned to turn over from his stomach to his back, but hadn't yet figured out how to go the other way.

J.J. had to laugh at this; he just wished he could see him in person. He showed the whole family the picture and everyone made wonderful remarks. Uncle Patrick said, "Well, ya, can tell that boy is Irish and Yankee, if they send him down here I'll have him splitting rails for the road!" Aunt Mary tuned in and said, "Yu'll do no sech thing Patrick Willard, Chris is going to be a congressman!" Uncle Patrick tuned back in and said, "They need to send him to me for a summer so as I can make a true Irishman out of him and teach him the Irish way!" Everyone laughed.

Uncle Patrick pulled J.J. outside and asked, "Son, are ye involved with either of these two young ladies?" J.J. replied no, they were just performers together. Uncle Patrick said that was too bad, cause that little Satin was sure a cute thing!

Then he laughed so hard, only the Irish can laugh at their own minds.

Gloria's letter was a little more disturbing to J.J. She told him all about this young man she had met, a Kim Dodge and that she had been seeing a lot of him. She hadn't told Papa about him yet, but she thought that when they got back from New York that she would. It seems that Kim was quite a carpenter and that his father owned a boat building business in Baltimore. He had seen her in a show and had been coming around every since. J.J. guessed that for her to marry a carpenter might not be such a bad thing. The way the country was growing and from what he saw along the riverbanks there was plenty of work for years to come. J.J. knew nothing about boat building, but looking at the *Mississippi Queen*, he figured there was money to be made doing that also. J.J. made his mind up right then, that during the Christmas shutdown period, he was going to go east and see everyone. He missed all of them so much.

They left New Orleans and headed back to Chicago. The *Mississippi Queen* was fully loaded with passengers and cargo. Captain Reed for being a young man was surely a good businessman. On the way north Captain Reed and J.J. and Mario were sitting on the deck one afternoon and Captain Reed told the both of them how pleased he was with their acts. He said that he had some news that he was sure they would both appreciate. They both pushed him and Captain Reed said, "Gentlemen, this boat is now free and clear or debt!" They both shook his hand and congratulated him on his success. He told them that he had four partners and that he hoped to have them all bought off by this time next year. He had an agreement with them each for a flat payoff. That at this point he was splitting the net profit five ways, plus he received a salary for being the captain. All the partners were very pleased with how things had gone for the *Mississippi Queen*. Each of them already had their investment back and from now on every thing they made was net profit. He was a full two years ahead of what they had expected.

They pulled into Chicago a full two hours ahead of schedule and this made everyone happy, the passengers all thanked the Captain for the wonderful journey and several even told J.J. that they were coming to see him at the High Hat Club. He knew this would make Glen happy. The *Mississippi Queen* was not due to leave Chicago until Monday morning at 10 am, so they had 3 full nights in Chicago. J.J. had a couple of the deck hands help him take his magic to the carriage. Actually J.J. had to hire a wagon because he filled it up, he took all his magic.

It was about two in the afternoon when they pulled up to the High Hat Club and the only person there was Glen. Thank goodness J.J. had hired the hands to come along and help at the club because Glen could not lift anything.

On the way to the club, J.J. and Satin had seen about ten posters saying:

James Willard the Magician
With Satin Lyons
Are appearing at the High Hat Club
on Friday and Saturday
Show time is 8 p.m.

It also had both their pictures with J.J. being prominent and Satin just a little behind him in her costume. Satin was the first to see it and she squealed like she had been shot. It scared J.J., he thought something had happened to her. He almost jumped out of the carriage. Then they both laughed.

Glen came out to meet them and he showed the men where to unload all the equipment as soon as it was unloaded J.J. and Satin started setting it up. One of the things about the High Hat Club was that it had a circular stage and there was an entrance from the rear of the stage. This entrance had a red velvet drape covering it and this made it easy for Satin to bring things from off stage and to carry them back. J.J. and Satin had everything set up for the first show by

Opening at the High Hat Club
WILLARD
THE MAGICIAN
AND COMPANY in a Bewildering Oriental Production
"Nights of Enchantment"
50 YEARS
SUCCESS
Unequaled for
MORALITY
INSTRUCTION
and
AMUSEMENT
High Class
WILLARD
THE MAGICIAN
A COMPANY OF FIRST CLASS ARTISTS
NELLIE
DAVENPORT
Some of Nellie Davenport's Many Marvels
MARVELOUS   MYSTIFYING
Wonderful Talking and Dancing Dolls Troup of Royal Martinettes

5 p.m. Glen told Satin to go home and bring her family to the show tonight. She left but first she checked with J.J. to see what time she should be back, he told her by 7 p.m. no later than 7:15. J.J. left and went to the boarding house and rented a room, Patricia and Mario were staying with relatives.

Satin came back with her entire family, her father John and mother Georgette and four other kids ranging in age from 5 to 14 and they were all there by 7 p.m. Frances took them to a table that was close to the stage and sat and talked with Georgette for a little while. Satin's father was a barrel-breasted man with lots of hair and a very rough appearance. One of his arms was as big as both of J.J.'s put together. The key thing that J.J. noticed about him was his eyes—they were warm and gentle, not at all matching the rest of the man. When he took J.J.'s hand John's hand almost swallowed J.J.'s and it truly felt like the hand of a man that worked really hard.

The house was really beginning to fill by 7:30 and Satin and J.J. went back stage to prepare for the show. Glen came back stage and he was so happy he was almost dancing, they couldn't get any more people in and they had people standing outside wanting to come in. He told J.J. that he had never ever had so many people in his club. He pulled J.J. to the side and asked him if they would be willing to do a second show that evening. J.J. asked Satin and she said you bet, as long as her palm got some green! Glen laughed and said, "Girl you sure do drive a hard bargain!" She laughed and said, "Why Mr. Falkenstein Sir, I learned from you!" Glen laughed again and said he would take care of both of them. Satin said, "Mr. Falkenstein, how about a split, you take 60% of the ticket sales and we will take 40%?" Glen thought a minute. He laughed and said, "Since it is a second show, you have a deal!" Satin then turned to J.J. and with a very coy smile said, "J.J., I'll split it with you!" J.J. smiled now it was his turn to laugh and he agreed.

Glen Falkenstein introduced James Willard the Magician and for the next hour he performed with Satin an almost perfect show. This was totally different from performing on the *Mississippi Queen*, these people were not stuck on a boat, yet he held them mesmerize for every trick. They gasped, they cheered and they applauded every single thing he and Satin did. He was called back for three "curtain calls", each time he performed just one more trick for them, after the third one he thanked them and appreciated their support and that he would perform different magic tomorrow evening and if they came back he hoped they would enjoy that show also. "He had not performed his "flying bird cage". He was saving that for the next evening.

Glen Falkenstein came back stage at 10:30 p.m. and asked if they were ready. J.J. told him they were and Glen went out and introduced them all over again. When J.J. went thru the drape he was surprised, the club was again filled to capacity. He immediately produced a bouquet of flowers he then went to a very pretty lady sitting near the stage and produced a real rose for her. This brought some *oohs* and *ahhs* from the audience. J.J. knew he had them and again, he and Satin performed an almost flawless show for the audience. This again was a wonderful feeling for J.J. Satin seemed to be floating when she was on stage. For J.J. time seemed to slow down and he saw every movement in slow motion, something he had never ever felt before. Just before he ended the show, he thought to himself that this was truly magic. The feeling was tremendous and he really did not want the evening to end. He and Satin took several bows and then exited thru the drapes. Back stage he hugged her and told her she was fantastic. She laughed and said, "And rich also Mr. Willard!" Then she laughed her little laugh and all J.J. could do was laugh also.

Satin went home with her parents and said she would see him tomorrow.

Glen came back stage and asked J.J. to come sit with him at his table. Everyone was gone except Frances and they all sat down to a large steak. J.J. was so wound up from the show that he was glad they had asked him.

Frances Falkenstein was very talkative and J.J. was sure that she must be a Willard because she chatted just like his sisters and his mother—of course his mother wasn't a Willard by birth. After dinner Glen and J.J. went out on a porch that overlooked the lake and smoked a cigar. Glen was so proud of what had happened that he just seemed to glow. The two men sat there both feeling that they had been apart of something that was wonderful. About 1:30 a.m. on Saturday morning J.J. walked from the High Hat Club to the boarding house, when he finally went to sleep that night he slept with a feeling of satisfaction.

Saturday night was a total repeat of Friday night, with one exception. Patricia and Mario had brought a bunch of their Italian relatives to the first show. The Italian's did not just clap, they hollered and cheered and there was so much energy in the club that J.J. could feel it in the air, it was vibrating. Satin, well, these Italian men certainly appreciated a good-looking blond. Every time she came out on stage there were a couple of them that were throwing money to her! She would give them a big smile and wink and pick it up and not lose one step in the performance. After the show was over Patricia and Mario insisted that they come out front and meet their cousins. J.J. shook many hands and Satin got kissed on both her cheeks more than she had ever been kissed in her life. They soon left and J.J. and Satin prepared for the second show, again, that second show was sold out.

The flying bird cage was the last trick of the evening for both the first and second shows, as soon as he finished that he would bow and go back stage. Satin would have his other coat ready and she would take the bird out and put it in its cage. He then would go back out and perform a card or coin trick as the new coat was loaded. He was thankful that he had a tailor make another jacket that was exactly like the one his mother had made, well, almost, if you didn't know, you could not tell them apart.

Satin and J.J. were exhausted after the second show. They packed all the magic and had it ready to load tomorrow. Glen asked if they would come to dinner on Sunday and they both agreed to be

there at one in the afternoon. Satin took a carriage to her parents' house and J.J. headed to the boarding house.

The next morning J.J. slept till 7 a.m. and then had breakfast. As soon as he finished he went looking for a wagon and a couple of men to haul the magic back to the boat. It was 10 a.m. before he found a couple of men and a wagon and they headed to the High Hat Club to load. J.J. had to go around back and get Glen to let them in. He looked at the lake and saw something that was strange. Where they were the lake was calm, but looking north he could see large waves, it was something he would never forget. Before Glen opened the back door a large gust of wind blew in and it was very cold wind!

They had the wagon loaded by noon and were headed to the *Mississippi Queen* and it was cold, with the wind blowing so hard that all three men could hardly see. When they reached the boat J.J. went and found George and asked if he would show the men where to put the magic. J.J. went to his cabin and got his heavy coat and then caught a carriage back to the High Hat. It was almost 1:30 when he got back but he knew all his magic was on board the boat. He and Satin had all day tomorrow to unpack it and set up for tomorrow nights show.

Satin arrived at 12:45 and she had on a real warm fur coat. J.J. asked her where she got such a coat and she just winked and said, "Oh, this ole thing, well, an Indian gave it to me!"
The High Hat was not open on Sunday and Frances had prepared a roast with potatoes and carrots that was delicious. After dinner Glen gave Satin and J.J. an envelope. J.J. just stuck his in his pocket because he trusted Glen and knew what they had agreed on was there. Satin wasn't that trusting and she opened hers and then she let out a big sigh!

She said, "Mr. Falkenstein, there is $300.00 in here, isn't that a mistake! Glen, with a lot of humor said, "Aw, Gee, let me see, well there must be a mistake, you should only have $10.00!" Then he laughed harder than J.J. had ever seen him laugh. "No cute little girlie, that is your 50% of the 40% that we agreed on for the second shows!" Satin ran over hugged him around the neck and kissed both his cheeks. Then she ran over and grabbed Frances and did the same to her She came to J.J., she hugged him and said, "Mr. Willard, I sure do like this magic business, this is more money than I could have made working here as a waitress in six months!"

J.J. told her that she should give Captain Reed at least $200.00 for him to keep for her until they came back to Chicago and she could put it in the bank. Glen told her he would deposit it for her if she wanted him to and she decided that would be best, she gave him $250.00 to put in her account and her deposit book so the bank would make sure and get it in the right account. She would pick up the book when they got back to Chicago. Satin then took a carriage back to her parents and said she would see J.J. on the boat in the morning.

Monday morning was cold and windy in Chicago. A cold spell had come in and the lake had waves on it that were at least four feet high, it reminded J.J. of the waves in the Gulf of Mexico when they were on the barge. He laughed to himself, at least this time he had no horses to attend to.

The *Mississippi Queen* left the dock at Chicago headed for New Orleans at exactly 10 a.m. She was fully loaded.

The *Mississippi Queen* sailed into New Orleans from Chicago with a full load of cargo and a full list of passengers. She had pretty much set a record from Chicago to New Orleans making the trip in less than two weeks. Captain Reed had really pushed the crew because he wanted to get back to Chicago for one more trip before the rivers and canal froze. Since the *Queen* was so new she handled the trip with no problems, but the crew was really tired.

Captain Reed told everyone that he would like to start back the next day but realized that the crew needed to rest, so, they would pull out on Wednesday at 10 a.m.

This gave everyone two nights in New Orleans. George told J.J. that he was going ashore to see a certain lady that he knew and that probably he would spend all that he had made over the last couple of months. J.J. convinced George that he should give him $30.00 to save for him. George thought about it and then said, "Yes sir, Mr. Willard, thas a good thought, here!" So J.J. kept George's money until they were back on the boat on Wednesday.

Patricia, Mario and Satin said they wanted to do some things while in New Orleans so it left J.J. free to go see his Uncle Patrick and Aunt Mary and of course his cousins. J.J. convinced his Uncle and Aunt and cousins to let him treat them to a restaurant meal, actually they were pretty easy to convince. Monday night they all dressed in their finest and went to Linda Prudhomme's Café de Paree. Linda called her food Cajun delight, which consisted of a bowl of gumbo, fried shrimp, fried catfish and fried oysters, with dirty rice and a salad.

It was totally impossible to eat all the food she put in front of you, but everyone sure tried. Mrs. Prudhomme was a short stocky blonde woman who had married a Frenchman, they had started the restaurant together. Then she had caught him messing with one of the waitresses and had kicked him out. Last anyone heard of him he had shipped out on a boat headed back to France. Despite this, Linda Prudhomme was a very happy person.

The evening cost J.J. $50.00 but he felt it was well worth it and his aunt and uncle very seldom went out to eat and they both seemed to really enjoy the evening.

The *Queen* left New Orleans on Wednesday morning at exactly 10 a.m. as Captain Reed had said it would.

They pulled into Chicago and it was snowing! Captain Reed told everyone that they were leaving at 7 a.m. the next morning, regardless if he had passengers or not. The cargo crew worked all night loading the *Queen*. Only Satin actually went on shore, she went to the High Hat and picked up her bank book and then went to the bank and deposited her money, she didn't go home but came straight back to the boat.

Winter seemed to be early this year, October it doesn't

normally freeze hard like it was trying to do. Captain Reed true to his word pulled out into the canal at 7 a.m. the next morning. Mario and J.J. had helped the crew during the night, when the *Queen* pulled away from the dock they were both exhausted. They ate a really big breakfast of eggs, steak and biscuits, then went out on the rear deck and watched the water for a few minutes. They both went to the cabin and slept till 4 p.m. that afternoon. That was something that J.J. never did, but Mario had done many times after spending a night entertaining one of the ladies on board. J.J. woke up feeling he had missed something by sleeping during the day. He also felt very tired and was glad that there were very few passengers on board. Captain Reed had announced that there would not be any entertainment that night, not because of J.J. but because the band members had also worked all night loading the cargo. Captain Reed believed in treating his people right and that was why everyone respected him so much.

When they reached St. Louis the booking agent told them that he had a lot of people that wanted to be on the *Queen*. As it turned out, the next day the boat was completely full. A boat being full has it good sides, but there is also a big down side possible. Satin and J.J. performed their show to a full house and then the gambling started. One person who shall go unnamed felt like he was being cheated at one of the tables. He pulled his gun and was going to shoot when a man that said he was a dentist shot the man from under the table. Apparently the dentist had a derringer that was in his lap. It didn't kill the man, but he had to be put off the boat at the next stop so that a doctor could take the bullet out. The dentist said he was sorry but felt if he didn't shoot the man, the man would have killed someone.

The dentist coughed a lot and held a handkerchief to his mouth. No one got his name. Mario had not been playing at that table and had seen the whole thing and he told Captain Reed that the dentist did the only thing he could. The dentist got off in New Orleans. Several years later someone said that it was Doc Holliday. J.J. never knew for sure if it was him or not. Actually it was a good trip except for that one small incident.

The telegraph informed Captain Reed that the canal and the river were frozen already and that there was no way they could get back to Chicago. Captain Reed then went to the cargo agent to see if he could get loads to St. Louis before it froze up also. He did get a load for St. Louis and so he told the crew that they would be pulling out for St. Louis in two days. J.J. went to the bank and then sent money to St. Francis de Salle in Houma, Louisiana. This was something that he had done every time since he had been on the *Queen*. It wasn't so much for religious reasons but he felt the priest there put the money to good use helping those that needed it.

J.J. was a good Irish Catholic, his mother had made him a true believer. She told him that they had been very lucky during the war and she felt it was because they all had an angel on their shoulders. She truly believed it! J.J. believed it also, because they had never gone hungry as many people had during that awful war. They sometimes only had rice and beans, but, they always had plenty of that.

On the way to St. Louis J.J. talked to Captain Reed about what his plans were and wondered if he would mind if he went east during the Thanksgiving and Christmas period. Captain Reed said that would be fine with him, that with the way the weather was turning he really didn't expect many passengers during the next couple of months. Actually Captain Reed told him that the way things were, it would help him not to have to pay entertainers when they didn't have a passenger load.

J.J. kept this to himself until the night before they would reach St. Louis. Then he called Mario aside and asked him if he and his sister wanted to stay in St. Louis until after Christmas. Mario, said, "You bet, we need a vacation, you know my legs wobble when we're on dry ground!" Then he laughed. That night after the show J.J. went to Satin and asked if she wanted to stay home in Chicago for the next couple of months, she said sure. When they docked, J.J. got Satin's money and then he bought her a ticket on the railroad. She was all excited about riding a train; she had never done that. J.J. told her that he would contact her after Christmas about what the plan was. When they reached the train station Satin did something that J.J. was not prepared for, she grabbed him and gave him a kiss on the mouth that was very exciting, then she said, "See, Mr. James Willard that is what you have to look forward to!" Leaving him standing there, she got on the train and gave him her big smile from the window as the train left the station. He just stood there and waved until she was out of sight.

That night J.J. ate at the Misuraca Italian Restaurant and was treated like a king. Momma Rose made him a special steak with lots of pasta and then he said goodbye to Patricia and Mario.

Riding back to the *Queen* in the carriage a deep spell of loneliness set in. These three people were his close friends and he was truly going to miss them. They had all been together only a few months but he felt like he had known each one for years. An emptiness set into his stomach. It got worse over the next few nights as he performed his magic without Satin. He kept thinking about that warm and wonderful kiss.

Docking in New Orleans J.J. went on shore and hired two men and a wagon to help him unload his magic and carry it to his Uncle Patrick's. He did not want his magic on board the boat without him there to watch it. George also helped and they loaded the wagon pretty quickly.

J.J. went back on board and told Captain Reed and everyone else he came in contact with goodbye and that he would see them after Christmas. He gave George $10.00 for helping him and also as a thank you for all he had helped J.J. with over the past few months. George was most appreciative, he wished Mr. Willard a very good Christmas and hoped he enjoyed seeing all his family.

When the wagon pulled up to Uncle Patrick's there was no one home, so J.J. and the men unloaded all the magic into the stables in a room that was empty. This was a good place because it was dry and in New Orleans that sometimes was hard to find.

J.J. paid the men and then saddled one of the horses and

headed to town. He went to the train station and purchased a ticket that would take him all the way to Baltimore, Maryland. The train would leave in the morning at 7 a.m. The ticket master asked J.J. if he was kin to Patrick and when he told him that he was his nephew the ticket master gave him the employee rate, this saved J.J. about $100.00 and he thanked the man. He then went to the bank and drew out enough money to last him, but he asked the President of the bank if he would give him a letter of credit in case something happened on the trip and he would need more. The bank president checked J.J.'s balance and was quite impressed and gave a J.J. a letter of credit for $1000.00, just in case he needed it. Bankers all over the states honored other banks letters of credits. They would give the customer the money and then wire the other bank that they had done so and the bank issuing the letter of credit would then send money to the other bank. This system worked well for men of means during this period. The bank that gave the customer money always charged a small fee, most of the time 10% of what money the client wanted.

J.J. went back to his uncle and aunt's and spent the night with them. They had prepared a lot of packages for him to take to everyone; special things for baby Chris and for Gloria, Madeline, Forrest and his mother and dad. The next morning at 5 a.m. Aunt Mary had a good breakfast for him. Uncle Patrick took him in the carriage to the station at 6:30 a.m. He looked forward to the trip and more in seeing everyone.

The train was considerably faster than the wagon J.J. and his family had come from New York to New Orleans in. The train was not a comfortable form of travel. No wonder people enjoyed riding on the *Mississippi Queen*. After two days and nights on the train he was starting to wonder if he would ever get to Baltimore. The seats were hard and there were two people on each bench seat. They faced two other people. You rode either facing the rear or facing the front of the train and either way it was totally uncomfortable. People on the train were friendly, but J.J. kept it a secret that he was a magician. He just told people he was going east to see his sister's new baby. The train would stop every few hours for water and fuel and at those stops is where you ate and went to the bathroom, sometimes just behind a bush.

J.J. had to change trains several times before getting to Baltimore; he never had any layover time. The most was about two hours and that wasn't enough to take a bath or clean up. At the end of the fourth day the train pulled into Baltimore. He stepped off and took a deep breath and immediately went to find a hotel.

As soon as he had taken a nice long hot bath and changed clothes he found a nice restaurant. The food was delicious and he was starved. He then went back to the hotel and slept for eight wonderful hours in a nice soft bed with clean sheets. He awoke refreshed and ready to continue his journey. First, he had never been in this area and decided to see Baltimore. On the *Mississippi Queen* a lot of the passengers had told him about the city, he wanted to check it out for himself.

He went out and hired a carriage and told the driver that he wanted to see Baltimore and especially Baltimore Cathedral. The driver told him his name was Lawrence Minmun. He knew a lot about the city, that really he should see the Cathedral but also the new city hall. So they headed toward the city hall first. It was indeed a wonderful building, 3 stories high made out of white marble and with a dome and a clock and a great bell. Lawrence told him it had just been finished in 1866 and that every one was proud of it because it was built under budget. According to Lawrence it was unusual for any government project to be "under budget!"

Then they headed to the cathedral. To say J.J. was impressed would be a total understatement. J.J. asked Lawrence to wait and he went in. J.J. had never seen such a beautiful church. He sat and just felt like he was in the presence of God, he was totally amazed at all the detail.

They then headed for Fort McHenry. J.J. wanted to see this fort because of the song *The Star Spangled Banner*. Of course they could not go in. He looked at it and in his mind he could just imagine the British ship sitting there and shooting cannons at the fort while Francis Scott Key watched from a British ship. For some reason this filled J.J. with pride that he was a citizen of the United States of America.

J.J. asked Lawrence if he knew where the Dodge ship building business was? Lawrence said he sure did and J.J. told him to head there. When they arrived J.J. was impressed, as there was a large ship under construction, a steel ship with a paddle wheel on the right side.

J.J. asked Lawrence to wait and then went to the building that looked like an office. There was one person in the office and J.J. asked him if a Kim Dodge was there or Mr. Dodge. The gentleman told him no, that Kim would not come to the yard until the ship was at the point of needing carpenter work on the interior. That Mr. Dodge Sr. was out trying to buy more materials. J.J. gave the man his card and asked him to please give it to Kim Dodge when he saw him. He was disappointed because he had hoped to meet this Kim Dodge so that he could decide if he was worthy of his sister Gloria, but that would have to wait for the future. The gentleman looked at J.J.'s card and asked him, "Sir, did you need a ship built?" J.J. told him no, that he just wanted to meet Kim. For a very short moment, J.J. thought about asking him how much it would cost to build a ship like the *Mississippi Queen*, then thought that would be foolish and a waste of his time and the man's time. He then went back to the carriage and asked Lawrence if he knew where Lancaster, Pennsylvania was and how was the easiest way to get there? Lawrence told him that he could take a train or a stage. Then J.J. told him that he actually was going to a farm that was south of Lancaster on the Susquehanna River. Lawrence told him if that was the case, he should rent a horse or a buggy. J.J. asked him to drive him to a place where he could rent or buy a horse or a buggy. This Lawrence did, and J.J. thanked him for the tour, paid him and entered the Baltimore Horse stable and Black Smith shop.

Inside J.J. met a man that was about 6'5" tall and big as a building by the name of James Prevott, one thing J.J. didn't want to do was make this man mad. They discussed the rental of a buggy and horse, but Mr. Prevott told J.J. that he might be better off buying and then they discussed prices. Mr. Prevott showed J.J. several horses and buggies. They discussed all the possibilities and J.J. finally decided that he would buy a horse and saddle. They haggled over the price for a little bit and finally reached an agreement. The horse was named Madam Grant and Mr. Prevott assured him that she was only four years old and was fully broke and would ride with a smooth gait. J.J. paid him and then saddled Madam Grant and gave her a test ride. She did have a smooth gait and was very easy to handle. J.J. got Mr. Prevott to throw in a few pieces of rope with the deal.

He then headed back to the hotel to pick up his luggage and paid his bill. He had two suitcases, one with his clothes and one with all the gifts for Christopher and a few items of magic.

After eating lunch and picking up a small snack and canteen of water he headed north toward Aberdeen, Maryland. Then on to Havre de Graca where he would cross the Susquehanna River. He entered Pennsylvania about dusk and decided he needed to find a place to stay. He saw a farm and went up and asked the owner if he would mind him spending the night in his barn. He told the gentleman that he was headed to the Edwards horse farm on the river just south of Lancaster. The man told him that he knew the Edwards, and that he was only a few miles away but he was welcome to spend the night. The man invited him to have supper with him and his wife, which J.J. did. He was pleased because he had already eaten all the food that he had purchased. He spent the night in the barn sleeping on several horse blankets that were there. The smell wasn't so great, but, J.J was so tired he didn't care and it didn't bother him.

The next morning he fed Madam Grant some hay and water and then saddled her and was about to leave when the gentleman came out with a cup of coffee and a biscuit. He explained to J.J. how to find the Edward's farm. J.J. thanked him for his kindness. It was almost noon when J.J. and Madam Grant turned into a road that was marked by a sign that said *Edward's Quality Horses*. On each side of the road was a fence and inside those fields were some very beautiful horses. Some of the younger ones would come to the fence, then run along the fence, as if challenging them to a race. After about a quarter of a mile, J.J. came to a house. It was a nice house, two stories high and had a very tiny front porch. He guessed people here didn't sit on the porch in the evenings the way they did in the south.

He tied Madam Grant to the post and went and knocked on the door, an older lady who he did not know answered the door. J.J. said, "Madam is this the home of Forrest Edwards?" About that time he heard a squeal and Madeline came running and grabbed him around the neck and hugged him hard. Then she turned and said, "Momma Edwards, this is my little brother James Jr.!" The woman's face turned to a warm glow, and she came threw the door and hugged J.J., then she said, "Young man, I have heard so much about you, welcome to our home!"

Madeline helped J.J. unload Madam Grant and she laughed when she heard the name of the horse she said, "With a name like that she is either a fighter or a drinker!" Then she laughed that wonderful laugh that J.J. had missed for so long.

They put the suitcases on the porch and then Madeline showed him around to the stables and they gave Madam Grant some oats and water. Madeline showed J.J. her son Christopher. Christopher was now a big boy. Blond headed, blue eyes just like his father and when J.J. picked him up the boy was solid as a rock. Chris Immediately pulled on J.J.'s ears, when J.J. laughed, Christopher laughed. Now J.J. really felt like an uncle. About that time Forrest entered from the back door, saw J.J. and ran and picked him up completely off his feet and swung around like they were dancing. When he finally put J.J. down, Forrest turned to his mother and said, "Mother, this man is not only a magician, but he is also a horseman, he helped me buy the horses that I brought back!"

About then an elderly man entered the back door, it was Forrest's father. Henry Edwards was a man in his middle 60s with gray hair, blue eyes and about 5'10" tall with a face with many wrinkles. When introduced to J.J. he had a very wonderful smile, even with the teeth that were missing, a very warm person.

J.J. suddenly remembered his suit cases and went out the front door and brought them in, he opened the one with all the gifts for Christopher and gave them all to Madeline. She opened every one and everyone *oohed* and *aahed* over each one!

Madeline then showed J.J. to a bedroom upstairs, and showed him where he could wash up. He did and then went down and they all sat down for lunch. J.J. was totally starved. The biscuit and coffee had long since gone away, the food was delicious. Mrs. Edwards was quite a cook. Her German heritage had taught her many delicious things to prepare and over the next few weeks J.J. enjoyed it all.

After lunch Forrest wanted to know if J.J. would like to go for a ride and see the farm, which of course J.J. did. They rode all the way to the river and Forrest showed him where they kept a boat for fishing, which they would do in the next few days. There was a large area of trees and Forrest told him that they would go there tomorrow, hunting for turkeys. He said it was sort of tradition that his family always tried to have a turkey for Thanksgiving.

The next few weeks seemed to fly by, first the snow, which came and covered everything. Then Thanksgiving day dinner. During this time J.J. helped Forrest and Henry take care of the horses. The world of entertaining on the *Mississippi Queen* seemed like another life.

J.J. enjoyed this life of living on a farm, taking care of the animals, the chickens and the pigs, well, maybe not the pigs. There was one big hog that every time J.J. fed them, this hog would just talk and talk to him. J.J. wondered if that hog really was intelligent enough to know what was happening around him. Of course he was

a boar and all he had to do was service the sows and eat and sleep. Guess that was why he always talked to J.J. Forrest said that Old Jed, as the hog was called, must have taken a liking to J.J., because he would follow him around the pen when J.J. was there, almost like a puppy. During this period J.J. almost felt like a kid again. Felt like he was playing all the time the way he had when he was a boy. He made a game out of feeding the animals and cleaning the stables. His mind was totally off magic and performing, well almost that is. At night after supper he would do a few things of hand magic, produce coins for Christopher or Henry and Mrs. Edwards, they all loved it, and it did keep his skills up.

On the 21st of December a two horse carriage pulled up to the front, James Sr., Elizabeth and Gloria had arrived for Christmas. When they saw James Jr. there was lots of hugging and laughing and talking. Every one of the Willards were all talking at the same time. Now J.J. really felt at home. This was truly a happy home and the Christmas was the best they had all had.

Forrest, James Sr., Henry and James Jr. all went into Lancaster on December 22nd and each did their Christmas shopping. Forrest took the ladies in the next day and they did their shopping. It was a grand Christmas with gifts for all, but Christopher got the most.

The boy had so many clothes, toys and all that of course he was too young to really know what was going on, other than he loved the things that made noise. His grandfather Henry gave him a red wagon and he was delighted when J.J. would pull him around the house in it.

After Christmas J.J. and Gloria got a chance to talk. She told him about Kim Dodge and how they were getting along, but with her cool head, she told J.J. that she was not going to do anything until she was at least sixteen. That Kim was in Philadelphia building a house for some rich man. That the house was going to take at least a year to finish. It was apparently a very large house on a hill over looking the river.

She said that his father had a ship under construction. Kim

would be going there to work on all the interior woodwork when it got to the point and was ready. In the mean time, she was saving all her money that their father was paying her for the shows they were doing. J.J. told her he had gone to the Dodge Ship Yard and had seen a large ship under construction there.

James Sr. and J.J. also talked. It seems that James Sr. had built a good reputation in the theaters and that they had plenty of bookings. James Sr. told J.J. that he was making more money than he had ever made in his life. They would probably buy a place some where near, so that Elizabeth could be near Madeline and Christopher. That it would be a while because of all the bookings they had. They might even settle in Baltimore. It was a nice town—with the railroads they could get almost anywhere to do their shows. J.J. told him about Glen Falkenstein and his High Hat Club and how great it had felt to do two shows a night there. His dad hugged him and told him he knew that feeling. One evening the two talked magic till everyone else had gone to bed. Each giving the other ideas about things they could perform.

J.J.'s mother Elizabeth wanted to know all about Satin, Patricia, Mario and the Falkenstein's. J.J. took the time to describe them for her and to tell her in detail about Dub and Dolly Smothers, the High Hat Club and the Misuraca Italian restaurant.

Elizabeth told him in detail about all her brothers, sisters and the Willards who were kin to them. Most of this info just went in one ear and out the other because J.J. couldn't picture most of them. A few that lived in Brooklyn he still remembered, but just barely. On January 2nd it was time to go and J.J. really had to force himself to leave. It was one of the hardest things he had ever done, but he had to go. He saddled Madam Grant and told every one goodbye and headed to Philadelphia. It took all day and both he and Madam Grant were cold. The roads were covered with snow and ice and the temperature must have been below freezing all day. When they got into Philadelphia it was dark. J.J. found a stable and boarded Madam Grant for the night, the owner was already gone home and there was just a stable boy there. J.J. went and found a hotel. After eating he went to the train station and got a schedule for the train trip. There was a train that would leave at 9 a.m. and with connections he would be back in New Orleans by January 7th. He would have an over night layover in Birmingham, Alabama. Thinking about this made him happy because he dreaded riding the train straight thru without having a stop to wash and change clothes and eat a decent meal.

He then went to the stables. There he found the owner and sold him Madam Grant, he really wished there was some way that he could keep her she was a good horse, but there was no way. Actually he was pleased, with the sale, he made $30.00 more than she had cost him. Which he felt like that was a wonderful profit since he had only owned her for a couple of months.

He then went to the station and caught the train south. They went thru Wilmington, Delaware, then Baltimore, Washington, D.C. He could see the capital from the train, in a way, he was sorry he could not stay a day of two to see all of Washington and finally into Richmond, Virginia. At Richmond he had a two hour layover because he had to change trains for Raleigh. After changing trains he again thought that the seats had not gotten any softer, they were still hard wood.

There was one thing he had done in Philadelphia and that was to buy two pillows, one for his seat and one for his head, he laughed at himself when he was changing trains, because he was sure he looked funny caring a suitcase and two pillows and a blanket. They really helped make his trip a little better or at least a little more comfortable.

Early the next morning the train pulled into Columbia, South Carolina and again he had to change trains for Atlanta, Georgia, they reached Atlanta in the late evening and again he had to change trains for Birmingham, Alabama, but this time there was only a 30 minute layover. They reached Birmingham late that evening and J.J. went and found a hotel. He took a long hot bath, shaved, which he was now doing every three or four days.

He put on clean clothes and went to eat. The hotel had a really nice restaurant and J.J. was feeling good after the bath, but the days on the train had him very tired. He headed to the room and slept hard till the next morning. Before he went to sleep he could feel the swaying of the train, he laughed and said to himself, "I'll take a boat anytime!"

The next morning he had a nice breakfast, used the indoor facilities and then went and caught the train for New Orleans. It left at 8 a.m. They went thru Tuscaloosa, Alabama then headed for Jackson, Mississippi. One of the things J.J. noticed about trains was that they seemed to back up a lot, then wait a lot for other trains to pass.

They pulled into Jackson late in the evening and J.J. again had to change trains for New Orleans. They left Jackson, Mississippi at 7 p.m. and would not get into New Orleans until early the next morning, with his pillows and blanket J.J. slept pretty good on the train that night, except that he woke up every time the train stopped, which was at every little town along the way, they finally pulled into New Orleans the next morning about 7:30 a.m.

J.J. stepped outside and yes, he was back in the south, it was warm, about 60 degrees, and truthfully, it felt good. J.J. headed over to a place near the station that stayed open all night and served coffee and donuts. Then he found a carriage and headed to his Uncle Patrick's. Aunt Mary was busy doing laundry and she saw him and gave him a big hug. He told her that he was just going to stay a little and then get someone to help him get his magic out of the stable. She said, "J.J. before you do that, maybe you should go down and see if the *Queen* is in dock!" He told her he hadn't even thought of that and she was right.

Chapter 9

Disaster on the Mississippi Queen

Sure enough there sat *The Mississippi Queen* she was in all her glory, but, wait, she was all draped in black! What did that mean?

He got out of the carriage with a very sick feeling in his stomach. He went on board and the first person he could find was George. George was sitting in a chair in the dining room and he was crying like a baby. He saw J.J., stood up and grabbed him in a bear hug and cried some more.

Finally J.J. got him to take a deep breath and tell him what was wrong! George said, "Mr. James, it was awful!" J.J. said, "George, what was awful?"

George, "That terrible gambler, he done shot Captain Reed dead!" J.J.'s knees buckled under him and he sat into a chair, he could not believe what George was telling him. All he could get out of his mouth was, "When?" George said, "The night before last, we was a comin' into NaOrlans and this man got into a fight with his table and he pulled a gun. Captain tried to calm the man down, Captain was a standing in front of ta other gambler who tha awful man was arguing with, when *bam*, the man shot Captain, right thar in the heart, killed him dead right then!" Both men cried like little babies.

John Thibodaux came in and went over and hugged both men, then he said, "James I am glad you are here, I need your help in arranging things. As the senior officer it is up to me. I have contacted the other owners. They are all coming by train and will be here tomorrow and the next day. But, we will have to hold the funeral tomorrow or no later than the next day. Can you help me make arrangements?"

New Orleans was overcast with gray and black clouds this gloomy day, the funeral procession wound thru the streets, the black carriage that carried Captain James Reed's body was followed by the *Mississippi Queen's* band playing solemn tunes. They were followed by the entire crew and behind them were most of the other owners of the *Queen*. The carriage went by the dock where the *Queen* was. Just as they arrived there the *Queen's* whistles started blowing. It was a very eerie sound. Included in the procession were dock hands, a lot of the railroad workers and a lot of the Irish. The procession was almost three blocks long with Cajuns, English, Blacks, Mexicans, Irish, Germans and many others. Captain Reed was a well respected man, a man that was known for keeping his word and treating everyone as equals. Flowers adorned the entire carriage, they had come from all over.

After the funeral the crew and owners went to the *Queen* and Jon Boudreaux had laid out a spread fit for a king. A lot of those that were at the funeral came as all were invited. Father Mahoney whom J.J. had got to do the service came and he and J.J. had a chance to talk. J.J. told him about the cathedral in Baltimore and how very fine it was. The father said that some day he hoped to see it. Father Mahoney said that he had been assigned to New Orleans from Ireland and he had come by boat direct to New Orleans. He really had not seen any other parts of the country.

By 2 p.m. everyone had left the boat except for the owners

and the crew. A Mr. Wade Young, one of the owners told them that if they didn't mind the owners would like to talk to them about the *Queen*. Mr. Young said, "Due to circumstances, the *Queen* is only going to carry cargo for the next few months, I realize that this is going to put some of you out of work, you Mr. Willard and the band and some of the waiters, but, we just do not have in us the heart to carry passengers. We are appointing Mr. John Thibodaux as captain and we do not want him burdened with the passenger problems. We have informed the booking agents along the river of our decision. The *Queen* has good cargo contracts for the next six months. Mr. Thibodaux has told us that he only wants to be temporary Captain, but that he will do it until we can find a new Captain! Are there any questions?"

Mr. Young caught J.J. as he was leaving and asked him to go on deck with him, when they got on deck Mr. Young told him that he was truly sorry. Captain Reed had told them all about how much business he had brought to the *Queen*, people booking a trip on the *Queen* just to see him perform. J.J. thanked Mr. Young, but then asked a very blunt question, "Sir what about Captain Reed's share of the *Queen*, what will happen to that?" Mr. Young took a deep breath and then he surprised J.J. with, "His daughter Virginia, will inherit his share of the boat and all the money he had saved!"

His daughter? J.J. didn't even know he was married so he said, "His daughter?" Mr. Young answered him, "Yes, his wife died four years ago and his daughter is eight and living in Illinois with his mother and father." All the times that he and James Reed had talked, he had not once mentioned that he had a daughter. J.J. said, "Then you are setting up a trust fund for her?" Mr. Young answered, "Yes, she will receive a little each month and when she is twenty the fund will be hers, and we will continue to put one fifth of the profits into that fund each quarter!" J.J. thanked him and left the boat.

The first thing he did was go to the telegraph office and wire Mario, Patricia and Satin that they were all out of a job. He said that he would write them a letter telling them all the facts.

Instead of a carriage back to his Uncle and Aunt's he walked. He had a very lonesome feeling, he was unemployed for the first time in his life, if it hadn't been for his relatives living there, he would have just got back on the train and headed back east. When he got back to his uncle's his Aunt Mary had supper ready, he ate and then asked if they had writing paper. He then sat down and wrote Mario and Satin long letters telling them all about Captain Reeds murder, the funeral and what Mr. Young had said.

He also wrote Gloria and told her all about it and asked that she pass it on to the rest of the family. He figured since she and his mother and father had all met the Captain that she could tell them about it. The next morning, J.J. got up, put a few clothes into his case and told his aunt he was going to Houma.

He caught the train to Houma and went to see the priest in St Francis de Salles. He had a long conversation with the priest. When he came out of church he felt better. Then he went to see Norm Newby. Norm all ways made him feel better. For the next week he went shrimping with Norm and his dad. Drank lots of beer and ate lots of shrimp. They told Cajun jokes that no one understood unless you were raised in that country. It only took J.J. a day to get his Cajun back and that is all they spoke for that week, no English at all. At night when they were in a bar the other Cajuns that he knew would tease him about being gone so long that now he spoke Cajun with an Irish accent. He needed this—it got him back into the real world—the world that he had to work in and make a living in.

He headed back to New Orleans and went directly to the theater where his family had played and asked the owner if he could have a job entertaining. The owner told him that he could, but that it would be two weeks before he would open. J.J. told him that was fine.

He then went to his aunt and uncles and asked Melinda if she would be his assistant for the next couple of months, she jumped at the chance. Aunt Mary made her a couple of costumes and then with Aunt Mary's help they trained her for the stage.

Melinda was a very pretty girl and she did have a warm

presence on stage, but she wasn't Satin. He would have sent for Satin, but, he did not know how long the show would last and wasn't sure he would make any money. Melinda was willing to work for what ever he could pay her. He took a couple of his posters down to the theater from the *Mississippi Queen* and asked the owner to adapt them to his theater. Two days later he saw posters all over town and they declared:

JAMES WILLARD THE MAGICIAN RETURNS!!

James had to laugh to himself, he really hadn't thought about his being away, but he really had been. Well, at least he now had a job again and he didn't even make arrangements with the owner about pay, but he trusted the man. He had always been fair with them as a family. Warren Salles was a fair man. J.J. and Melinda played the theater for the next six weeks, a show Friday night at 8 pm, a show Saturday afternoon at 2 p.m. and a show Saturday night at 8 p.m. and then a show on Sunday at 6 p.m. They made on average a $100.00 a show and J.J. paid Melinda $20.00 of that. He had to pinch himself, he was sorry Patricia wasn't around to pinch him, he was making on average over $300.00 a week after he paid Melinda and she was making $80.00 a week. Aunt Mary showed Melinda how to do the spirit cabinet, the same way she had showed J.J.'s mother Elizabeth. They started doing that only on Saturday night. It really added to the show.

Many people that would come on Friday night would come back on Saturday because of the spirit cabinet and also J.J. did different tricks, his Friday night and Saturday night shows were totally different. J.J. paid his Aunt Mary $30.00 a week for room and board, she didn't expect it, but was grateful when he offered it. His bank account grew nicely.

Warren Salles the owner of the theater brought another owner from a theater in Baton Rouge to see J.J. and Melinda. He told that owner that he worked with them on a 60/40 split and that he could only talk to J.J. about playing his theater if he promised to be honest with J.J. and work on the same split. The man agreed and so then Melinda and J.J. went to Baton Rouge for three weeks. The first two were real good but the third week was slow. They had come to Baton Rouge in his dad's wagon and it still said "Willard's Magic Elixir" on the side. J.J. got some black paint and painted over that. He sort of hated to, but it was not the image he wanted. He then hired a sign painter and had "James Willard Magician" painted on both sides of the wagon.

When they closed in Baton Rouge he asked Melinda if she wanted to go to Houma, she said you bet, so they packed up and headed to Houma. They went to the theater there and asked if they could play there for a couple of weekends. The owner was more than happy, as he had nothing going on except rehearsals for a play that was to open in four weeks.

J.J. took their poster from the New Orleans theatre to a printer and with the help of the artist at the printers they made a poster that they could use from then on at any theater. When it was finished J.J. had them print 100 for him, then he and Melinda went through out the town putting them up where ever they would let them.

Thinking ahead, J.J. sent wires to a theater in Alexandria, Louisiana and to Shreveport, Louisiana to see if he could book them. He got wires back from them both and each gave him dates that he could play there. J.J. immediately wired each back that he accepted the dates and was mailing them posters to put up. He then mailed each of them ten posters. He felt like he was living under a lucky star! The first booking date was Alexandria and then Shreveport. He went back told Melinda that they had work for the next three months, she laughed and said that was great, she was really getting into being an entertainer. J.J. and Melinda had developed a good relationship and the audiences loved her. Melinda was not nearly as flirtatious on stage as Satin was, but she was efficient and she had a wonderful smile which she displayed ever time she came on stage.

After they packed up they all went to Norm's grandfathers

restaurant for a fish dinner, the restaurant was full of people and when they walked in every one stood up and clapped. J.J. and Melinda both took bows, then one of the Cajuns said, "Hey, J.J. we was a-clapping for Melinda!" Everyone laughed and so did J.J., then in his Irish Cajun he said, "Watch out Pierre, she is my cousin!" Everyone again laughed and several applauded appreciating that J.J. was one of them.

J.J. bought a round of beer for the house, it cost him $12.00 but this endured J.J. to the people of Houma for the rest of his life, this and of course the fact that he had gone to school here and learned their language.

The next morning they left the hotel and headed toward Alexandria; it would take them two days by wagon to get there.

When they arrived in Alexandria they found the theater right next to the river and next to the bridge that went across to Pineville, Louisiana. They located the owner of the theater and he told them that the hotel really was sort of a rough place, but that there was a real nice boarding house just a block away.

After unpacking the wagon they headed to the boarding house. The lady that ran it was a Cajun woman. When J.J. spoke Cajun to her she was impressed. She had a stable where he could board the horses and since they were staying with her she only charged them 50 cents a day for the horses and because J.J. spoke Cajun she gave them each a room that over looked the river toward the east bank and they could see Pineville. They could also see the place where the battles had taken place between the north and the south, in that area a lot of the trees were cut off about half way up and J.J. figured that was from cannon fire.

The Cajun woman's name was Marie and she confirmed that the trees looked like that because of cannon fire. She said, "The noise was terrible; you'd be sound asleep and then *boom, boom, boom*! Many men died on both sides—it was awful; I'm glad that it's over. Both sides were thieves!!" Then she laughed, "Soldiers on both sides come here and take what they want without paying. They were

James Willard
Magician

robbers, we people were lucky that we could hide rice, that is about all that kept us from starving!" From the meal that Marie put on the table that night you wouldn't think anyone had ever been without food. It was delicious. They played four nights in Alexandria. The take wasn't that good, they only cleared a total of $200.00 after their expenses; Melinda got $40.00 so this left J.J. with $160.00. To him, the way he looked at it, that was $40.00 a night, he still felt that was good for such a small town. While there J.J. talked to the owner about other theaters that might be close to Shreveport or Alexandria. The owner told him there was one in Jackson, Mississippi but said he wouldn't go there, those people were too poor for live theater and that his best bet was Memphis.

J.J. sat down with Melinda and talked about the traveling, she said she had no problems as long as they could be back in New Orleans before it got too cold. She didn't want to spend the winter sleeping in the back of the wagon! J.J. wired the owner in Memphis and got a reply back the next day. The owner knew him from the *Queen* and was eager for him to play his theater. J.J. sent him ten posters and told him they would be there by the middle of August.

They only played Shreveport for one weekend. The crowd was good, but the owner told them that it was not a town to come back the following weekend. So they packed up and headed east toward the Mississippi. They went thru Monroe, Louisiana, it was really no more than a general store and a few houses. When they got to Tallulah, Louisiana they headed north to Lake Providence. J.J. knew the riverboats stopped there and he felt it would be cheaper to travel by boat.

They lucked out, the next day the *Delta Queen* came by going north, the captain knew J.J. from the *Mississippi Queen*. The Captain said he wouldn't charge them one penny if they would put a performance on for his customers that night, they agreed and the horses and the wagon were put on the boat. That night they performed for just about an hour, they only dug out a few things from the wagon. It was just an overnight trip up the river to

Memphis. There were only about 50 people on board. J.J. told them that they would be appearing at the theater in Memphis for the next few weeks.

They arrived at the theater a full week ahead of schedule but the owner was glad to see them. He said they could start performing Friday night. They got settled into a boarding house that was about three blocks from the theater. Got the horses boarded at a stable for $5 each a week. J.J. never contacted the theater in St. Louis, they played to sold out audiences as many as four nights a week in Memphis. Riverboats docked there for the night and when the word spread that James Willard was performing in Memphis, people came from all over. Boats made sure that their passengers knew where the theater was when they docked.

J.J. felt like every night he was playing the High Hat Club in Chicago. They did performances on Wednesday, Thursday. Friday and Saturday. Melinda was making $150.00 a week and J.J. was averaging over $500.00 a week. They liked Memphis!

After all the expenses J.J. was still clearing over $400.00 a week. They played there until the first week in November, the owner told them that his door was always open to them just to wire ahead and he would confirm dates. Nine weeks at over $400.00 a week was tremendous money during this period, especially for a 18year old boy and a 20year old girl.

The *Mississippi Queen* had stopped twice during their stay in Memphis, she still was not caring passengers only freight. John Thibodaux was still the Captain, he chose to stop in Memphis so the crew could go see J.J. J.J. talked the owner into comping their tickets, after all it was Wed and they were not sold out. He told him about Captain Reed and the owner remembered, so he comped the whole crew. When they stopped the next time, which was about the middle of October J.J. pulled Captain John over and asked him if the next time they were headed south if they could hitch a ride with them. J.J. told him he had the wagon and two horses. Captain John didn't hesitate, he said, "Son, your more than welcome, I'll stop by

Queen of the Mississippi

on the way north and let you know when we'll be back!" He was a man of his word and he did just that.

Then the *Queen* came back, they loaded the horses in the stable area and the wagon on the deck and headed south. There was a new cook, but besides that the crew was almost the same. Jon Boudreaux and George had left the *Queen* to set up their own restaurant in St. Louis. Now J.J. had more friends in St. Louis. He told Melinda, "If we ever get to St. Louis, we'll have two wonderful places to eat. We can eat Italian one night and French the next night." They both laughed. Then Melinda, with a twinkle in her eye, said, "J.J. don't you know any Irish restaurants?" J.J. laughed and said, "Melinda, who in the world would pay to eat stew and boiled potatoes?"

They both laughed and she said, "You have a point my dear cousin!"

Captain Campbell, in honor of Captain Reed, kept the black drapes on the back of the *Queen*. When they arrived in New Orleans it was cold, the front had caught them at about Natchez, Mississippi and it was getting colder all the time. New Orleans is great town but not when it is cold, because it is so damp it goes right through you.

They unloaded, J.J. and Melinda both thanked Captain John and then they headed to Uncle Patrick's. Melinda was home for the first time in months.

Chapter 10

A New Boat–the Memphis Belle

Thanksgiving was a wonderful time in New Orleans, between J.J.'s aunts and uncles all getting together for one big meal, which consisted of deep fried turkey, something you would only find in Louisiana, mustard greens, potatoes, corn, green beans, rice and pork. The desserts were fantastic, cakes of all descriptions, pies, pumpkin, chocolate, pecan, apple, J.J. tried some of it all and was so full he thought he wouldn't have to eat for a month.

The day after Thanksgiving, J.J. went into New Orleans and did his Christmas shopping. He was amazed at how many new shops had opened just since he and Melinda had left. He bought gifts for everyone back east, his mother, father, Gloria, Madeline, Forrest and Chris. All those gifts he had boxed into two boxes and then he took them to the train depot and shipped them in care of Forrest at Lancaster, Pennsylvania, at the same time he posted a letter to Forrest telling him to go to Lancaster and pick up the boxes, they should be there in about a week.

When shipping the boxes J.J. had the biggest urge to take the train and head toward his family, but, he then remembered how miserable the train ride had been and decided that he would just stay with his Uncle Patrick and Aunt Mary.

J.J. then went to the theater and talked to the Warren Salles to see if they could play a couple of weeks there, but the Warren said that business was so slow this time of year that he was just going to close the theater until after the first of the year. He asked J.J. if he wanted to play the month of January and J.J. told him that he would let him know in a few days.

J.J. headed down to the boat's ticket booking agent to find out which boats were taking passengers, there were only two— the *Delta Queen* which was an older boat and really didn't have a theater and the new and larger boat—the *Memphis Bell*. J.J. did not know the owner or the captain of the *Memphis Bell* and asked when she was due to dock. She would not be back for about a week. When he got back to Uncle Patrick's there was a letter for him from Satin. She told him that she had appreciated working with him, but she had met someone and was getting married on Christmas day. This saddened J.J., because in his mind he had hoped that they would become an act again, but also he was glad for her. The next day he sent her a telegraph wishing her all the happiness in the world. He also went to a shop and bought a nice set of dishes and had the shop owner ship them to her for a wedding present.

J.J. now felt he was at a turning point in his life, he really thought over the next few weeks what he wanted to do. He had a long talk with Melinda and it was obvious that his cousin really didn't want to do what they had done the previous year, she said she didn't mind playing New Orleans and maybe Houma or the small towns around New Orleans, but did not really care to go north like to Memphis.

Just before Christmas the *Memphis Bell* docked and J.J. went down to talk to the Captain. His name was Dick Mentzer, a fellow of German extraction, actually he was the one that had come to America. He was a very nice gentleman, he told J.J. that he would hire him, but since he had limited cabin space available that he would have to sleep in a cabin with one of the band members and that there was no room for a female assistant. Captain Dick had heard of J.J. and told him that he could only pay him $200.00 a week but would expect only 3 shows a week, Wednesday, Friday and Saturday nights, Captain Dick also said that they would give it a try for two trips, New Orleans to Memphis and back, after the two trips the two men could talk about it and see if they wanted to continue. Since J.J. really had no idea of which way he was going, he agreed to this arrangement. J.J. felt that this would at least give him some income while he was deciding what he wanted to do!

J.J. discussed it with Melinda, and she actually told him she was relieved, she wanted to stay home and do some things, what those were J.J. never found out.

Uncle Patrick agreed to keep the horses and wagon for J.J. J.J. agreed to pay him for the keep, as it turned out, that was $5.00 a week and $2.00 to his cousin Mary Jane to exercise and feed and water them. She thought this was great to be able to do something and get paid for it. J.J. gave his Uncle $20.00 for the month and also gave him Mary Jane's money so that he could give it to her weekly.

When he boarded the *Memphis Bell* he did not carry any of the illusions that would require an assistant, he carried only tricks that he could perform solo.

J.J. actually liked working the *Memphis Bell*. Captain Mentzer ran a tight ship like Captain Reed had. The two men became friends and like when he was on the *Queen* J.J. spent time in the pilot house helping navigate the river, he actually knew the river better than Captain Dick and almost as well as a couple of the pilots.

Winter turned into spring and in the spring the *Memphis* started heading for Chicago as soon as the spring floods were over. One of the men said that the river was as reliable about flooding as it was sure to turn cold in Michigan. You could count on her to flood starting in April and lasting till the first of May. If it was a bad year and she was mad, the Mississippi might even flood till June.

When they docked in St. Louis for the first time, J.J. headed first to Misuraca's Italian Restaurant. There he found John and Rose, the mother and father of Patricia and Mario, but no Mario and no Patricia. Since neither spoke good English one of the customers interpreted for him, it seems that Patricia and Mario had gone to New York to dance and while they were there, Patricia had met another Italian and had married. Mario had decided to take his savings that J.J. had helped him to save and opened an Italian restaurant and called it Mario's. J.J. was sad that he had not seen them, but, also was glad that things were working out well for them.

John and Rose insisted that J.J. eat with them and they fed him the usual great meal and J.J. performed for their customers, with much fanfare from Rose to all the customers about how great he was. Since the waters above St. Louis were still too rough for the *Bell* to travel they headed back to New Orleans. When they reached New Orleans J.J. deposited his money into the bank, checked his balance and sent the church his regular deposit to Houma.

He then paid his Uncle Patrick for another month for the horses including another months' salary for Mary Jane. She had done an excellent job taking care of them. J.J. told her how good she was doing and she just beamed with pride. For exercise she was riding one horse in the morning and the other in the afternoon. He slipped her an extra five dollars and told her that was because she was working so hard. She gave him a big hug; her actions reminded him of Gloria.

The *Bell* only spent the night in New Orleans and the next day they were off and this time they had cargo for Chicago. They also had an overnight in St. Louis and this time J.J. went in search of his shipmates, George and Jon Boudreaux. He found them at Boudreaux's French Cuisine Restaurant. George saw him come in the door and immediately ran and grabbed J.J. and picked him up in a big hug almost squashing J.J. and laughing all the time. Jon came out of the kitchen all dressed in white with a big white stove of a looking hat, he also picked J.J. up and swung him around then sat

him down on his feet and kissed him on both cheeks.

The restaurant was full of customers and Jon banged a pan to get their attention and introduced J.J. saying, "Ladies and Gentlemen, this is James Willard the Greatest Magician that there has ever been!" J.J. laughed and took a bow, everyone applauded. George took J.J. to a table. He did not ask J.J. if he wanted to eat. He just sat him down and in a very few minutes started bringing in food. Of course it was all food that J.J. liked, George had not forgotten.

J.J. stayed till all the customers had gone and Jon, George and he could talk. They told J.J. that they were partners, 75/25. George said, "How about that Mr. Willard, I am a part owner in this restaurant! Who would have ever thought that a poor black slave could become a partner in such an elegant place?"

Jon told him that George was responsible for hiring and firing the waiters and taking care of the dining room and that he Jon took care of hiring cooks and buying the food and setting the menu. They had been open only six months, but that they were doing great and were making money every week, a lot more than they had made working on the *Queen*.

They had spent a lot of money on the décor of the restaurant. They had imported French chandeliers and mirrors and totally remodeled the building that they had bought. Instead of leasing and that their plan was to have it free and clear in the next year. It was a two-story building and they had living quarters upstairs.

J.J. told them that they had even exceeded the High Hat Club in Chicago as far as décor and that their food was really a lot better. He left and headed back to the *Bell* and was content that his friends were going to be successful and make lots of money.

Their restaurant was right in the middle of town and on the corner of two of the busiest streets. Boudreaux's had all the makings for being a long running enterprise.

The *Memphis Bell* docked in Chicago. As soon as J.J. came on deck, he knew he was in Chicago. The wind was really blowing, you actually had to lean forward in order to walk into the wind, yep, this was Chicago. After checking with the Captain on how long it would be before they headed south, the Captain told him two days. J.J. rented a carriage and headed to the boarding house. He felt like he needed a couple of nights sleep in a bed that wasn't vibrating from the engines. After getting a room, he went and took a nice long "hot" bath. Put on some clean clothes and headed for the High Hat Club. Glen and Frances were glad to see him and welcomed him with open arms. He stayed at the club till it closed and then he and Glen spent a couple of hours talking on the porch and smoking a cigar.

Glen told J.J. that Satin was pregnant the last time she had come by the club and was probably about ready to have the baby. He said she seemed very happy and that her husband made a good living working at the Union Stock Yards. Glen then asked J.J. if he wanted to go with him tomorrow to see something that Glen had invested in? J.J. said sure and what time, they agreed to meet in the morning at about 8 a.m. J.J. asked what this investment was, and Glen just smiled and said he would see the next day.

The next morning Glen picked J.J. up at the boarding house and they headed south toward the train yards. When they arrived they were at a train yard and there were train cars under construction. They went into the office and Glen introduced J.J. to a man named George M. Pullman. Mr. Pullman was very cordial and asked J.J. if he knew anything about his cars? When J.J. said no, Mr. Pullman then took him and Glen out to where they had five different train cars under construction. The first was a car he called the Pioneer, this car had separate compartments and in each was a seat that made into a bed and then a second bed would drop down from a compartment that was hung from the ceiling. Mr. Pullman was proud of this and told J.J. that he held the patent for it construction. Actually he held several patents for different aspects of this car. His favorite was a car that was all beds, two high on both sides of an isle. They had curtains that gave you privacy.

Mr. Pullman then took J.J. to see another car under construction.

When they walked into this car, Mr. Pullman said, "This car is the one that Mr. Falkenstein helped me to design, this is a dining car, we built our first one in 1868 with the help of Glen!" J.J. was completely amazed, had these two cars been available when he took the long trip back to Pennsylvania he would not have been so worn out when he got there and when he returned to New Orleans.

The three men went to lunch. J.J. was totally fascinated by these inventions. Mr. Pullman told him that he had built two sleepers but the railroads were not anxious to accept them, that he had then moved to Colorado and opened a general store, but his friend Ben Field had convinced him to come back to Chicago and try again, that is why they were called the Pioneer, after Mr. Field. They were eating at the High Hat Club one evening and that is when Mr. Pullman and Mr. Field got the idea for a dining car, so who better to ask for help in the design than a man that knew the restaurant business and the requirements it would take to make good food.

J.J. said, "Gentlemen, I think what you have accomplished is amazing, but, please satisfy my curiosity, how much do you sell these cars for?" Both men laughed, and Glen said, "That is the beauty of this J.J., we do not sell them, we lease them to the railroads and they pay us a monthly fee to use them, we keep ownership of the cars!" Then Mr. Pullman said, "J.J. we now have orders from the different railroads for all the cars we can produce for the next three years, our biggest problem is trying to figure out how we can produce more, faster!"

Mr. Pullman excused himself and headed back to the office, Glen and J.J. headed back to town. On the way Glen told him that he owned five percent of the company and that every time they built a new car they improved it, there was always a difference in every car, they just kept finding new things to do to them.

J.J. found out that there were two railroads out of Chicago that had both cars on their runs, one was a train that went to New York City and the other one went to Washington by the way of Baltimore. When J.J. heard this, he made up his mind that the next time he went to see Forrest and Madeline he would leave from Chicago and take one of these trains.

The *Memphis Bell* made six more trips to Chicago that year and on two of them J.J. performed for audiences on weekends at the High Hat Club. J.J. was becoming very tired of working on the *Memphis Bell*. It had become so routine that J.J. was not getting that feeling of excitement that an entertainer gets any longer and felt that he needed to have a change.

J.J. talked with Captain Mentzer and they agreed with no hard feelings that J.J. would leave the boat in Chicago in October. J.J. wrote Madeline a letter and told her that he planned on visiting them in November.

In New Orleans J.J. paid his Uncle Patrick for six months for the horses and also gave him the money to give to his cousin. He told them he was going east but would be leaving from Chicago. He told his uncle about the sleeper cars and the dining car that they were making in Chicago. To his surprise his uncle knew about them and said that there were plans to add those cars to the long routes in the south, as a matter of fact, they were already ordered.

Before leaving New Orleans J.J. bought gifts for all his family there and had them wrapped for Christmas, he then gave them to his Aunt Mary and asked that she give them to everyone at Christmas. J.J. also went to his bank and got a letter of credit to take with him and checked out a sufficient amount of money to be gone for several months. A lot of this money he had his Aunt Mary sew into the lining of his stage coat, not the coat that he wore everyday. He also hid some of the money in some of his tricks. For some reason when he left Uncle Patrick's and Aunt Mary's he felt that it would be a very long time before he ever saw them again, he had no idea why he felt this way, but he did.

He packed an extra case of magic and took it with him. Some where in his mind he was thinking that maybe he would find a new assistant and these tricks would come in handy.

When the *Memphis Bell* docked in Chicago J.J. said his good byes to everyone. He took his magic and hired a carriage to take him to the train station. Instead of carrying all four large cases he shipped them to Lancaster. He then purchased a sleeper ticket to Baltimore, the train would take only two nights to get there.

Chapter 11

Going Back East Again

J.J. settled into his Pullman sleeper compartment, he really looked forward to this ride. It was going to be different from his last train ride. A black porter by the name of Henry helped him and told him that in the evening he would come and make his bed for him. Henry was a very polite person with a very warm smile that actually made J.J. feel like he was in Henry's home and that he was a special guest.

As soon as the train left the station J.J. was up and out of his compartment walking thru the train. There were actually three sleeper cars, then two just seating cars and then the dining car. It was 7:30 a.m. and J.J. had not eaten so he sat at one of the tables and a waiter came with a pot of coffee and a cup. J.J. thought to himself, this is the way people should travel, not only enjoying the view from the windows but able to eat. He had a very large breakfast, two flapjacks and two eggs with sausage and toast. There was a rhythm to the train, a rocking and a clicking noise as the steel wheels rolled from one piece of steel track to the next. At first it was distracting

but only after a few minutes you really didn't hear it anymore unless you thought about it. It was also wonderful to sit there eating and looking out the window at the countryside.

The train stopped about every 20 miles to take on water. These stops were usually for only ten or fifteen minutes but long enough for passengers to relieve themselves. Most of these water stops had outhouses for them to use. J.J. thought that it would be nice if the train had a toilet, but he was sure they couldn't do that as there would be no place for the waste to go. A person they called the conductor would always check to make sure all the passengers were back on the train. Usually with the same way of calling, "All aboard!" Which every time J.J. heard it he would laugh because it sounded to him like you were getting on a ship.

There was something very nice about having a private compartment. Just one thing made it wonderful, that was being able to look out the window as the train rolled along thru the countryside. It was amazing at how the scenery changed, from land that was plowed to pastures with cattle, horses, sheep and goats. Compared to his last train trip, this was wonderful.

At lunch all the tables in the dining car were filled. There was only one seat available and the other three people there were very nice. J.J. was comfortable sitting at the table with strangers and eating. They struck up a conversation and J.J. even did a couple of coin tricks for them. After lunch J.J. returned to his compartment and read a book that he had brought along. J.J. was a good reader and he loved getting ideas from books. Many times books had helped him with some of the things that he said on stage.

The train pulled into Baltimore and J.J. then caught a train to Lancaster, at Lancaster he rented a carriage and picked up his baggage, lucky for him all his cases had already arrived, in a way this sort of amazed J.J. that his shipment had actually beat him there, even though he had a thru train that went directly to Baltimore. The baggage master told him that his baggage had been transferred to a different train in Pittsburgh here it had gone to Harrisburg and then to Lancaster, there had been no stops for people from Pittsburgh.

When J.J. arrived at the Edward's farm everyone was out to meet him. He was amazed at how much little Christopher had grown. But, Madeline had her hands full with Chris, he bounced everywhere on the run.

Thanksgiving and Christmas came and went much too fast for J.J., now the New Year was here and it was time for J.J. to decide what he was going to do.

His father, mother and Gloria had to leave as they had bookings in Georgia and several other cities. James Sr. wanted J.J. to come with them, but J.J. really thought that it was time for him to be back on his own working and making money.

Since his father was traveling and performing on the eastern states, J.J. felt that his area was the western states but yet, he really wasn't anxious to perform.

After his father and mother left he had a chance to sit down with Forrest and talk about the future. Forrest gave him an idea that he had never thought about, that was, why didn't he go to New York and see if he could get a job on one of the ocean liners that were now hauling passengers to Europe. He could work, make money and travel to places that he had never been. This excited J.J., he thought about it for a couple of days and the more he thought the more he liked the idea.

He had heard about some magicians in London and Paris that he would really like to meet and wondered if that would be possible. He loaded up the carriage and Forrest drove him to Lancaster where he caught a train to Philadelphia and then on to New York.

New York City had grown so large since he had left Brooklyn in 1861, he couldn't imagine where all the people had come from and after being at the Edward's farm in Pennsylvania he couldn't imagine why people wanted to live in a city. He knew a lot of these people had no idea how wonderful the country could be.

J.J. gathered his baggage and hired a carriage to take him to the docks. There he found that there were really only two lines that were carrying passengers. He went to both and at the White Star lines he met the booking manager who told him that there was a good possibility that they would hire him. J.J. was to come back the next day and talk to a Mr. David Kersh about performing.

J.J. checked into the hotel that was closest to the docks and then wondered around looking at New York, when suddenly he remembered that Mario had a restaurant there in the city. What was the name? Then he remembered that Mr. Misuraca had told him, Mario's Italian Restaurant. It was starting to get dark and he hired a carriage that the driver told him he knew exactly where the restaurant was.

New York in January is not a warm place, it was cold, there was snow everywhere and the wind was blowing off the ocean, it definitely was not the type of evening that you would expect people to be out dining. When the carriage pulled up to the restaurant, J.J. could see thru large glass windows that the place was packed.

J.J. entered the restaurant and was greeted by a man in a tuxedo and asked if he had reservations. J.J. told him no and the man checked his table seating and found a place for J.J. to sit. Immediately two other waiters appeared and one brought him water and asked what he would like to drink and the other person put hot bread on the table with butter and a napkin and fork, knife and spoon and lit the candle on the table. J.J. was seated where he could observe everyone in the room. There were ladies that were dressed very nicely and all the male customers had on suits, all were very well dressed. J.J. made his selection from the menu and almost as soon as he had, the waiter came with coffee. Considering the weather outside the coffee tasted delicious, actually, J.J. had never tasted coffee so good. The atmosphere of the restaurant was very elegant, it had red and gold tapestries, pictures of Italy hung in several places on the walls and the chandeliers were crystal.

Suddenly there was a scream that was so loud that most of the ladies dropped their forks and some of the men reached for weapons! J.J. saw Mario coming at him and before he knew it he was up in the air and being whirled around with his feet off the ground. Both men started laughing and Mario realized that he had caused a big commotion in his restaurant and scared his customers, he put J.J. down and said, "Ladies and Gentlemen, I apologize to you all, but this man is the one and only Mr. James Willard the greatest magician that has ever performed on a stage and it is because of him that I have this wonderful restaurant."

There was so much catching up to do that the two men ended up in Mario's apartment that was above the restaurant and talked until almost 2 a.m. Many times Mario repeated to J.J. that he sincerely felt that his good fortune had started with J.J. talking him into giving that gambling money to Captain Reed. He laughed and said, "You know J.J. that when we received your telegraph that Captain Reed had been killed, that my family draped the restaurant in black in St. Louis and we had a real mourning period for such a great man!"

J.J. told Mario, "I have never enjoyed entertaining the way I did when the four of us were doing shows on the *Queen!*" This was the first time J.J. had said that and it was the first time he had realized it himself. Mario told him that he had actually saved almost $15,000.00 working and gambling on the *Queen*. When he came to New York he bought this building for eight thousand and by the time he had remodeled it and purchased all the equipment he had a barely enough to buy the supplies for the opening day. Then he laughed and said, "If people hadn't have come, he would probably be in jail for not paying the waiters and cooks." Then Mario said, "But now, J.J., I clear over one thousand a week and I have a lot of money saved in the bank, isn't life wonderful?"

J.J. said, "Mario, you and I have been blessed by the little people. Who would ever expect two men growing up in a country during a terrible war to be as lucky as we have been?" Actually both men had made their own luck by working hard and saving their money and using it wisely.

Mario insisted that J.J. spend the rest of the night in his spare bedroom. The next morning they had breakfast together downstairs in the restaurant and J.J. went to the hotel to change clothes, shave and freshen up. He then went to the ship company to talk to Mr. Kersh. When he arrived, Mr. Kersh was in his office. He was a big man about 6' 2" tall and weighed about 200 pounds; he had on a very nice suit and a big cigar that he smoked continually.

J.J. presented him with his letters of introduction from all the theaters that he had performed in. J.J. had asked every manager or owner to give him a letter when they finished playing at the theater. He had them all in a book. In the book also were letters he had received from people that had seen his show. Mr. Kersh seemed to go back and read the one from the High Hat Club the most. He would read a couple of the others and then go back to the one from Glen Falkenstein. Finally Mr. Kersh looked up and said, "Mr. Willard you have very good references, especially the one from Mr. Falkenstein, I know him personally and if he tells me you are the greatest he has ever seen, I believe him, you see, I know Glen is a magician also, so you really must be good!" Then out of the clear blue Mr. Kersh asked him, "Sir, are you kin to the James Willard Magician that has performed here in New York at the Opera House?" J.J. answered, "Yes, sir, that is my father!"

Mr. Kersh then said, "Then sir, let's you and I discuss terms of an agreement for you to entertain on the White Star lines." What they worked out was that J.J. would entertain as a solo magician for three round trips on what ever ship they wanted him on, then the line would give him passage one way to either Liverpool or a port in France, which ever one he chose, he would entertain on that ship and then when he was ready to return to America he would entertain on that ship on the way back. They would pay him four hundred a week for all the trips. Mr. Kersh told J.J. that he was a first—the first entertainer besides a band to be hired to entertain their customers while crossing. They had been thinking about hiring entertainers, but until now they were not happy with any that had applied.

Mr. Kersh told J.J. that he would leave on the *Oceanic* on

January 30th for Liverpool and then he gave him a caution, "Mr. Willard, you have been on boats on the Mississippi, but this is a ship and the Atlantic Ocean is not a river, I hope your sea legs are good!" With that the Englishman laughed from the bottom of his stomach so hard that J.J. thought the man might burst a blood vessel.

J.J. caught a carriage and headed to Mario's and told him the good news. Mario told him that it was over a week before he would ship out and that because of that he did not want him to stay at the hotel. Mario said, "J.J. I have plenty of room and you should stay with me, I insist on it!" There was no arguing with the man, so J.J. went back to the hotel and paid his bill and moved to Mario's apartment. During the next week J.J. went back to Brooklyn and saw some of his relatives, his mothers sisters and brother and some of the other Willard's that were there. He actually was glad that his father had moved them to New Orleans. The way the Irish lived in Brooklyn was awful—some of the families were six or seven in one bedroom flats. Streets were nothing but big holes and mud and rats were everywhere. He truly felt sorry for all those people, but mostly they were a happy people. They laughed at things, even laughed at themselves for living like this. J.J. wished that there was some way that he could help them, but he knew they each had to help themselves.

The time went by fast, all of a sudden it was January 30th and time for J.J. to go aboard the *Oceanic*, he bade farewell to Mario and took all his luggage to the ship.

They sailed at 2 p.m. in the afternoon with a band playing on the dock and a band playing on one of the decks. Everyone seemed in high spirits. J.J. talked with the Captain and the Captain told him that he did not have to perform until the third night. The captain was Captain John Campbell.

He had retired from the British navy and had been sailing for the White Star line for five years. The first night out J.J. got acquainted with the ship and where everything was. The theater was like it had been on the *Mississippi Queen*, a riser made the stage and it actually was the dining room for the first class passengers. It was not as nice as the *Queen's* had been and not as large.

J.J. figured that they could seat a 100 people and there was a balcony that another 50 or so could stand in. Behind the riser there was a curtain that separated a small room from audience area. At J.J.s request they put his two cases of magic in this room.

The next day was a rough one, the ocean seemed to be saying, *you're not going to cross me, you're not going to cross me!* It was hard to walk down one of the halls without bumping from side to side. J.J. knew what David Kersh had been laughing so hard about, and he was right. Never on those riverboats did they rock and roll the way this ship was doing. J.J. went up on deck and there were several people at the rails that were sick. It almost made J.J. sick to see them, but he composed himself and did not get sick, thank goodness.

The third day was much smoother, but the ship still had a strange rolling motion, that you truly had to get used to. He went to the band and introduced himself to all of them and then asked if they minded doing a rehearsal with him. They were all very nice men and said they would. That night he performed for the audience for the first time and actually enjoyed it. The seating area was full and so was the balcony.

He saw Captain Campbell in the balcony watching and wondered if he enjoyed it? The audience gave him a standing ovation and brought him out for one more trick.

The next morning Captain Campbell had him summoned to his quarters. J.J. went in not knowing what to expect. It turned out that the Captain was very pleased with the performance. He told J.J. that he truly did not know how people would take to having an entertainer, but that Mr. Kersh had convinced him and that the company had told him to try it. He then said, "Mr. Willard, you did an excellent job and many of the passengers told me so, I am pleased with your work!" That was the last time J.J. spoke to the Captain during the whole 12-day trip.

The *Oceanic* docked in Liverpool and it was not at all what J.J.

had imagined. The *Oceanic* would not leave for two days. One of the band members told J.J. about a little hotel that was in the heart of town. From what he had seen at the docks, J.J. wasn't really anxious to see much of Liverpool. He did want to get off the ship for a couple of days.

The cabbie, as a carriage driver was called, took him to the hotel but was only too proud to point out the two main buildings of Liverpool—St. George's Hall, which had opened in 1854 and the Town Hall which had been built in 1795. Since the next day was Sunday J.J. asked the driver if there was a Catholic church? The driver looked at him in a funny way, but said yes, there was a small church.

Liverpool was not really a place that you would want to live. The streets were very narrow and with the exception of the two buildings he had seen. There were not very many impressive things about the city. The hotel was an old wooden frame building that was not in great condition, but the rooms and the bath were clean. In many ways J.J. was surprised at the differences of the two cultures of the English and the Americans. He went looking for something to eat, and was told that he needed the Lion and Wolf pub. They didn't have a menu, the waitress told him what they had to eat. For the most part J.J. couldn't recognize a single thing that they offered. He finally told her that he would like to have some sort of steak and that he preferred it to be medium. With that she gave him a funny look, sort of like the one that the cabbie had given him when he asked about a Catholic church. The steak when it came was almost burnt and had beans and potatoes. The beans were good—a variety that he had not eaten before but they were tasty, the potatoes were fried and were in squares but were also good. The steak was awful, J.J. wondered if it was a steak or maybe it was shoe leather. Other than the waitress no one spoke to him and he wondered if maybe he had a big sign on his forehead that said "American"?

The next day J.J. had a really good breakfast at the hotel, the only meal that it served, he ate a lot because he was afraid what he might find to eat that day. He then went to check out St. George Hall. Here J.J. felt like he had found a jewel among the thorns. It was beautiful, a plaque stated that it was finished in 1854 and was designed by Harvey Lonsdale Elmes. This was a beautiful building. Inside had frescoes that were painted on walls and ceilings, stained glass windows, almost like a church. J.J. decided that someday he would perform here.

The ship headed back to America with about 60% capacity, this naturally did not make the Captain happy. The other thing that J.J. noticed, the English seemed to enjoy his shows, but they were restrained in their applause. He really had to look at their faces to see if he felt like they were grasping his magic. After the third show of the voyage he deliberately stood near the exit to hear what they were saying. Several of them came over and shook his hand and told him that he was the best they had ever seen. He presumed that they must have liked his performance.

The *Oceanic* next headed from America to Le Harve, France. J.J. was performing for Americans on the way over and truly, he enjoyed it. Americans always let a performer know if they thought he was good or bad, of course J.J. was never bad.

When they docked in Le Harve, J.J. looked at the town from the deck of the ship and thought to himself, "Now, this is what Europe is suppose to look like!" The buildings were either rock or brick, it had several wide streets that looked like avenues and from the deck the town looked very clean. Le Harve is about two hundred miles from Paris. J.J. sure wished that he had enough time to go to Paris. The *Oceanic* was only spending one night before she would sail back to America.

He contented himself with hiring a carriage and asking a driver if he could tell him about the town. Actually had to talk to four different men before he found one that spoke enough English that he could understand what he was saying. His Cajun did come in handy because it at least allowed him enough knowledge to sort of know what they were saying in French.

There were several things in this small town that were really worth seeing, for one was the Cathedral of Notre Dame, the other was Round Tower of Francis I, and of course a beautiful theater. J.J. was amazed at a town so small had such a nice theater. The driver informed him that just a short distance away was a resort that many people came and spent the summers at, so actually the theater did opera, ballets and plays. J.J. asked him if magicians ever performed there? The driver said that he could only remember one about five years previously but could not remember his name.

J.J. returned to the *Oceanic* and when he was back on board realized that he only had one more round trip to make to complete his contract.

On the return the ship was at 80% capacity and almost all were French. For all his performances, he tried to clean up his Cajun and spoke in English and Cajun and was surprised at how many of the French understood his Cajun banter. They seemed to be a happier group and much less reserved as the English had been. They applauded loudly when they liked a trick, on the third night he did the flying bird cage and they gave him a standing ovation.

In New York the *Oceanic* had a three-day lay over and so J.J. first went to Mario's and stayed the nights with him. He then went in search of a European Booking Agent. He found one with an English name, Wallace Agency; he felt like he needed someone that could at least book him into some locations in England and maybe even Scotland and if really lucky, France and Ireland.

J.J. in his normal manner appeared at the Wallace Agency at 9 a.m. with his letters of introduction, his posters and a few tricks up his sleeve. He even had two letters from the ship line. One from Captain Campbell (it had surprised him that the captain wrote such a glowing letter about him) and one from David Kersh whose letter also was a surprise. He had been interviewing passengers of the ship to find out what they liked about the voyage. Kersh told J.J. that he was amazed at how many times his name came up in these interviews.

Entering the office he was greeted by a man that was sitting behind the desk, the desk was covered with papers and the man had his head down. Without looking up the man said, "Can I help you?" J.J. replied, "Yes, I am a magician and I am looking for someone to book a tour for me in Europe!" Still not looking up the man said, "Are you now, Governor? What makes you think that the people of Europe would pay to see a bloke perform magic?"

J.J. without hesitation replied, "Sir, they are already paying to see me!" Then putting on an air of superiority, "But, if you're not interested in making money, I shall do it on my own and you will not make a penny!" He turned and started out the door.

The man stood up and said, "Sir, just a minute, I will see if Miss Wallace is interested in talking to you, please have a seat!" He then knocked on the door that was behind him and went inside, he was gone only a minute and returned, "You may go in now sir, Miss Wallace will see you!"

J.J. tipped his hat to him and entered the office. He was not prepared for what was coming around a desk to greet him! He had expected to see an older gentleman, fat, sweating with a cigar in his mouth. Instead, he was being greeted by a beautiful blond woman in her early thirties who looked just like an older Satin.

She said, "Sir, my name is Shannon Wallace, I am the booking agent!"

J.J. just stood there for a moment looking into the bluest eyes he had ever seen, then he realized that he must have his mouth open and said, "My name is James Willard the Magician!" She giggled like a schoolgirl and said, "Well, that is a strange last name—MAGICIAN!" J.J. laughed and said, "I am sorry, you caught me so by surprise, I was expecting to a large fat man chomping on a cigar, I am a magician!" She returned to behind her desk and then said, "How can I help you Mr. Willard and why has it taken you so long to come and see me?"

J.J. 's only answer was, "Long?"

Miss Wallace said, "Yes, Mr. Kersh told me about you about

BOOKING AGENT

a month ago. He said that surely that you were a pot of gold at the end of the rainbow!"

J.J. could only just look at this beautiful woman, she was about 5'1" tall, her skin looked as white as ivory and her lips were full. Her smile was so warm that J.J. could feel the heat all the way on his side of the desk. Finally he said, "I only have one more round trip to complete my contract with the White Star lines, then they have agreed to give me passage back to Europe as long as I perform three times on the voyage over. What I want is to play the best theaters in London, Paris and elsewhere in Europe for at least a year or maybe two, if the money is good!"

Miss Wallace stood up from behind her desk, walked around toward J.J. She sat on the corner of the desk, in doing this it exposed her left leg to above the knee as the motion of sitting on the edge pulled the long dress up. J.J. had seen legs before, but hers were gorgeous, he had to force himself not to stare, instead he looked directly into her face.

"Mr. Willard, it takes time to arrange a tour the way you are speaking of and it also takes a percentage of what you earn!" Miss Wallace said.

"What is the percentage you are speaking of?" J.J. asked.

Miss Wallace replied, "For this type of tour I would require 25%, because I will have to pay a percentage to the agents in the other countries and of course you will have to pay all your own travel and hotel expenses, I will try to at least get hotel and maybe even food in some of the cities."

"That is perfectly acceptable to me!" J.J. said happily.

Miss Wallace, stuck her hand out. "Then Mr. Willard, we have a deal, please come by tomorrow and I will have a contract draw for you to sign and leave me all the promotional materials that you have. I will have a printer make copies and return the originals to you."

Shaking her hand J.J. said, "Please call me James or J.J., all my friends call me J.J. and my father is also a magician and he plays here in New York!"

The next day J.J. returned to the office and was disappointed that Miss Wallace wasn't there, only Stewart her secretary. He read the contract and saw nothing that might be a trick in it, actually it was very plainly worded and anyone could understand that she was actually working on his behalf. Stewart told him that Miss Wallace had asked that he contact her as soon as he returned from the next voyage.

He assured Stewart that he would check with them as soon as he docked.

The *Oceanic* went to Liverpool; the voyage over was fun, but all J.J. could think about was performing in the great theaters of Europe. Then all of a sudden one night after performing he realized that a lot of his magic was in New Orleans and for what he was wanting to do he was going to need an assistant, maybe two. He did not sleep that night; the sun came up before he ever fell asleep. For all of the rest of the trip his mind was on the production that he wanted to put on in the theaters.

When the ship docked in Liverpool, he didn't even go ashore. He sat at a table with writing paper and wrote out every trick he would perform. He had enough, if he could get his magic from New Orleans to do five two hour acts and would repeat just certain tricks each night, for example, if he did a trick on Monday, he would not do that trick again until Wednesday. He would intersperse them into different parts of the performance so that very few people would catch that he was repeating a trick.

As soon as they docked, he first went by Mr. Kersh's office and thanked him for the opportunity of performing for the White Star line. Mr. Kersh said that they could make arrangements for J.J. to work for them again in the future.

The next thing he did was to go to the telegraph office and send a message to his Uncle Patrick and asked him to ship all the magic that was in the wagon to him. J.J. told him he would pay for all the crating and shipping and to please send him a telegraph as to when he had shipped it in care of this office in New York.

With that taken care of, J.J. then headed to Miss Wallace's office. Stewart was his normal cheery self when J.J. entered, but Miss Wallace heard his voice and came out of her office, she ran over to J.J. jumped up and grabbed him around the neck and gave him a big kiss on the cheek. J.J. felt like he was turning four colors of red!

Miss Wallace said, "James, I have wonderful news! Agents in Europe have heard of you and they are booking you into all the best places, you start with London in a month and a half, then Paris, then Vienna, Rome, Madrid, Cairo, Brussels, Glasgow, Dublin. Mr. James Willard you are going to be gone for at least two years, maybe longer. When you return you are going to be one rich man!"

J.J. slumped into a chair, he couldn't catch his breath, he couldn't believe what he was hearing, then it hit him—a month and a half! Out loud he said, "A month and a half?" How could he possibly be ready? He had to train assistants, he had to get all his magic from New Orleans. Again he said it out loud in the form of a question, "A month and a half?" He got up, laughed, kissed Miss Wallace on the cheek and said, "I must get busy, you are an angel, I will check with you in one week and we will discuss all this!" He left her office floating on a cloud, he didn't even remember hiring a carriage to take him to Mario's.

The next day he received a telegraph from Uncle Patrick telling him that the magic was on it's way and should arrive in a week, that he had shipped it freight collect but had used his railroad discount so it wouldn't be expensive. J.J. then wired his sister Madeline and asked where his father was playing. He asked Mario where he could find a good tailor to make him some clothes. After he had the name, he went directly to the tailor and had three sets of tails made, exactly alike and to special specifications. He showed the tailor the coat that his mother had made for him and that he had been wearing for the last two years. He told the tailor he wanted all the secret compartments in the tails exactly as they were in the coat.

The tailor said he would and that he would have all three sets ready in one week, but, he wanted Mr. Willard to come back for a fitting in four days.

He also ordered a dozen shirts from the tailor, two of silk or satin.

He then went to a hatter and ordered two hats, and each hat he explained to the hatter just what he wanted inside. His last stop was a shoemaker, here he ordered three pair of shoes, two black and one brown. Then he wondered again about assistants, he would discuss that with Mario. Mario always had good advice.

That night he and Mario talked until early morning again, Mario's one key advice was about assistants, he told J.J. not to hire them until he was in Europe. His reasoning was simple, they would know the customs of the people, He should hire four girls. J.J. mouth fell open and he said, "Four girls?"

Mario said, "Yes my friend, one English, one German, one French and one Italian!"

J.J. asked in a very simple voice, "Why so many?"

"In London you have only one, one that you totally train, she will understand your language and she will travel with you. When you reach France you hire another girl, a French girl, you train her to do just a few simple things. Then when you go to Spain you hire a Spanish girl and you train her to do something else and the same with the German girl. The German girl will help you in Germany, Switzerland and in Austria and Holland. In each place you explain to the girl that her job will only last for a few weeks, with the exception of the English girl." Then with a wink Mario said, "I would suggest that you find a nice English girl that you can sleep with!"

Then he laughed very hard. When he stopped laughing he said, "Seriously, my friend, make sure that all the girls know that they are employees. That you will terminate their employment if they step out of line and that their job is only for a few weeks!"

When they finally turned in J.J. was exhausted, he slept very sound and did not wake up until almost noon. He felt like he had wasted a half of a day. When he went downstairs the restaurant already had lunch customers. He sat at a table and the waiter brought him coffee without saying a word, then came back with a plate of scrambled eggs and bacon and toast, he saw Mario talking to some customers and Mario waved and winked.

He went to the telegraph office and there was a message from Madeline. His father and mother were playing in Boston. J.J. decided to go to Boston; he took a carriage to the train station and got the times that trains would leave to go to Boston. He found that there actually was a Pullman that would leave New York and go to Boston. The car would actually change railroads and engines as it went from one railroad to another. The car would be what he bought a ticket for and he would not have to physically change trains. J.J. headed back to Mario's and talked with him and told him of his plans to go see his mother and father for a couple of days or maybe even a week. Mario in his normal jubilant manner said that J.J. should go see them because the next time he saw them he would be a rich man, then laughed.

J.J. boarded the train at 6 p.m. and by 6:15 the train was on it's way. They went up to New Haven; there the train engine changed and a couple of cars were added and to J.J.'s delight a dining car. From New Haven the train traveled to Providence, Rhode Island. J.J. did not see Providence; he was sleeping soundly. He was awakened when the train changed engines again because of the large jolt that the car took as the new engine connected. He ignored it and went back to sleep.

They arrived the next morning at about 8 am, J.J. had already eaten a large breakfast and immediately hired a carriage and gave him the address of where Madeline had told him his mother and father were. It turned out that they had taken a house in Quincy on the Quincy Bay and it was a long carriage ride which the driver did not informed him of. When they arrived the driver demanded $10.00. J.J. felt it was high, but paid the man anyway. He had learned a lesson that would serve him well later in Europe, always find out the cost before you take a carriage; he didn't forget that lesson.

J.J.'s mother Elizabeth greeted him with hugs and kisses at the door, then his father James Sr. was next and finally Gloria, who was now grown and a very pretty young lady. J.J. noticed that she was a full six inches taller than her mother, as he was a full four inches taller than his father.

They spent that day and evening talking about all the family everywhere. The next day, they took his father's carriage went through Boston. His father was proud of Boston College, a Catholic college that had been established a few years before. He also showed J.J. where the Boston massacre had occurred and the church where the lantern had been lit for Paul Revere to make his ride. And of course all the ships that were in Boston Harbor. J.J. wasn't really impressed with Boston. The streets were very narrow and muddy and even though it was an old city, there didn't seem to have been much planning in the layout of it. Buildings made out of wood set next to brick buildings, many were in bad repair.

That evening he sat down at the dinner table with his family and told them about his adventures since he had last seen them. His travel to Europe on the White Star lines and what he thought of that part of the world and how the people acted.

Then very calmly he asked his father if he had heard of the Wallace Agency. James Sr. told him he had. He had heard it was run by a very talented young lady that was really great at getting entertainers that qualified bookings in Europe. That is when he told them, "Well, Miss Wallace has me booked on a tour of the best theaters in Europe, London, Paris, Berlin, Madrid, Rome, Edinburgh and Dublin!" The three of them just sat there with their mouths open! J.J. took pride in the fact that he had amazed his family.

From their silence the Willard trait could not hold back, all of a sudden all three were speaking at the same time, all with different questions and too many for J.J. to answer at the same time. He held up his hands and laughingly said, "Please, please just one at a time, but let me tell you my plans and how I am going to do it."

Everyone laughed all at the same time, then set back down in their chairs and waited for him to talk. "Father, Uncle Patrick has shipped all the illusions that I have accumulated to me by train, they will be there when I return. Mother I have ordered three suits that are being made for me now, with tailcoats and two hats and three pairs of shoes. Gloria, I shall hire an assistant when I reach London and she will be my main assistant. Then I shall hire one in France in addition to the English girl, one in Spain in addition to the other two and one in Germany in addition to the others. So by the end of the journey I shall have four assistants. Then before I go to Edinburgh I shall dismiss each of them except for the English girl who will work with me until I am ready to leave Dublin. Now, does that answer most of the question?" James Sr. said, "J.J. there is a man performing in New York that I wish for you to go see, his name is Alexander Hermann!" J.J. 's mouth was now the one to flop open.

"You mean the brother of Carl Hermann?"

"Yes, Carl was here also for a period of time and they have been performing all along the east coast, but Carl felt like he preferred to go back to Europe. These two men are really great magicians and they have really made people stand up and think about the art of magic!"

J.J. assured his father that he was a real admirer of the Hermann's and he would certainly go to see Alexander. That he had his brother's book and was doing a lot of the things that were in the book. James Sr. said he also had it and was also using some of the illusions that were there, but that he was not nearly as proficient as the Hermanns were.

That night sitting on the porch facing the Bay was his first chance to talk with Gloria and to ask her about Kim Dodge. She told him that they were corresponding by letters, but with her being way up here in Boston that she had not seen him for the last six months. She was sure that he was the man for her, that is, if he ever decided that she was the woman for him. In his letters he had said so. She felt like any thing could be said in a letter, and that when he asked her father for her then she would know he was sincere. Gloria always seemed to have her head on straight.

The next morning his father carried him to the train station and he headed back to New York. He gave them Shannon Wallace's address and told them to write to him in care of her and that she would forward them to him.

He also promised his mother that he would let her know where and when he was going and promised to write her a letter from each city. Gloria insisted that he do the same for her.

There was no Pullman going back to New York on a timely basis. J.J. had to take the regular trains, hard seats, no privacy and change trains three times before he got back to New York, which wasn't until the next day. He was actually exhausted when he arrived, very little sleep, he went straight to Mario's, had dinner with him then took a nice long bath and went to bed, he slept till the next morning at 6 a.m.

He had breakfast with Mario and then went to check on his clothing. The tailor had one jacket to the point that he needed to check it for fitting, this done he was told they would be ready in a few days. He then found out what theater Alexander Hermann was playing at and went there and purchased tickets for the show, he bought two, one for Mario.

That night he and Mario went to the performance. Mr. Hermann put on a very wonderful performance, he actually did many of the things that J.J. was doing but his style was tremendous. He had a wonderful grace with his moves and he commanded the audience's attention by his very presence.

J.J. gave one of the ushers his card and told him that he would like to speak to Mr. Hermann, the usher disappeared and came back shortly and told J.J. to go back stage to the dressing room. Mario and J.J. went through the door to the back stage area and found his dressing room.

As it turned out, Mr. Hermann was a very gracious man. J.J. asked him to have dinner with them at Mario's restaurant, which he accepted and they headed to Mario's. At Mario's J.J. told Alexander that he was fixing to head to Europe and would appreciate any tips that he might give him. Alexander told him his brother was performing in Paris and said that he was sure his brother would like to meet him. He told J.J. to come by the theater the next day and he would give him a letter of introduction. Alexander loved to hear his own voice and J.J. was more than willing to listen; he had learned that you gain a lot more from listening than from talking. J.J. learned several very valuable tips on things in Europe that night; it was well after 1 am when Alexander took a carriage back to his hotel.

At 9 a.m. the next day J.J. went to see Shannon Wallace. She was her normal girly self and they spent the entire morning going over details. The key thing was she wanted J.J. to open an account in a bank there in New York. Actually two accounts, one with only J.J.'s name and one with her name and J.J.'s. All monies received would be put into the joint account and then she would deposit her share in her own account and deposit the rest to J.J.'s. This sounded reasonable to J.J. so he and Shannon went to the Empire State Bank and opened the accounts. J.J. put only $100.00 into the joint account and then he gave the banker the letter of credit to put that money $2,000.00 into his personal account, this would still leave J.J. with over $2,000.00 in the New Orleans bank. They then went to Mario's for lunch and J.J. introduced Shannon to Mario, it was an immediate attraction. The two could not keep their eyes off each other. Normally Mario would be circulating around the tables making sure his customers were happy. Not today, he sat down at their table and did not leave until they did.

They returned to Shannon's office and she gave him all the dates that she had booked. London for two weeks, then a small town outside of London in southeastern England. She said it was a resort area for the rich. Paris for 3 weeks and then to Berlin for two weeks. Vienna, Austria for twoweeks, then Zurich for three weeks. She told him that she would mail him a list of the next performances to Berlin.

J.J. left her office and headed to David Kersh's office. There he made arrangements to sail and the date he would leave. He then went to the rail station and picked up all the cases his uncle had sent, instead of opening them, he just had a man deliver them to the steam ship line with the date of sailing. He would open them when he got to London.

For the next three days he really was just on sort of a vacation, there wasn't anything that he could do. His clothes were being made; he didn't sail till the next week. He went to see where George Washington was sworn in as the first President of The United States of America. He took carriage rides all over the city; at night he attended several shows and plays. Some were good and some were not very good, but they helped him pass the time. Actually he was anxious to get going, he was really looking forward to the future and all the people he would meet.

Finally his clothes were ready, his shoes were done and his special top hats were finished, all had done excellent work. The hats had the special compartments that were totally hidden, you could actually look into the hat and not see them, the same with the tail coats, the tailor had really taken special care to do them exactly the way J.J. had wanted them.

The day of sailing arrived and J.J. bid farewell to Mario. When he got to the dock, Shannon was there to see him off. He was glad that she was. For some reason this created a trust of her in him. He had not really doubted her, but he had not really known her before walking into her office. She gave him a letter of introduction to the owner of the first theater in London.

One of the sailors carried his three bags to his cabin and J.J. stayed on deck and watched all the festivities on the dock, the band playing, people dancing and waving goodbye to friends and relatives.

Chapter 12

Touring Europe

The ship docked in Liverpool, the voyage had been uneventful, J.J. had performed for three nights and as usual with Americans, they applauded loudly and seemed to enjoy his performances.

J.J. found a wagon and two men to help him get all the boxes loaded and taken to the train station. There he shipped them to himself in care of London and boarded a train. These trains were different from the trains in the United States. They had individual compartments with room for six people and they had nice cushioned seats. Only two other people joined him in the compartment and the journey only took five hours to London.

J.J. had two men at the train station help him with all the boxes and they loaded them into a wagon. J.J. paid the men. He told the wagon driver where he wished to go. Riding next to the driver as they drove through London J.J. was amazed at this city, and was also very pleased. It did not look like Liverpool. London had some very beautiful buildings and lots of churches, many of the churches were very large and very old.

The driver pointed out Buckingham Palace, as where Queen Victoria lived; poor Queen, her husband had just died last year and now she was alone, except for her children of course. J.J. had to listen very hard to understand what the man was saying. He was speaking English, but with a manner J.J. had not heard. It seemed that he cut off every word, as if saying the whole word was too much trouble.

No one knows for sure where the name "London" came from, but probably from the Romans, maybe some Roman general or god; they have found a jug that had the inscription "Londini Ad Fanum Isis" which meant Londinium at the Temple of Isis.

J.J.'s head could not take in all the sights as the wagon went through the city. Westminster church, then Trafalgar Square with its very tall monument to Horatio Nelson. Piccadilly Circle and finally the theater. J.J. could not believe that he was in a city that had so much history, he actually felt like it was the city that the English language had begun, which was probably true, but to hear the wagon driver you would not think so.

They finally arrived at the opera house where J.J. was to perform. He went in and found the manager a Mr. George Carman, a very big man, about 6'3" and over 200 pounds and smoking about a ¼ of a cigar, switching it from side to side when he talked. J.J. gave him the letter from Shannon Wallace and his attitude totally changed from being a gruff person to a nice person as soon as he read it.

George had two men help J.J. get the boxes and they stored them in a room that J.J. could lock. J.J. thanked George for that, explaining that he did have tricks that were his secrets. George replied, "Sir, that is a common courtesy here, the blokes in this area will lift your shirt buttons while you're wearing it!" Since there was an opera going on there was no dressing room available and George told him that there would not be until the day before he was to perform.

J.J. enlisted George's help in finding an assistant. George looked him square in the eye and wanted to know how many girls he wanted to interview, or did he just want George to find him one.

J.J. said he would like to maybe talk to eight or nine and George said. "If that is all, how about 9 a.m. tomorrow morning?"

Shannon Wallace had made arrangements for J.J. to stay at a boarding house that was only 3 blocks from the theater, it was very clean and the lady that ran it was a very nice person. Probably in her middle fifties, a little on the heavy side but with a very easy laugh and a great cook. She would change the sheets once a week and the water closet (bath room) was always very clean.

The next morning J.J. headed to the theater to see if George was a man of his word, sure enough, he was. There were about fifteen girls there waiting to talk to him by 8:30 a.m. J.J. wondered how in the world George had done it and asked him. George replied with a wink, "Sir, it is me charm!" Then laughed. Only three of the girls stood out when J.J. was looking at them, a girl with really dark black hair, a girl with blond hair and a red headed girl. Out of courtesy he did talk to all the girls, some of them had the same accent that the wagon driver had the day before.

He released all the girls except the first three, he asked each of them to enter from stage left, turn and then exit stage right. George sat a few rows back and watched.

J.J. then interviewed each girl, giving them the details of the job, how long it might last and their pay in as much detail as possible and that they would be expected to start tomorrow and rehearse for three hours every day until they opened. The redheaded girl told him that there was no way for her to start the next day or the next, so he thanked her for coming. The blond had that cockney accent and it was very hard to understand her, so he also thanked her for coming. He had pretty much decided that he liked the black-headed girl the most anyway. She had told him that she could be there as much as he needed her. Her name was Wilma Banfield, she was about 5'2" or 3" tall. Nice figure in the dress and very pretty dark eyes. She had been the best at taking directions and also she seemed very comfortable on the stage, all those things went into his decision. Actually the deciding factor really had been her easy laugh and the smile that showed the minute she had stepped on stage.

J.J. went back to George and ask him what he thought of his decision, George answered, "I was worried that you were going to pick my girlfriend, the red head!"

Then he laughed in his normal manner, like he knew a dark secret.

J.J. needed a bank and a costume maker. George told him where to find both and Wilma and J.J. left the theater. He went to the bank, changed his American dollars into English pounds, shillings and half pennies. He had no idea how to figure out the money, it was strange. Then he and Wilma went to the costume maker and they ordered three costumes for Wilma. With Wilma's help, her laughing at him, J.J. paid one half of the cost to the costume maker who said they would be ready in three days. One half was 7 pounds, which J.J. figured out was about $20.00 or so, as close as he could come.

Wilma met J.J. every morning at 9 a.m. and they practiced until noon. She was really a fast learner and by the time her costumes were ready, she was ready to perform. The hardest thing to teach her was the "Spirit Cabinet", but they worked on it every day and he soon had complete confidence in her performance.

J.J. had been so busy training Wilma that time had flown by and he had not really had time to worry until the day before their opening. He and Wilma had lunch together which by now he was also getting familiar with the food and knew that there were certain things he would not eat, like blood pudding, just the thought turned his stomach. The English acted as if it were a real treat! When Wilma left they agreed to meet the next evening a 5:30 to get the props for the show ready.

The last three rehearsals the crew had rehearsed with them at the insistence of George who wanted it to be perfect. The men at this theater took a great deal of pride in what they did. J.J. made sure that he let each one know how much he appreciated their work.

It was show time! J.J. and Wilma had everything set up, they were ready, J.J. looked thru the curtain to see if they had an audience. He was amazed, it was a Friday night and the house was full. About 1500 people, more than he had ever performed for at one time. All of a sudden, for the first time in his life, J.J. became a very nervous person. His knees felt weak, his stomach felt like he needed to throw up. His hands were actually shaking, he had never in his life felt this way.

Wilma saw this, she saw his hands shaking. She came over, took his hands, looked him right in the eyes and told him they were going to have fun! Then she giggled!

Her giggle and her giggle alone did the trick; just the sound of it calmed him down. He still felt like throwing up. Wilma lead him to the center of the stage behind the curtain and all of a sudden he heard George proclaiming: "Ladies and Gentleman, we are honored to bring to you for the first time, America's most wonderful conjurer of magic, Mr. James Willard the Magician!"

The curtain went up and James looked at the audience and immediately his stomach calmed down and he started performing. As he had on other occasions, he felt like everything was in slow motion, that he was watching himself from up in the balcony. Wilma, she was wonderful, she did not miss a cue and she was an immediate hit with the English. Unlike the English on the ships, these people applauded and several times they stood and applauded. J.J. had not held anything back that night—they did the spirit cabinet, the flying bird cage and the doll house. After each one of these the audience stood and applauded. Every single trick went smoothly and he and Wilma looked as if they had worked together all their lives.

After the show, George came back with a tremendous smile on his face, no cigar and asked J.J. and Wilma to go out to eat with him, which they did after packing everything and storing it in the lock room. At the restaurant George had his girlfriend the redhead. She told J.J. that she was sorry she wasn't the one picked, but that Wilma had done a wonderful job. Probably better than she would have done. George laughed and said, "Honey, Mr. Willard couldn't pick you, how would I live if you were gone for months abroad?"

They both laughed.

The next day at the boarding house Mrs. Willoughby had all five London papers at J.J.'s table; they were all turned to articles written about him. J.J. had not even thought about reporters being there. Every single one had a glowing report about the Yank that was a skilled conjurer, how smooth his performance. How wonderful and beautiful his assistant was—a Miss Wilma Banfield of London. One of the papers even quoted his stage line: *I perform tricks that are to entertain you not by magic but by skill!* Well, this was the first time J.J. had seen his name in print, and it made him feel good. Their praise also was a burden, as he knew he could never do a bad performance now.

At the end the second week, George came to him back stage and asked that as soon as everything was packed, he wish to speak with him. J.J. went to George's office and sat down, he was actually exhausted. George smiled and said, Mr. Willard, you have set box office records here in this theater, he handed J.J. a sheet of paper with figures on it. J.J. looked at it, but, since the dollars were in pounds he was not sure that he understood them. He asked George what they meant. George said sir, what they mean in the simplest form is that you have earned for yourself the sum of $2,100 pounds for the two-week period according to the contract we signed with the agent here that works with Miss Wallace. I have been instructed to give you what ever you need, to send 10% of this money to the agency here in London and then to send the balance to the James Willard/Shannon Wallace account in America.

J.J. told him that he would need a 100 pounds and that the rest should be dispersed the way he was instructed, then J.J. asked George, "George in American dollars do you know how much this is?" George replied, "Yes sir, that is about $16,000.00 American. I believe sir the rate of exchange right now is about eight American to one British pound." J.J. was totally amazed. George told him that he had asked the agent to book J.J. again before he went back to America and that he had been told that it would be at least a year, but, if he wanted positive schedule they would forward it to him with in thirty days. J.J. stood, shook his hand and told him that he had really enjoyed performing there and looked forward to the return. George gave him the copy of the accounting and said he would send a copy to the agents. They all went out that night and J.J. bought dinner for everyone, including all the crew.

The next morning Wilma met him at the theater at 8 a.m. and they took all the equipment to the train station and headed for Brighton. It was only two hours south of London and was truly a very pretty place, but, it was the "upper crust" the rich of England that was there. It had been a resort city ever since one of the Kings, a George IV or so had made his home there. The largest audience they had was 200 and when they finished the week they had only made 90 pounds. George instructed the manager to send the 10% to the English agent and the balance to the joint account in New York along with copies of the tally sheets. J.J. and Wilma then caught a boat for France. They landed at Le Harve and immediately caught a train to Paris.

J.J. and Wilma both enjoyed looking at the scenery out of the train windows. The trains were the same as in England–six-person compartments and J.J. and Wilma were the only ones in their compartment. It was nice.

Paris was really a city, it was huge, massive buildings everywhere and you could see the church for miles before getting there. J.J. told Wilma, that they were going to spend at least one-day sight seeing. She said she really wanted to. That she had heard about so many things in this city that she wanted to see.

J.J. had to hire two carriages to carry them to the theater; the boxes of equipment took up one entire carriage. They found the theater and J.J. found the manager a man by the name of Pierre Fontenot, a very nice gentleman who spoke really good English. He had two men help and they stored all the boxes in a secure area. He then showed them to their dressing rooms, which were very nice. He gave each a lock and key for their dressing rooms. J.J. talked to him about needing to hire another assistant. Pierre, like George, asked him how many he would like to interview.

Here there was a difference between George and Pierre. Pierre told J.J. to come to the theater tomorrow afternoon at 3 p.m. and he would have some ladies for him to interview. J.J. told him that one of the main requirements was that they speak both English and French. He and Wilma then went to the hotel, now this hotel was really a luxury hotel.

They each were on the 6th floor, they each had a balcony and they could both see the church of Notre Dame and their rooms adjoined. The way their balconies faced they could also see the river Seine. Since they were on what was called the east bank the afternoon sun setting was beautiful. J.J. asked the bellman for the name of a good restaurant and then he and Wilma went to eat about 8 p.m. They both had a filet of beef smothered in wine sauce that just melted in your mouth it was so tender. He told Wilma that he loved England, but that they had no idea how to fix beef. This was the best steak he had eaten since leaving America. She agreed, said that in all her life she had never tasted steak as good as this was. They each sat out on their own balconies and looked at the city and the boats on the river that evening.

The next morning J.J. was up and at breakfast when to his surprise Wilma came down. She told him she had always been an early riser. They headed for the cathedral of Notre Dame. It was really something. They spent three hours just taking in all the sights of this magnificent building. J.J. could imagine all the knights that had prayed here. The kings and even the poor people, he was sure that it had given most of them the same feeling that it did him.

They had lunch at an outdoor café along the river and then went to the theater and sure enough, Pierre had seven girls for them to interview. J.J. first asked all the girls to make an entrance from stage left, then do a spin and exit stage right. After this was done, he interviewed each person and then Wilma interviewed each. They were both looking for a girl that spoke clear English and French and that they felt would work well with each of them. They decided on two of the girls and then J.J. talked to each girl and explained the job, that they would have two bosses, he and Wilma.

He and Wilma again discussed the two girls and they both decided that Lavelle Tabler was their choice. J.J. thanked the other girl and told her that she was very pretty and appreciated her coming. Lavelle was very happy; also she knew where there was a lady that made costumes.

Instead of J.J. going to the costume shop he sent Wilma and gave her the money to have two costumes made for Lavelle. He figured if the two could get along during this trip that then they would get along for the months they would be together. Lavelle was a green eyed blond and had a fair complexion. J.J. could see that there would be a nice contrast on stage look wise of the two girls and no one in the audience would confuse the two.

Lavelle had a wonderful voice and the next afternoon, J.J. decided that for the first few days all he wished for her to do was to stand stage right and relay in French to the audience what he was saying. They went thru a few card and coin tricks and both he and Wilma were impressed with the projection she had of her voice. It turned out that she had studied to be an opera singer.

They learned one more thing about Lavelle, she also spoke Spanish and Italian, amazing, they now had one person that could translate in three maybe four different countries. She apologized that she could not speak German. J.J. laughed and told her she had two months to learn! For a minute she thought he was serious, then she understood he was kidding her.

They had three days till opening and Wilma and J.J. were satisfied that Lavelle could handle it. Even on things that she hadn't seen, so with the help of Lavelle they saw Paris. It was wonderful. One evening she took them to a different part of town and they saw some very risqué shows. J.J. was very uncomfortable in these.

He was not used to people being so open and sexual, he was glad when the evening was over. The next evening they went to the opera and there they all enjoyed the music and the singing. The story, even though it was in French, J.J. 's knowledge of Cajun helped him and Lavelle explained it all to Wilma. They opened in the first night with only an audience one third the capacity of the seating. This disappointed J.J. Pierre assured him that it would change and change it did, word in France spreads fast and the next night and all the rest of their performances were standing room only. When they finished the three weeks Pierre called J.J. in the same as George had done and they went over the figures the same as he had done with George. That extra week in Paris had really paid off; he had made for their part over $20,000.00. This kind of money in the 1870s was something that J.J. had never imagined he would make. He had Pierre give him what was the equivalent of $1000.00 in French francs and handle the rest per the instructions he had received. He paid both girls, then he took Pierre and the crew out to dinner that night.

One thing that had happened during the second week was Charles Hermann had come back stage and told J.J. that he really enjoyed his performance. He then asked J.J. if he would like to meet Monsieur Houdin. J.J. assured him that he would do anything to meet the other man that had written so much about magic. The next morning Mr. Hermann picked J.J. up and they went south of the city to a Châteaux where the great Houdin lived. He was not in good health, but, he was a very gracious man and he spoke English, which J.J. was glad of. The three magicians of three different generations talked until almost four in the afternoon, the gracious Houdin showed J.J. some of his illusions and granted J.J. a letter of permit to use any that he saw fit. Most of these were not in his books. J.J. hated to leave; he felt like he was leaving a father, the man had been so kind. Mr. Hermann was also very kind, and told J.J. that he hoped that they would meet again. J.J. told him he looked forward to seeing him perform. They compared schedules and they would not cross paths until maybe London, J.J. hoped that would be the case, he had seen the younger brother and he sure wanted to see the older Hermann perform.

They left Paris for Berlin. They were lucky—there was a Pullman like car that they could take that would take them all the way. J.J. was really happy about this because it was a two-day train trip to Berlin and then they would only have three days before they would perform. Plus they had to find a girl that spoke English and German.

The two girls shared a compartment and J.J. had one by himself. They all enjoyed the trip. The dining car was good with excellent food and this train was on time forever stop and every departure. Berlin was also a large city. It was an industrial city, many manufacturing plants. It also had wide avenues and many building that were made of rocks or bricks. The theater was surrounded by a park; this was very unusual but it made for a very peaceful setting.

Their hotel was nice and was about a mile from the theater. J.J. felt lucky that the manager of the hotel spoke good English.

Hans Rummel was the theater manager and he also spoke good English. J.J. explained to him that he needed another assistant and Hans like Pierre and George asked him how many he wished to interview? Unlike Pierre, he told J.J. to come to the theater the next morning at 9 a.m. J.J. laughed to himself, so, the German people were early risers like the Americans and English, he was learning about these cultures as he went. He was also seeing the differences, but those differences are what made it so much fun.

The next morning he and Wilma went to the theater, Lavelle said she wanted to explore Berlin and see what she could. At the theater there were only three girls and those three were all very attractive. J.J. had them do the entrance from stage right to stage left and then they each talked with the girls. J.J. and Wilma then conferred and they had both decided that Carol Loessberg would be the one. Before letting the other two go, J.J. sat down with her and explained the travel, the pay and the details of what her duties were to be. She said immediately that she wanted the job.

So, J.J. thanked the other two girls and set a rehearsal time with Hans. J.J. pulled Hans to the side and asked if he knew about this girl? Hans said, "Yes, she had performed in several productions at the theater and was a nice girl." J.J. then asked Hans if he could pay him to sit and listen to the interpretations the next day and see if she was grasping what was going on. Hans agreed as a courtesy at no charge.

J.J. asked him about a costume person. Hans took J.J. upstairs to a part of the theater where they had many costumes and introduced him to a lady that did all their work.

J.J. had the two girls go up and had Wilma tell the lady what they needed for Carol. The lady said that she would have one costume ready for opening night and the next would be ready in a couple of days after that. With the material and the time she said the cost would be about 20 marks, the mark and the dollar at this time were about equal so J.J. thought that was a good deal.

J.J. was quiet pleased with the look of his girls. Carol was a real red head with a very creamy complexion and she was tall—5 feet 11 inches. She also spoke three languages, English, German and Italian. This gave the performances a very versatile look. They could change girls around in certain spots and have them doing things that would also help keep them interested.

The two weeks in Berlin were wonderful, Carol had a wonderful sense of humor and she expressed this to her people in the audience. They loved her and they loved the performances of J.J. Hans and J.J. did the same thing he had done in London and Paris. He went to Hans' office and was given a written accounting of the monies taken in and their share of it. Two weeks, twelve performances and J.J. had earned twelve thousand marks, J.J. just thought in dollars so that was $12,000.00 to him. He asked Hans to give him 1000 marks and do with the rest as he had been instructed.

The four of them left Berlin for a two week stand in Vienna, Austria. True to her word Shannon had sent him more of the schedule. After Zurich, they were to return to Munchen, Germany for two weeks. Then to Madrid, Spain for two weeks, then a week in Malaga, Spain and a week in Valencia, Spain. Then back to France to

Marseille and then to Monaco. J.J. really had very little idea where a lot of these cities were, but he was ready. Shannon's letter was full of praise. She had received letters from people that had just seen their performances and were talking about how great he was. Every agent was already talking about another tour for J.J.

He thought that was funny, he hadn't finished this one and had no idea where he was going. With her letters were also letters from Gloria, his mother and Madeline.

Madeline sent a picture of Chris and Forrest and herself. J.J. cherished that picture; it gave him fond memories. The girls all went on about how cute little Chris was.

Wilma worked out some things with the girls so that each of them would be part of the show. She taught each of the other two almost every trick, except, the spirit cabinet. She kept that one for herself alone, which was okay with J.J.

Zurich was fun, the audiences were great and Lavelle and Carol both had to do translations each night because the audiences were mixed with French and German speaking people. To amuse the audience, J.J. would speak then he would make a big issue out of pointing first to Lavelle and then to Carol. Then he would point to Wilma and she would throw her hands up and walk off the stage.

This worked every night so much so, that they added it to where ever they went for at least one trick. The Mediterranean Sea was a wonderful, beautiful place. Monaco especially, there the Prince attended every one of their performances. He invited the entire cast to his home for dinner one evening. The man was so well educated, he spoke French to Lavelle, he spoke German to Carol and of course English to Wilma and J.J.

J.J. went to the gambling casino but he could not understand what was so great about it. Every one was dressed formal, they did not holler when they won, actually you couldn't tell who was winning and who was losing.

For sixteen months the four of them went from country to country performing, it became very routine, except for one thing—

that was the money he was making. It was so hard for J.J. to accept that he was making thousands. He would give the girls extra money when they had an exceptional week. One time, he gave each girl an extra $100.00—you should have seen their faces. They all gave him a big hug and each kissed him on the cheek and he turned red. The girls had kidded him a lot about not making passes at them and Carol, well, she loved to play little tricks on him. Like touching him in the wrong place and then lowering her eyes and saying, "Oh, so sorry, is that tender, maybe it needs some gentle care!" Then she would laugh. J.J. knew she was just teasing; besides, his mind was always on the performance. He did not spend much time thinking about that. They had finally played all the cities they were booked for and it was time to head to Scotland.

J.J. knew he had told Lavelle and Carol that when this part of the tour was over their job would end. He had grown used to how they all performed together and decided to ask them if they wanted to play Scotland and England with them. Both girls said yes immediately, so off to Edinburgh, Scotland they all went.

They were a big hit in Scotland and the manager there asked them to stay for an additional week, since they had two weeks before playing London again, they agreed. J.J. even picked up some of the brogue and so did all three girls. The last week they did their translation thing but this time instead of exiting Wilma would put on an air of indignation and in a heavy Scottish brogue, "What sort of lass do ye think I am, Mr. O'Willard?" Then she would storm off the stage, the audience loved it. One night out of the clear blue, she came back to the edge of the curtain and started hissing at J.J. during the middle of his trick, naturally he turned and when he did she took her fore finger and crooked it toward him and said, "Mr. O'Willard, Sir, please come behind this curtain and I shall show ya the type of lass I really am!" Then she winked so that all the audience could see. J.J. followed her instructions and when he got out of sight behind the curtain, Carol and Lavelle went running over to look. Wilma told him that she was going to drop all the pans and when she did for him to fall backwards holding his face. She dropped them and he flew backwards, Carol and Lavelle caught him, turned him to the audience and both said at the same time, "Poor Mr. O'Willard, she is a mean woman!"

The audience laughed so hard that J.J. thought some of them might choke, since this was totally unrehearsed on J.J.'s part. The girls had apparently worked it out so he could only react and apparently he did a good job.

They kept that as part of the act in London and all the papers raved about it, in the words of one, "It is wonderful to see a conjurer who is not so stuck on himself that he can actually make light of some things to lighten up his audience." Of course in London they dropped the Scottish brogues.

One thing that happened was that the minute that George Carman laid his eyes on Carol Losseberg it was love at first sight. They were not separated a single night, George told J.J. that he had finally found a redhead that was the only one for him!

They did even better in London the second time than the first. When the performances ended, Carol told J.J. she was staying with George. Wilma and J.J. took Lavelle to a boat headed for France. J.J. gave both girls a $500.00 bonus and told them both how much they had meant to the show. He also dictated a letter of reference for them both. He and Wilma were really sad to see them leave, but they still had Dublin, Ireland to play.

Dublin was something else, the first night was awkward it was the first time in months that Wilma and J.J. had performed as a duo since they had left London so long ago.

The second night was much smoother, but after the performance, J.J. had relatives coming out his ears, family on his mother's side that he didn't even know their names, first cousins, first cousins once removed and the same on the Willard side.

He and Wilma did not have to buy a meal the rest of the time in Ireland, they went to this cousins house for breakfast, then to another for lunch and finally another for dinner. It was wonderful.

He was given letters to pass on to his mother and letters to be given to his father. Pictures of people, which he had them all put the names and the dates on the back. He knew he would never remember them all without those notes. Several nights after the performances he drank much more beer than he should have, but hey, it is hard to turn down happy relatives. Every morning he would wake up with an awful taste in his mouth and a headache and swear he would never do it again.

Finally the sad day came, the tour was over and it was time to go back to America. He had breakfast with Wilma and asked if she knew what she was going to do. She said she wasn't sure, but that she knew she enjoyed performing and was sure that was what she would do. J.J. gave her a $1000.00 bonus and bought her boat ticket back to England. He actually stayed at the dock and waved to her until she was out of sight. Then he took all the boxes to the ship company and marked them to himself in New York. He had two weeks before a ship would sail, so he toured Ireland. He saw everything that he could. J.J. even kissed the Blarney Stone.

The first week he kept thinking of Wilma Banfield and how good a friend she had become, he truly hoped she would have a good and happy life. He missed all the girls—they had been his constant companions for the last two years, but especially Wilma. He knew Carol was going to be happy, she had George. Lavelle was also a person that was sure of herself and she was such a talented person he hoped she would be fine.

Finally he was back on the White Star line and headed back to America. It seemed to take forever, but actually it only took nine days, but, they were long nine days and of course per agreement with David Kersh, J.J. performed three nights for the passengers. After the big shows he had been doing, to perform solo with only small things almost seemed like child's play, he enjoyed it. He could circulate down into the audience and perform things close up and watch their expressions.

When the ship docked, J.J. gave one of the porters $10.00 to store his boxes in the White Star freight area, he would pick them up later when he knew what he was going to do.

The first thing he did was to stop at the telegraph office and send a wire to Madeline and tell her he was home and to wire him where his mother and father were. The second thing, he went to see Mario. He walked into Mario's and the second Mario saw him, he hollered and ran and hugged him like a brother, actually J.J. felt like Mario was a brother. From the corner of his eye J.J. saw something in blue flying at him, he turned just in time to catch the full blunt of Shannon flying into his arms! J.J. turned red from his neck to the top of his head, the restaurant was full and everyone was laughing.

All of a sudden, Mario said, "Unhand my wife you scoundrel!" J.J. laughed and then it dawned on him, he looked at Shannon's left ring finger and sure enough, there was a ring, then he looked at Mario's left ring finger and yep, there was a ring there too.

Then with a Scottish brogue J.J. said, "Sir, men are always entitled to kiss the bride!" With that he kissed Shannon square on the mouth! The restaurant customers were almost in tears they were laughing so hard. Mario laughed and then said to all his customers, "This is James M. Willard, the Greatest Magician that has ever performed!" J.J. took a bow and everyone applauded. The three of them then went to a table in the far back. J.J. said okay, when did this happen and why didn't you write me? Mario took Shannon's hand and said, "Sir, this beautiful woman said yes and married this poor Italian man six months ago!"

Shannon spoke up, "You see sir, he knew that I was making so much money off a certain magician that I would need help spending it!" Then she laughed, they all laughed. J.J. looked at Mario and said, "Why you low life Italian, I should report you to the Pope, I bet you have even been spending my hard earned money!"

Shannon, said, "Oh, no, your kind sir, all your money is safe in yonder bank!"

Chapter 13

Heading to San Francisco

J.J. woke up at 5:30 am, he dressed and went down stairs, he was still in a daze that he was really in New York. Mario's breakfast cook was already busy in the kitchen.

Henry Holly, the cook, said, "Good Morning Mr. Willard, how are you?" J.J. mumbled a reply and sat down, one of the early waiters brought him a cup of coffee.

Henry was a very large man, about 6' 2" and about 340 pounds, always had a beard and it was gray. He could prepare anything you wished for breakfast and when he did, it seemed to be effortless. The man was good-natured and laughed at life as if it was a big joke. J.J. asked him what time Mario came down in the mornings. Henry said that now that he was a married man, it normally was around eight or nine.

J.J. ate and left the restaurant, he went first to the telegraph office, there was a message from Madeline. J.J. 's father and mother were with them in Pennsylvania, this was great, J.J. could see them all at the same time.

He then went to a warehouse company and arranged for all his boxes to be brought from the White Star storage area to the warehouse. He needed time to decide what action he was going to take. He went with two men to White Star because there were several boxes that he had presents in. While in Europe he had purchased gifts for everyone, including Mario and Shannon. It struck him funny that he had packed Mario's and Shannon's in the same box before he knew they were married.

He took all six boxes with him in a carriage. Two of them were actually crates and went to the train station. There he shipped four of them to Pennsylvania and one to New Orleans, he then took the one for Mario and Shannon back to the restaurant.

Mario and Shannon were still not down, so with the help of one of the waiters he carried the box up to the apartment, they left it in the middle of the sitting room.

J.J. then headed to the bank, it was open and when he entered the President of the bank recognized him from over two years earlier. This impressed J.J.—that a man could remember someone from such a long time that he only met for one day.

J.J. told him that he was there to see what his balance was and that he did not have his deposit book. The man assured J.J. that he did not need it unless he was going to make a withdrawal, which J.J. was not, not at this time anyway, maybe later. The man got out a large book that was marked "W" on it, opened it and said, "Mr. Willard, your current balance is $212,430.60." J.J. shook his hand and thanked him and went outside, it was all he could do to contain himself. In his mind he just kept saying, "I, James Willard have over $200,000.00!" There was an old box sitting next to a building. J.J. sat down on it, his knees were weak. Then he thought to himself, "I am only twenty years old and I have $10,000.00 for every year of my life!" The bank was about half a block from where he was sitting and he looked at its sign, Empire Bank and Trust Company. He laughed. "I have an Empire!" Then it hit him. "What am I going to do with all that money? Banks fail, I can't leave all of it in one place, they are liable to go broke and I will lose it all? What am I going to do?"

He then checked his wallet and what he had was the following: $22.00 American, one pound English, ten francs, 50 lire, 20 marks. Sitting there looking into his wallet, he started to laugh and people walking by sort of went around him thinking he must be a crazy man. It was a full twenty minutes that J.J. sat there, then he hired a carriage and headed back to the restaurant.

Shannon was sitting at a table drinking coffee. He didn't see Mario. He went over and kissed Shannon on the cheek and sat down. She said, "Well, Mr. Magician you have been a busy person this morning, thank you for the gifts, Mario and I thought that it was Christmas!" J.J. looked her square in the eyes and said, "Shannon, I wish to thank you from the bottom of my heart for all you have done for me, you are an honest person, I had not kept any tract as to the money I had made and I just came from the bank, I was astonished at the balance!"

Shannon dug into her purse and handed him two bank books, one was his account and the other was the joint account, he looked at them, then handed her the one that was the joint account back, "You keep the joint account book, we will do business again I am sure and you will need it!" Then she showed him that there was a balance of over $1,000.00 in that account. He told her that was fine, just to leave it there until one of them needed it.

Shannon then said, "What are you going to do, J.J.?" J.J. said, "Shannon, I am going to go see my mother and father and sisters and then I am not sure, I have seen Europe, there are some really beautiful places there, but I haven't seen the west. I sort of think I may go out west, I have heard a lot about it, maybe San Francisco!"

He went up stairs and got his things and when he came down Mario was back from his buying trip, the two men hugged he then hugged Shannon and left.

First he went to the Empire Bank, there he got a letter of credit for $25,000.00 and he also withdrew $10,000.00. The bank had some gold coins, so they gave him 50 of these that were worth $5.00 each.

J.J. knew that in some areas they wouldn't accept paper money. He kept five of these coins in his pocket, then spread the others into his other clothes, making sure that the coins would not touch each other to make a noise if someone was looking for them. He then went to the railroad and purchased a sleeper to Philadelphia, he would arrive there the next morning and then he would take a regular train to Lancaster.

He arrived in Lancaster about one in the afternoon, he rented a surrey and the finest horse that they had, the man wouldn't rent it to him until he told him that he was the brother-in-law of Forrest Edwards, then a big smile came on the man's face and he said, "Then you must be Mr. James Willard the Magician?" J.J. laughed and said that he was, the rental for one week was $5.00, so J.J. reached up behind the mans head and produced a gold coin. The man laughed and said, "Yes, sir, you sure enough are him!"

It was almost dark as he drove up to the Edward's farm, driving down the lane there were some very fine colts that ran along with him and his horse. Before he could bring the horse to a halt Madeline was out the door running to greet him, followed by a Chris who was now about three feet tall. J.J. got down, hugged Madeline and then picked up Chris. What a handsome boy, blond headed, blue eyed, the only way you could tell there was any Irish in him was by his build, he was stocky like so many cousins that he had seen in Ireland.

J.J.'s mother Elizabeth came running out the door, followed by his father James and then Forrest, Forrest's mother and father, but not Gloria.

Chris looped the horse reins around the post like he was really a horseman. They all went inside, supper was on the table and immediately they sat down at the table to eat. Mr. Edward's gave the blessings and then the questions started. J.J. had so many stories to tell them about Europe, meeting Mr. Hermann, and Mr. Houdin and the Prince of Monaco and Queen Victoria.

The men moved out on the porch and that is when J.J.

remembered the horse was tied and hadn't been watered. He and Forrest took his things out, including all the boxes that he had picked up at the train station that had the gifts for everyone. They took the horse and surrey back to the barn, watered the horse and put the surrey in the barn. They had added a new barn and silo. J.J. remarked that they must be doing real good. Forrest in his normal manner said, "Yep!"

Before going back, J.J. asked Forrest where Gloria was. Forrest said, "J.J., she ran off with Kim Dodge, they are married and living in Baltimore and he is working with his father in the ship yard. She did it two months ago and your mom and dad were not real happy, but they went to Baltimore and they like Kim!"

J.J. sat down on the porch with his dad and Mr. Edwards again and smoked a cigar with them, what a wonderful peaceful feeling he had, sitting there by his father and the two of them talking. Gloria never came up in the conversation that evening not until he was with his mother the next day.

The next morning he woke early, Forrest and Mr. Edwards were already sitting at the dining room table drinking coffee. J.J. asked what their plans for the day were and Forrest said he just had to check some fences. Mr. Edwards said he was going to clean out the barn that had the stalls. J.J. said he would help him with those after he had talked with his mother. Madeline came in and for the first time, J.J. noticed that she was pregnant, he patted Forrest on the back and said, "Looks to me like you have been working a little over time brother-in-law!" Everyone laughed.

Elizabeth came in, kissed J.J. on the cheek the way she had done when he was a small boy. For that minute, he was nine years old again, she even ruffled his hair like she used to.

After breakfast J.J. and his mother (Elizabeth) went out on the front porch, the sun was up and it felt warm, from the porch you looked east and could see the scattered trees and the fields, some under cultivation. It was May and spring and being outside felt so very good. J.J. asked his mother when they were going to perform again.

Elizabeth said, "J.J. we didn't write to you because we knew you would be home soon, but, your father and I lost everything in the fire in Boston last Nov. 9th. We have no illusions, we have no money to start over, the bank where we had our money in Boston, it burned down too!" Then she started to cry. J.J. got up and hugged her and then he said, "Mother, there is no need to worry or cry, I have plenty of money and I have plenty of illusions!"

Elizabeth looked at her son with a big question mark on her face. J.J. said, "Mother, I, your son, little James Jr., have over $150,000.00 in the bank!"

Her mouth fell open in disbelief that her little J.J. had so much money. He continued, "I also have a lot of illusions that you and father can have to start over. I am going to head out west and see the country and it will be a while before I even think about performing again, right now, I am performed out!"

Having said this, he realized that it was true and he laughed.

James Sr. came out on the porch and Elizabeth jumped up and hugged him in happiness then she blurted out, "James, our little J.J. is rich, he is going to loan us the money to perform again and all his illusions!" James Sr. sat down with a big sigh, as if he couldn't believe it. He looked at J.J. and said, "What does she mean you're rich?"

J.J. said, "Father I am, when I returned from Europe, I had over $150,000.00 in the bank, the Empire Bank and Trust Company of New York!"

James Sr. repeated it, "Over $150,000.00!"

"I have decided not to perform for awhile and I have all my illusions stored in a warehouse in New York. Father you can have all of them! I am going out west maybe to San Francisco, who knows, maybe even to Alaska. There is something that I want to give you and mother, I want you to go back to Ireland and see everyone. I have pictures from so many people that claim to be our kin. They were warm and so wonderful to me, you must go back to Ireland and see them, will you do that?"

Elizabeth said, "Back to Ireland, that would cost so much!"

Then she and James Sr. looked at each other and then they hugged and then they brought J.J. into their hug and all three just stood there on the front porch feeling the warmth of each other and the spring sun.

They talked for another hour and then J.J. went and hitched the horse to the surrey and he and his father went into Lancaster. In Lancaster he wired David Kersh and asked when the next ship was leaving for Ireland, that he wanted his father and mother to go. They walked around town for a little while and then went back to the telegraph office, there was an answer from David.

Oceanic sails June 1st STOP If your father and mother will perform their passage is Free STOP Answer needed today STOP.

They telegraphed back, with a very simple message: *Contract accepted! STOP.* They then checked the train schedules; J.J. wanted his mother and father to travel first class. He found that they could connect with a Pullman in Philadelphia the next evening at 7 p.m. J.J. bought the tickets. Riding back to the Edward's farm J.J. felt really great. He was able to finally give his mother and father something after all the hard work they had done for him and his two sisters. The suffering of leaving Brooklyn and going by wagon to New Orleans. Making sure that none of them were ever really harmed during the war, it was a great feeling. James Sr. kept his arm around his son for the whole ride back.

The whole house was in an uproar, the ladies were washing clothes and ironing and trying to get things ready, clothes were all over the place upstairs. The men just sort of watched and stayed out of the way. J.J. went out to the pig pen and Old Ned started talking to him, J.J. actually felt the hog had missed him. J.J. penned two letters, one to his bank that he wished for them to give his father $10,000.00. The other to the warehouse company that would give his father permission to check out the boxes he had there. The next day after lunch, they loaded up the surrey and a carriage and took James Sr. and Elizabeth to the train station. J.J. had sealed the letters and on the outside they were addressed to who they were going to, he gave them to his father. It was a very happy time, and J.J. was both happy and sad. His mother hugged him for the longest time and then his father hugged him and for the first time in years he kissed him. J.J. then took the rest of the family to a restaurant in Lancaster for supper.

J.J. and little Chris were getting along tremendously. No matter where J.J. sat, Chris would either crawl up on his lap, or pull a chair up next to him. That also was a good feeling, to have some one that thought you were great. Chris rode in the surrey with J.J. back to the farm and J.J. let him have the reins, Chris handled the horse like a real horseman, for a fiveyear old, J.J. was amazed.

That night he and Forrest had the chance to sit on the porch and talk, Madeline had already told him how much he had made, Forrest wondered if J.J. had enjoyed it or was it a strain performing so much. J.J. told him about the three girls and how much they had done. Forrest's next question was natural, "Which one were you sleeping with?" J.J. said, "Believe it or not, none of them, they were all beautiful girls but he wanted to maintain a professional level with them and knew that would affect the relationship."

Forrest said, "For a young man of only twenty J.J., you are a very smart man, not very many eighteenyear olds would be that smart!"

The next morning J.J. was packed and hugged everyone and headed to Lancaster to catch a train to Baltimore. He wanted to see Gloria and to meet Kim.

He arrived in Baltimore about 3 p.m. and took a carriage to the Dodge Ship Building yard. There he met Mr. Dodge, a gruff sort of man, but when he learned who J.J. was he was immediately cordial. He took J.J. to meet Kim. Kim was working on the inside of a very large iron ship—it was huge. Mr. Dodge pointed out that this was the largest ship ever built in America and that it was using the new stern twin propellers and was the first to do that. They had to go up three flights of stairs to get to the top and then there was no deck yet and had to go down two flights to get to where Kim was working. It was inside a cabin, where he was installing the wood paneling. From what J.J. could see, it was going to be a beautiful cabin.

Kim dropped what he was doing when his father told him there was a man to see him. Then the elder Dodge said, "by the strange name of James Willard." Kim turned and stuck out his hand with a big smile, then said, "You must be J.J.!"

J.J. felt a kinship to him right then and knew they were going to be friends. Kim turned to his dad and told him that he was leaving for the day.

They took a carriage to an outer part of the city, actually out of the city to a farm. J.J. was quite surprised that they were actually living outside the city. He didn't know why this surprised him, but it just did. When they turned down the lane to the house Kim said, "Gloria said she wouldn't marry me until I owned a home, so I bought this place, it has 300 acres and the house is only forty years old and in good shape!" Gloria came running out of the house giggling like a schoolgirl. She jumped and had her arms around his neck hugging him.

J.J. spent the next three days with them, one day he spent the entire day working with Kim at the shipyard. This huge ship fascinated him; he wondered how something so heavy could actually float. In Germany J.J. had purchased a set of china for Gloria, so it turned out to be a great gift, perfect for a wedding present and since they only had everyday dishes it was even better. When she opened it there was only one cup broken out of twelve, which J.J. had worried about, he was afraid with all the shipping the whole set of twelve would be broken, but, they weren't.

When he left, he was happy! It seemed to him that his whole family was happy and that both sisters had someone that loved them and would take care of them. He caught the Pullman from Baltimore to Chicago, that night he blessed Mr. Pullman for inventing something so nice.

It was early afternoon when he arrived in Chicago, he could not believe what the city looked like, the fire had destroyed so much of it. The carriage driver told him that the High Hat Club wasn't harmed, the fire was north of it, he hadn't heard from Glen so he was glad. The boarding house where he had stayed had been burned down. He asked the driver if there was a clean boarding house with rooms anywhere. The driver took him to one that was on top of a hill, it was made of bricks and was brand new, inside, he found that it was the same lady that had owned the other one, it had taken all her savings and a loan from the bank to build this one, but it was so much nicer than her older one.

She was really glad to see J.J. With a wink she said, "Well, Mr. Willard, I guess I can expect that you will be cavorting till late hours every night?" J.J. in his best Irish accent answered, "Aye, lass, I will probably close down several of the pubs in this fair city!" They both laughed. One thing that amused J.J., in each room was a tub and toilet. Complete privacy, you did not have to go down the hall. He said, "My, my, aren't we the fancy place now, indoor plumbing and right in your own room, I must be in one of those deluxe fancy hotels!" She answered, "Don't be ye going with that glib tongue of yours young man, this room cost you an extra two dollars a night!" J.J. answered, "I had better not stay too long then or I'll be one broke Irishman!" They again laughed.

Mrs. Susan Shoultz was a lady with a German background; her specialty was cooking pastries, pies, cakes and rolls. She was originally from Petersburgh, Indiana and had come to Chicago with her husband, a fisherman. He was one of the many that had been caught in a storm on Lake Michigan. People do not think of a lake as being dangerous, but, Lake Michigan is really a sea and many men have lost their lives in boats on it. Susan is a person that faced life and enjoyed it regardless of things that happened.

J.J. got to the High Hat Club at about 7 p.m. He was surprised to see that there were not many customers. Frances was the first to see him and gave him a big hug. One of the waiters that had been there a long time saw J.J. and went and told Glen.

Glen came from the back with that big smile on his face and

grabbed J.J. and gave him a big hug. Then he said, "Well, the Prince of Europe has returned!" Both men laughed. Glen then stood off a little from J.J. and took a good look at him, then he said, "Look at you, you left a boy and you have come back a man!" Frances said, "Glen, don't you think he has become a real handsome man?" J.J. turned red. All three laughed.

Glen and J.J. went and sat at a table and Frances went to check on some things.

J.J. asked, "Tell me about the fire, I saw how awful it looks?" Glen said, "Well, you have probably heard that your cousin's wife, Patrick O'Leary is being blamed for the fire, or at least their cow. I am not sure of that, we had been in a drought for months without rain and every thing was so dry. When it started and it got out of control so fast, our fireman tried hard to contain it, but they just didn't have the right equipment. Good things are coming from it though, the government is now setting up some building codes and most places will have to have brick or concrete construction and also must have fire escapes if they are two floors or more!"

J.J. "Did you know my father was wiped out by the Boston fire?"

Glen: "No, I had not heard, were they hurt?"

J.J. "No, but he lost all of his illusions, plus, the bank they had their money in burned so they lost everything, but, lucky, I made plenty in Europe and have sent them to Ireland to see all their relatives! When they return they are going to use my illusions to start again."

Glen: "Won't you be needing them to perform yourself?"

J.J. "Glen, I am not going to perform for awhile and I am headed out west to San Francisco and maybe even Alaska!"

J.J., Glen and Frances talked until midnight and then J.J. headed back to Mrs. Shoultz's after agreeing to come see Glen early the next day.

Breakfast at Susan's Shoultz's was the best he had in a long time. He told her so, that her cooking was something that brought him back to Chicago. Susan said, "With this new kitchen, I can out cook the chefs of Europe!" J.J. told her that was truly a real fact.

Before going to the High Hat J.J. went to the docks to see if there was a riverboat that would be leaving for the south soon. Luck would have it, the *Mississippi Queen* was there and she would leave the next morning. John Thibodaux was no longer the captain, he was back to being the first mate, the new captain was a man by the name of Patrick O'Malley, an Irishman. J.J. saw John Thibodaux and John took and introduced him to the captain. Captain O'Malley told him he would give him free passage to St. Louis with a cabin if he would perform one night for the passengers.

J.J. told him he really didn't have any magic but he could do card and coin tricks if that would be okay. They agreed and J.J. told them he would the there the next morning.

J.J. and Glen spent the day going around Chicago and seeing all the damage and talking to people. Glen was on the city council and it really was part of his job. So many people poor and rich alike had lost everything. Many had just abandoned their property and moved. Without the churches many of these would have starved. Churches were preparing two meals a day for the poor.

When they returned to the High Hat about six they were covered in black soot and their faces looked like they had been digging in the coal yard. Frances told them they had to do a major cleaning before they could come in her dining room. Neither of them realized how bad they looked until they looked into the mirror. Then they had a good laugh. J.J. went to the boarding house and took a bath and put on clean clothes then went back to the High Hat Club.

J.J. asked Glen if he had any hand magic that he might buy from him, something that was fun but he could carry in a bag. Glen took J.J. to his magic storage and there were several things that he could use, Glen would have given them to him, but J.J. insisted on paying, so, Glen took $20.00.

The next morning J.J. had breakfast at Susan's and gave her a big hug after paying her and headed for the *Mississippi Queen*.

It was July and as he rode the carriage to the docks, he could smell the lake and also the smell of charred wood, but it felt normal to be going to the *Queen*, almost like home.

John Thibodaux had arranged for J.J. to have his old cabin, so this really did feel like home. They left the docks at 9 a.m. Their was a band playing on board the ship, but none of them were the same as the old band and they had a totally different sound. More of a brass sound, where the other band had been more of a string band, guitar, banjo, bass fiddle and drums. This band was trumpet, clarinet, bass fiddle and drums. They sounded good. J.J. performed that night for the passengers, he told them he felt like he was home and that he had performed on this boat the very first time it had sailed up the Mississippi river. Since he had no illusions, except for his flying bird cage, he saved it till last and he would do a trick and then he would talk about Europe. Another trick and then a little more chatter about Europe. He finished with the flying bird cage and since he had no bird, he borrowed a gentleman's watch from the audience and had it swinging from the little perch in the cage. The audience loved it, especially when he then produced a watch that was all broken and told the gentleman he was certainly sorry. The audience loved it and they really laughed. J.J. then produced the gentleman's watch and the man was happy. They gave J.J. a standing ovation.

He had to admit to himself that he couldn't give up performing, it was part of his life, it was who he was. Well, he was just going to consider himself on vacation for the next few months, after all he had worked continuously for four years, he deserved it.

When they docked in St. Louis, J.J. told Captain Patrick that he appreciated his courtesy.

Captain Patrick said he was welcome any time, John gave him a big hug and told him to say hello to Jon and George for him. He would see them as soon as they had an overnight in St. Louis.

J.J. headed for Boudreaux's French Cuisine Restaurant. It was about six in the evening and he was actually hungry. George saw him first and gave him the big bear hug and then Jon Boudreaux came from the kitchen, and his exact words were, "Hey, Magician, No birds in My Restaurant!" Then all three men laughed. J.J. spent the night with the two men in their apartment above the restaurant and they talked till almost 1 a.m.

The next morning he went to the train station and there was a train that would be leaving at 1 p.m. for the west. In talking to the station manager, J.J. found that yes he could get to San Francisco by train, but, he was going to have to change lines six times! At each change he would have to buy another ticket, he was sorry America had not combined all the railroads the way Europe had. At least there as long as you were in the same country, it was the same railroad. Oh, well, he was going to see the country and it looked like he was going to see plenty. He went back to Jon and George's and got his stuff, told them they could expect to see him when they saw him coming.

J.J. dressed as comfortably as he could for the long journey, comfortable jacket, no tie, cotton pants and shirt. He knew this was going to be worse than New Orleans to Philadelphia. The train headed from St. Louis to Kansas City, it arrived there about nine at night, there was a hotel across the street from the station and J.J. stayed there for the night. After breakfast he boarded the train headed for Topeka. One nice thing, the train from Topeka would run all the way to Colby, Kansas and there was at least a dining car on the train. There also was a stop or a town every twenty miles, sometimes only ten miles. Colby, Kansas had no hotel, but it did have a boarding house. The train arrived there at 6 p.m. and the train leaving wasn't until 7 a.m. the next morning. J.J. spent the night in the boarding house, it left a lot to be desired. The next morning breakfast was served at 6 a.m. and if you weren't there you didn't eat.

They left for Denver and arrived there at four in the afternoon, here again the train he needed would not leave until seven the next morning. At least Denver had a very nice hotel and J.J. took advantage of being able to take a nice long hot bath. Denver also had great food. Of course after three days of only average food, probably any well cooked balanced meal would have tasted great.

Going through the mountains reminded J.J. so much of Europe and the alps. He sat looking out the window and it made him wonder how Wilma, Carol and Lavelle were doing, it also brought back memories of the performances they did in places like Zurich and Munchen and Vienna. Since they were going thru the mountains they didn't arrive in Rocksprings, Wyoming until the next morning.

All there was in Rocksprings was a café and not a very good one, but they did have a washhouse and the food was edible.

J.J. had only one and a half hours before the train left for Ogden, but, that really was more time than he needed, he thought to himself that he would be glad when George Pullman leased sleeping cars to these lines. He changed rail lines again and headed for Ogden, Utah. They arrived at Ogden at 3 p.m. and by this time J.J. was actually very tired. The scenery had kept his attention but now it was starting to get to the point he just wanted to get there, wherever there was. The train for Salt Lake would not leave until the morning. One of the main reasons most of the trains were not traveling at night was simple, animals on the tracks at night were a danger to the train, trains had been wrecked because of a bear or elk on a track.

Ogden had a nice hotel, but, J.J. had to laugh, the cost was twice what a nice hotel in Chicago or New York would cost. It did have a nice dining room and the food was very good. He would say one thing for the hotel, they had really comfortable beds and again he got the chance to take a nice hot bath. From what they had told him this would be the last chance to bathe until he reached either Sacramento or San Francisco.

The next morning they left Ogden at 7 a.m. and arrived in Salt Lake at 11 a.m. Salt Lake was something to see, J.J. sort of wished he had the time to explore it, but decided to stay on the train. He could see the massive church setting on the hill and told himself he would come back and see that one day.

The train arrived in Sacramento, California at 8 p.m. that night, it was going on to San Francisco but for some reason, J.J. decided to spend the night in Sacramento, he did not know why. He found a nice hotel about a block from the train station and welcomed the hot bath and clean sheets.

The next morning after breakfast he walked around the city, it wasn't a large city but it was the capital of California. After seeing Washington, D.C. and London it wasn't very impressive, but was nice. He was standing on the corner heading for the river when a carriage went by with a large white man, a dark woman that looked Indian and three girls varying in ages, the girls had olive complexions. One of the girls waved at him like she knew him. J.J.s first thought was, that is the most beautiful girl I have ever seen! He waved back like he had known her all his life. Long after the carriage was out of sight all he could think about was that long black hair, flashing eyes and that smile. He figured that must have been the reason he stopped in Sacramento. He wondered if he would ever see her again and then thought probably not.

He went down by the river and he was amazed at how fast the water was running, he loved swimming but there was no way he would try it in current that fast. He put his hand in the water and it was ice cold. A man standing there fishing said, "Yep, it is cold, comes right out of the snows in the mountains!" J.J. asked him how the fishing was and the man pulled a string of fish up that had five on it and they were all at least a pound.

J.J. headed back to the hotel and had lunch and then caught an afternoon train to San Francisco. He arrived at about 7 p.m. and when he stepped off the train, it was cold. This was August—it didn't make sense for it to be so cold. He caught one of the street cars that were being pulled by mules and it took him to the top of a hill where there was a hotel. It was a very deluxe hotel, six stories high and built out of stone and bricks. When he entered the lobby it was decorated the same as many of the hotels in Europe. J.J.'s room was on the fourth floor and it was very nice. His view looked out toward the bay and even though it was night he could tell that there was an island in the bay. It had been a long journey and J.J. decided that this first morning, he was going to sleep in, which he did till 8 a.m. When he awoke he looked out his window and couldn't see anything, there was fog covering the entire city. He had seen fog in London, but this seemed thicker than London fog.

He went down and had a very good breakfast, it was served in a buffet style and you got what you wanted. J.J. had scrambled eggs, two kinds of sausage, bacon, biscuits and jam topped off with wonderful coffee. He thought the coffee was the best he had ever had. Maybe it was the fog. He then went outside to go for a walk and immediately decided that he was dressed wrong. It was as cold as winter in New Orleans. Had he slept for a couple of months? Boy, it was cold; he went back in the hotel and asked the desk clerk about the cold. The desk clerk told him, "Yes, sir Mr. Willard, this time of year we get a cold breeze from the ocean, that wind can cut right through you, but, tomorrow will probably be nice!"

J.J. went to his room and put on some warm clothes and looking at his clothes, he decided that they should be washed, so he took them to the desk and asked him to please get them done for him. His stage clothes were in a different suitcase and they had not been worn.

He sat in the lobby of the hotel till noon reading the papers, it seemed there was a lot going on. There were two theaters and they both had plays and then there was the Opera House and tomorrow evening they were doing an opera. J.J. decided to venture down to the docks and see what was happening there. The desk clerk had been right, the wind cut right thru you. At the wharf he found a nice restaurant and he had fish for lunch. He laughed; it wasn't fish and chips the way they served in England. The fish was baked and the potatoes were mashed, it was delicious.

He caught the trolley back up the hill to the hotel. Those trolleys were a great idea, some one was making money because they always seemed to be full, it took four mules to pull them up the hill. Even though he couldn't see anything for the fog, he felt that San Francisco must be all hills.

The next day as the desk clerk had said, was beautiful, still very cool but the sky was clear and when you were in the sun it was warm. From the front of the hotel J.J. could see the Fort on the island, he wondered if they were still holding confederate prisoners there, he hoped not. It did not look like a very nice place. He could also see that in the harbor there were three ships that were three mast sailing ships. Then there were a couple of steam ships and one rear paddle riverboat. He could also see a ferryboat going to the north side of the bay, he wondered what was on that side.

J.J. decided that since he had been to the docks the day before, that today he was going to explore other parts of the town. He caught the trolley heading south and asked the person taking the money what might be an interesting place to go? The money taker told him to get off in China Town, that there was a lot to see there in the shops. He was also told if he liked to eat Chinese food that the best place was a restaurant called the Maverick's Hong-Fong. The money taker and J.J. had a nice conversation. He told J.J. that he was here from Texas and that his name was Oliver Mills Johnson from Mason, Texas.

So, J.J. got off in China Town, if you didn't know you were in San Francisco you would think you were in China. The men and the women were dressed in traditional Chinese attire. The women wore long silk dresses that were very tight at the ankles. They were in vivid colors with flowery prints on them, their long black hair braided and hanging to the middle of their back.

J.J. wondered from shop to shop looking at everything from silks to glassware and to jewelry. In one shop he found some hand dyed silk that was just beautiful and it was about 3 feet wide and about 30 feet long, he couldn't resist it, he knew that he could use this on stage performing. He purchased it for only $15.00; that price amazed him. He had looked at some similar in Europe and they had wanted $200.00. He laughed to himself. Okay, now you have it, what are you going to do with it?

He found Hong-Fong Restaurant, it didn't say Maverick's but he went in, a very kindly looking Chinese man greeted him when he entered. J.J. asked him if this was the Maverick Hong-Fong? The man said, "Yes, I am Maury Maverick Huey II." For some reason this struck J.J. funny and he laughed. Who ever heard of a Chinese man being the "second"? The man asked what he thought was funny and that is when J.J. told him he had not heard of a Chinese man being a second.

Mr. Huey after seating J.J., told him, my grandfather came from China, he worked for a man in Texas that's name was Maverick. That man Maury Maverick helped my grandfather start his own restaurant. His grandfather named his first son Maury Maverick after the man, since we have had such a good life owning restaurants my father named me after Mr. Maverick also and I also have a son with my wife Beverly who's name is Kenneth. J.J. told him that he meant no offense and was pleased that they had a good life.

J.J. sat there looking at all the décor and all of a sudden he saw the young lady from Sacramento sitting at a table across the room! He truly could not believe that this was the same girl, but it was. She glanced up and saw him looking and gave him that same smile she had given him from the carriage. J.J. was not normally a bold person with strangers, actually usually very shy, but this time he was not going to let this chance meeting get away without knowing who she was. He got up and went across the room to her, when he reached her table, he bowed and said, "Miss, I saw you in a carriage in Sacramento three days ago; if it wasn't you, you have a twin!"

She stuck out her hand to shake and said, "No, I have no twin, it was me, I was with my father, mother and two sisters!" With that she laughed, a wonderful, blissful laugh that made J.J. feel good. J.J. said, "My name is James M. Willard, I am from New Orleans, New York and all points east!" She laughed and said, "Mr. Willard you certainly cover lots of territory, my name is Lucy Mae Keefer, I am from Chico, California, would you like to join me?"

J.J. did not wait for her to repeat it, he immediately sat down at her table then he asked, "What are you doing in San Francisco?" Lucy replied, "I am here attending school, my father and mother insisted that I learn to be somebody!" Then she laughed. J.J. could not take his eyes off her; he had never been so taken with the beauty of a girl before. Not Satin, or Amber or Carol or Lavelle or Wilma. This girl took his breath away with her dark eyes, olive complexion and dark hair that hung to the middle of her back in two braids. He was so caught up in her beauty he did not hear her ask him what he was doing in San Francisco.

Lucy Mae repeated, "Mr. Willard, I asked what are you doing in San Francisco?"

This time he heard and said, "I am here on a vacation!"

Lucy Mae asked, "What is you normal occupation, besides staring at girls?"

J.J. laughed. "I am sorry, truly I am Lucy Mae Keefer, but, you are the prettiest woman I have ever seen, I am a magician!"

Lucy laughed and said, "Oh, a conjurer of the slight of hand and the mysteries of the far east, but how do you do that with eyes that are so bad?"

J.J. laughed and said, "Lucy Mae, my eyes are perfect, I see things the way they are!"

The waiter brought J.J.'s food to the table and he ate and he really has no idea what it was, but, it was delicious, he thinks, but isn't sure because he doesn't remember eating. Lucy said she had to get back to school, so J.J. went with her. They caught a trolley back to the center of town. When they reached the school J.J. asked her if she would go to the opera with him that night? She accepted and told him where to call for her that evening.

J.J. dressed in his tails for the evening and picked her up at a large brown stone house on one of the hills. She told him her father owned it. J.J. and Lucy Mae went to the opera, but he has no idea what it was or what it was about. The next day he picked her up at the same house and they spent the entire day seeing the sights of San Francisco. The next day Sunday, they attended the Catholic mass together in a beautiful church.

Sunday night Lucy Mae told him she wouldn't be able to see him during the week, this disappointed him, but she said that she had to take test and needed to study for them. If he would like to meet her family for him to come to Chico the next Saturday and she would introduce him to them. J.J. asked a very simple question, "How will I find your home in Chico?" Lucy Mae answered, "Oh, just ask where the Keefer ranch is!"

It was a very long week for J.J., all he could think of was Lucy Mae, he had seen her father and he was a big man. Would that big man like him or throw him off his ranch or maybe just shoot him as soon as he sat foot on the ranch and asked for Lucy Mae, it was a very long week.

On Thursday J.J. found a Chinese theater that was doing traditional Chinese dance and also there was a female magician. She did a thing called the "Tien Chie Thumb Tie"; this totally fascinated J.J. After the show he asked if she spoke English, she didn't so that ended him finding out how she did it. Maybe later he would find out how it was done. She also did some things with silks that gave J.J. ideas how he could use the silks that he had purchased.

Friday finally came and J.J. checked out of the hotel and went to the train station and caught a train to Chico. He had to go back thru Sacramento and it was late in the afternoon when he finally arrived at Chico, California. It was a beautiful area, lots of orchards, fruit trees, nut trees and fields of cotton and corn. The corn had already been picked and was being plowed under. The cotton was ready to be picked and it made J.J. wonder where they got the laborers to pick it.

He found a boarding house in town and checked in and took a hot bath. Then he walked around the town, he asked one man if he knew where the Keefer ranch was. The man said, "What ya want to see that Indian lover for?" J.J. thanked the man and walked away.

He had never been one who tolerated prejudice and felt it better to go unsaid. He found the livery stable and asked about renting a horse, the man told him it would be five dollars for a day or a week. J.J. asked him how to find the Keefer ranch. The man said, "Just head out the Redding road for about a mile and a half and you can't miss it."

The next morning after breakfast J.J. went and rented the horse and saddle, the saddle cost an extra dollar. He carried a box of cigars for Mr. Keefer, Lucy Mae had told him that her father smoked cigars, so he had bought the finest the store had. He also had a silk scarf for her mother. He was very nervous about this meeting and he could not think of why he was so nervous.

He could see a large house about a quarter of a mile before he got to it. There were large fields on both sides of the road then he saw another road that he had to turn down to get to the house, before entering that road, he had to get off the horse and open a large gate. Above the gate was a wrought iron sign that said "Keefer", so he knew he was in the right place. He laughed to himself because it looked like the house was still a quarter of a mile away.

In a fenced field to his left were horses, some of the finest he had seen. He thought of Forrest and that he bet he would like to have one of these beautiful animals. One thing for sure, these were thoroughbreds probably used for racing at the county fairs. Just as he was approaching the house two riders came racing around at full speed and almost ran him over, suddenly he realized that it was two girls and that they were riding bare back; he watched as they kept going, they were bare footed, their hair was not in braids but flying in the wind of the race. Both were laughing as they went around the side of the house and out of sight. After they were gone J.J. realized that one of those girls was Lucy Mae!

He rode up, got off his horse, tied it to a post and went up to the door. When he knocked a Chinese man came to the door, with an accent the man asked J.J. what he wanted. J.J. told him that he was there to meet Mr. Keefer, the man showed him to a room

that was full of books, with a desk and several different style chairs around the room including a couch and a beautiful fireplace.

After what seemed like an eternity the man J.J. had seen in Sacramento entered the room. J.J. told him that he was a friend of Lucy Mae's and that he had come from San Francisco to meet him. Mr. Keefer looked him square in the eyes and then looked at him all over, then stuck his hand out and said, "Lucy has told me about you, you are an entertainer from back east!" J.J. gave him the box of cigars. The man motioned for J.J. to sit, which he did, the cigars seemed to have broken the ice. At least J.J. hoped so. Mr. Keefer then asked J.J. why he was in California and where he had entertained.

J.J. and Mr. Keefer sat for about an hour and J.J. talked about his magic, where he had been and the many things he had done, Keefer seemed to really be interested.

Just about the time J.J. was running out of things to say, Lucy and another girl entered the room. They were still barefoot and their hair was still loose, J.J. stood and as usual he couldn't take his eyes off Lucy. Lucy said, "J.J. this is my little sister, Blanche, we are sorry we almost ran you over! We were racing and as usual Blanche beat me!" Blanche was about twelve. Blanche came over and stuck her hand out, J.J. shook her hand then reached behind her ear and produced a nickel. J.J. said, "Blanche do you always store money behind your ears?" She laughed and even Mr. Keefer laughed. Mr. Keefer said, "See there little Indian, I told you that bathing was necessary!" Then he laughed.

Out of the blue, Mr. Keefer asked J.J. if he would like to see the ranch. J.J. told him he would enjoy that. They went out back to a stable and Mr. Keefer saddled a horse, along with Lucy and Blanche, they went touring. J.J. noticed that he could see a mountain off to the north, he asked what mountain it was. It was Mount Shasta.

Lucy said, "There are a group of men that live on that mountain, they are suppose to be holy men, friars or something." Mr. Keefer said, "You only see one of them occasionally when they need supplies, they come down and always pay for what they need with gold." J.J. asked, "How far away is the mountain?" Lucy answered, "About a hundred miles." J.J. having seen the alps knew that was probably true.

Mr. Keefer showed him where he used to have a stage stop before the damn railroads came, he then took him to the mill, actually you could see the mill from the stage stop. Lucy said, "Daddy has won the blue ribbon for flour for three of the last four years at the state fair in Sacramento!"

On top of the hill above the mill in a large field were some pens with cattle in them. Mr. Keefer explained that this was where they brought their cattle and branded them and also where they kept them when buyers were coming. They started back toward the house and Lucy said, "Want to race back?"

Mr. Keefer said, "Son, you don't stand a chance, both girls will beat you and you will be covered in dust!"

J.J. laughed and kicked his horse into a run; this caught both girls by surprise.

About half way back they caught him and passed him like he was standing still.

When he got to the ranch house they were both sitting on the front porch, laughing.

Lucy asked, "What took you so long, Mister?" Then she and Blanche both laughed.

J.J. said, "Oh, I stopped to see if my horse had lost a leg!" Both girls laughed and about that time Mrs. Keefer came out of the house. She said, "You girls picking on a poor Irishman from the east?"

J.J. got off his horse and said, "Mrs. Keefer, my name is James Willard, it is a pleasure you meet you." He took off his hat and bowed to her. Mrs. Keefer said, "Young man no need for that bowing around here, can't you tell by these foolish girls that we sure do not do things in a formal manner, Lucy has told me all about you, welcome!" She stuck out her hand and J.J. shook it.

J.J. had supper with them and he met her other sisters and her two brothers, one sister was older and of course Blanche was younger and the two boys were in between Lucy and Blanche. The boys were pretty rough, but when Mr. Keefer said something, they listened. Because of the Spanish land grant, Mr. Keefer was referred to as Senior Keefer, his grant was for 3000 acres.

It was obvious that Mrs. Keefer was an Indian, there were also other Indians on the ranch, there were several houses that they lived in. J.J. noticed that they all treated Mr. and Mrs. Keefer with respect. The Chinese man well, he was something, his name was "High Chinaman". J.J. asked Mr. Keefer about him and his name. Mr. Keefer told him that when High Chinaman came over on the boat that he could speak no English, so on the boat people kept saying to him "High Chinaman" so when he landed and they asked him his name, he really didn't know what they were asking so he told the immigration man in San Francisco that his name was High Chinaman and that was what was on his papers. Mr. Keefer then said, "To answer your other question, my wife is Cherokee, her father and mother came out here with her and her two brothers when all the mess started back east."

Sunday Lucy came into town in a carriage and picked J.J. up and they went to church, it was a Lutheran church, the service was different than J.J. was used to because he actually understood what the minister was saying. After church they had a picnic that Lucy had prepared. Then she took him and showed him the Indian reservation.

They rode the train back together that night to San Francisco, arriving about 7 p.m.

J.J. hired a carriage and took her to her house. She recommended that if he was going to stay in San Francisco he should move into a boarding house. The next day he did just that, he moved into a boarding house that she recommended that was close to her school. J.J. found a small theater and started performing magic on Thursdays and Fridays.

His income from these performances was not really great but it paid for his room and board and gave him pocket money to take Lucy

Mae to lunch and dinner. They went to see the ballet one evening, it was a traveling troupe and the lead dancer was a beautiful dancer by the name of Margaret Miller, she truly had the grace of a Swan. It was amazing that this town that had been such a rough and tumble place just a few short years ago would have so many people come to a ballet to see something so sophisticated.

Lucy Mae Keefer and James Michael Willard were married in Oroville, California only six months after they met. They became entertainers traveling the United States and Canada. They had four children, three sons and one daughter. All their sons became magicians. They moved to San Antonio, Texas during WW I where they bought a nice home.

✳✳✳

There is much more to the story, but that is for another time. It's been nice talking to you. 'Til next time, Adios!

The Author

Billy grew up on ranches in South Texas around Beeville and San Antonio. Yes, in the 40s and 50s there were still ranches close to San Antonio! He went to Northside High School and was President of the 1954 class. He was drafted into the army in November, 1954, and served two years in Germany. After the army he went to San Antonio College at night while working during the day. He married Madeline Willard in 1957 and they are still married. They had two sons, Christopher and Forrest. Forrest died on Dec. 9, 1994. Billy worked in middle management in corporations including WWGraingers, Westinghouse and Southwestern Bell, before starting his own businesses. Billy and his wife opened Opulent Advertising in 1976 and purchased San Antonio Fine Arts Center, a children's live theater production company, in 1978. They opened the Melodrama Playhouse and Saloon in 1982 and Billy wrote plays for both theaters—several of which were repeated several times. Billy opened Copeland Insurance Agency with his son Christopher in 1995, and sold the agency in 1999 when Billy retired. This book had been running around in his head for many years and in 2000 he finally had the time to write it.

www.ingramcontent.com/pod-product-compliance
Lightning Source LLC
Chambersburg PA
CBHW050517190726
48284CB00003B/841